Self vs. Soul ... a novel

Book I

Love & Fear

J. Ronald Clements

ISBN 978-1-64468-159-6 (Paperback)
ISBN 978-1-64468-160-2 (Digital)

Covenant Books, Inc.
11661 Hwy 707
Murrells Inlet, SC 29576
www.covenantbooks.com

For my friend… Dr. C. O. Simpkins
Despite Selma, bombings, and jail, he stood his ground
with love and service…and his Soul Won.

Life is a competition within oneself that can only be endured. It can't be judged or valued by the accumulation of pleasure, painless moments, or good works. Wealth and power are meaningless. A life can only be graded by the performance of the soul versus the instinctive needs of a human.

J. Ronald Clements
March 2017

1

CHAPTER

1954

The four-foot lad stumbled, then fell facedown as he ran through the grassy lot across the street from his frame home. His two friends sprinted ahead, graceful, almost gliding across the thick Bermuda on ballerina feet. But not Steven; he lay on the wet ground dreading that he might have to tell Mama that his overalls were torn once again. Catching a boot on a rolled cuff, he fell a second time as he tried to get up too fast, scrambling, hoping to catch his friends who were already climbing in the pecan trees up ahead.

Minutes later, his chest heaving, Steven made it to the trees on the two-acre lot that served as the boys' sanctuary. Green and heavy with foliage on the hot summer days, they climbed as high as they dared into the deep shade, searching for that little breeze to cool their beet-red faces and hide from any parent who might come looking.

Steven climbed higher than Lawrence and Big Henry, pushing himself and instinctively calculating his positions as he dared to stretch for limbs that seemed unreachable at first, then perched above and doused with unbridled joy, he reveled in each magical moment, a toothless grin beaming from his fresh face.

By late November, his summer haven stood barren and gray as the wet cold pierced any and all with its northwest fury. The once-dominant leaves, tossed like an orchestrated cacophony by discordant winds now carpeted the Bermuda, hiding a bountiful supply of the thin-shelled nuts. Steven felt the late-evening cold across his shoulder blades and drew them forward, tightening his skin against the brutality. It would be time to go home soon.

"We need ammunition," he heard Lawrence saying. "There might be another war and we can shoot these pecans at the enemy."

"Augh…there ain't gonna be no war," Big Henry said. "My daddy says Ike's got everything under control now."

"Might not," Lawrence argued. "Besides, if it ain't no war, we can eat the pecans any time we want."

Steven looked from one to the other, not worried about a war but thinking that he could use a stockpile of pecans for the slingshot that he'd carved from a discarded wooden apple box that he scored in the alley behind Wilson's Grocery. If he were careful when he took the apple crates apart, the thick end pieces wouldn't splinter, and in the fall of 1954 he had the best slingshot in the neighborhood— maybe the best in all of Richland County, and anybody who was anybody in his world knew that, including Big Henry Watson who tried to rule that corner of Elm Street.

"We need to get lots of pecans and store them in the fort," Lawrence said.

"Not in the fort, you dummy," Big Henry said, sneering. "Rats and squirrels will haul off every one we put in there. We got to seal 'em up in one of those five-gallon buckets with a lid that Papa keeps in his shed."

Big Henry's family lived in a six-bedroom white house that sat on the corner, adjacent to the lot with the pecan trees. It was a brick house that had smooth plaster on the exterior walls and large columns all across the front. You couldn't actually see the brick. But it was still a brick house. Big Henry told Steven and Lawrence that.

"But I want mine where I can get to them," Steven said. "I'll use 'em in my special slingshot."

"You ain't got no special slingshot," Big Henry fired back. "That's just some old apple crate slingshot that ain't worth nothin'. My daddy bought me one from the mail-order house. It's made of shiny wood, and it'll shoot further than anything you got, that's for sure."

Steven's face turned red. He wanted to bull-rush Big Henry and tackle him, but that didn't seem wise. Still, Big Henry shouldn't have insulted his slingshot; that was out of bounds. Even if it wasn't made of shiny wood, it would shoot a long way…and straight too.

"You already got this fancy slingshot, or are you just shootin' off your mouth like you always do?" Steven asked.

"I got it. It's better'n anything around here, no matter what you say. I keep it in my sock drawer, and I'll put some of these pecans in there so I can shoot the burglars when they come."

"And what about the rest of us? What if the burglars come after us and we don't have any pecans for ammunition? That ain't right," Steven said.

"Is too," Big Henry said. "These are my pecans. All of them. They're from my daddy's trees, and that makes them mine."

Steven glared at Big Henry, grinding his teeth before he dropped the half-dozen pecans that he'd been carrying in his rolled shirttail. His face flared as he stared at Big Henry. Slowly, he began to mash one of the loose pecans into the muddy, black soil with the heel of his leather boot, almost daring Big Henry to brawl. Steven didn't necessarily want a fight that he would almost certainly lose, but he couldn't chicken-out. Not now, even though he knew that he could always say that he was just planting a tree.

The cold numbed his hands and Steven laced his fingers together at his waist, standing ramrod stiff, slowly working the pecan into the ground. Big Henry watched him at first, glancing from the leather boot, then up to lock eyes with Steven, then back to the boot again. Steven saw him ball his fists and take a deep breath. He braced for Big Henry's charge, thinking that he would sidestep and trip him, then pile on top and pound him with his fists. Big Henry's jaws flexed; his face reddened, and he gritted his teeth. Steven saw Big Henry swallow hard, then narrow his eyes readying himself. He held his breath and stared without blinking, boring into Big Henry's soul before he tensed his shoulders, still visualizing the move he would make. Big Henry's chest swelled, and his face got redder still as Steven stared down on him. Steven tried to imagine the pain of being hit so it wouldn't be a shock to him. He swallowed hard, getting ready, then at the last second Big Henry twitched just before he shifted his eyes to the side. He spat a short breath from flared nostrils and bent to gather the loose pecans that Steven had dropped.

Steven watched Big Henry rake in the bounty without a squabble, knowing that he would wait until the other two were inside and come back to collect his own ammunition in the late dusk, just before the black of night. They wouldn't see him then, not them nor anyone else.

Steven looked up slowly; the pecan was down in the soil now, flush with the surface. He'd been careful not to crack the shell, thinking that it might indeed be a tree one day, that is, if Big Henry's Uncle Dillard didn't mow it down when he came to cut the grass with his big, slobbering diesel-powered lawn mower.

Steven watched Big Henry finish gathering the piles of pecans and pack them in his leather sack with drawstrings that now wouldn't close. He took a breath and held it; then without saying a word, he turned and walked away.

Steven didn't look back. He didn't threaten Big Henry or let the indignant pain within him turn to rage and insult. The five-year-old simply took one small step after another, not feeling his feet touch the ground but thinking that it was much colder than he expected. He wondered if Mama would light the big propane heater that night. He'd overheard her saying something to Dad about how expensive the propane had gotten, but he really wanted her to light the big heater. Their little rented house would feel warm and safe then, even if she didn't leave it on for very long.

"Where *are* you going?" Steven heard Big Henry shout behind him. Steven didn't respond and kept walking. "You gonna be here tomorrow, Steven?"

Still, Steven didn't turn back or answer.

"Maybe," he finally said after walking further with almost measured strides, still looking ahead as he reached the shallow ditch between the lot and the street. "If it's not too cold."

"You better be here tomorrow. You hear me? Just two can't play Tag. We need three and you know it!" Big Henry yelled.

Steven didn't answer this time, but as he crossed the street, he remembered that the withered old men who spent their daytime hours in the barbershop reading newspapers and telling stories had mentioned that it should be warmer tomorrow. He smiled at that, wondering if Karl, the butcher at Wilson's Grocery might have a little extra beef kidney that he could get when he knocked on the alley door. Nobody would pay solid money for beef kidneys, and Karl would sometimes give them to the boys who liked to go after the catfish. If the wind didn't blow from the east, Steven thought that it could be a good day on the creek. He would need Dad to help clean them, of course. It scared him when they wiggled; plus, the bloody mess of death bothered him, even if it was just a catfish.

Steven stopped on the top step just before the screen door that led to the front porch. He scowled, puffing his cheeks a little as he stood still, holding on to the door handle, then turning to stare at the pecan grove where he'd last seen his friends.

Big Henry's words annoyed him. He deserved some of the pecans. They all worked to find them in the leaves and thick grass. Of course he knew the trees belonged to Big Henry's daddy. Everybody knew that. Still, it would have been fair for him and Lawrence to get a share, maybe not as many as Big Henry, but at least some. Without thinking, he gritted his teeth and glared into the night before shuddering.

The wind's icy moisture stung his face as he stood on the step. His jaws tightened as he braced against the cold, realizing that it must be near freezing by now. He pulled the earflaps on his cap down and tied the string under his chin as he looked back down the hill toward Big Henry's house where all the windows were lit and smoke drifted from the wood-burning fireplace. Maybe Mama had the heater lit by now. He shivered again, the thin sweatshirt and patched overalls no match for the nasty wind and the cold it delivered.

Steven imagined Big Henry and Lawrence warming in front of a fire or at a kitchen table having a bowl of hot Texas chili by now. He swallowed again. To them, he was just a renter's kid living in a small wooden house that never had enough heat or insulation on those icy nights when the wind sent its incessant waves of cold through the once-proud shiplap boards, now shrunken and cracked with time. He knew that Big Henry and Lawrence couldn't know how he felt, nor did they have the focus to care.

Steven dropped his chin to his chest, seeing the red brick steps below and thinking that someday Big Henry and Lawrence would regret keeping all the pecans. He was sure of that.

Another gust from the northwest pummeled him, and he tensed his body and held his breath, hoping to insulate himself from the pain. That didn't work, of course, but when the wind settled and he began to breathe more regularly, he nodded his head almost imperceptibly, agreeing with himself about Big Henry and Lawrence.

He couldn't fault them. They didn't know what it was like to stand before Abraham's Council and plead for a life. He'd suffered through three contentious reviews before they finally agreed to give him his chance. Now he had to survive the relentless battles with himself, fend off the dregs of humanity, and find Sarah...somehow.

Steven shuffled his numbing feet, then shook himself a little. He could still remember some of his life before birth, but he didn't know if he could do what he was sent to accomplish. A Level Three in the heavens, he was now trapped between a child and a man on earth, and he knew that his enemies wouldn't rest until they broke him.

Ten minutes prior, the dusk had faded to a moonless night, and another bitterly cold minute passed before he released a deep sigh and lifted his eyes, opening the screen door to go inside.

2
CHAPTER

The Snack Jack boxes depicted an airplane that would actually fly, and Steven wanted a plane even more than the slingshot that he'd made for himself. The pictures showed a full-bodied red-and-blue plane with a propeller that would spin and take it airborne. It wasn't just a model to sit in the window; it would really fly, and that was big stuff for a renter's kid. Best of all, it was almost free. Steven only had to save the tops from ten Snack Jack boxes and mail them to the company, and they would send him a plane.

Steven was certain that it was a real plane; he'd studied the box, but it seemed too wonderful to be true. Worse, he didn't know how the plane could work. He wondered if he would have to assemble the plane. Did he need glue? How much would that cost? A D battery would be heavy, but the plane would need lots of power for the propeller motor. And how would the propeller mount on the plane to give him control so he could make it fly straight? It just didn't seem possible, but every time he bought a fresh box of Snack Jacks he studied the picture again. It was supposed to fly; that was clear to him, and the plane on the box was definitely full-bodied. None of this seemed logical, but Steven hoped the advertisement was correct. He wanted to believe that. He couldn't conceive that a big company like Snack Jack would trick a kid, but still, he was suspicious.

It seemed like he'd never get enough box tops to qualify. Snack Jacks weren't cheap, and even though he didn't actually like them much, he bought a box every week when he got his allowance. By the time he had enough box tops to qualify for the plane and mail the letter, there were four uneaten boxes in the pantry re-sealed with tape so the critters wouldn't get into them.

He was sure that he would have a plane to fly, and nobody else had one of those, not even Big Henry with his brick mansion and all of his daddy's money. When he'd told Lawrence about his plan, Steven felt important, even privileged in a special way that he couldn't necessarily explain.

Steven was the first to get to the mailbox every day, always walking back up the hill, head down when the package—he knew it would have to be a big package—didn't come.

The daylight hours were short on the Friday evening when he stretched to look in the mailbox that sat on a fence post across the street from their screened porch. It was the thirtieth day since they'd mailed the box tops and the letter, and his heart surged when he saw the logo and the brown envelope.

Then fear shot through him. The "package" was just a stiff ten-inch-wide envelope with something inside, maybe a quarter-inch thick. He pulled it out of the mailbox slowly, confused and staring as he turned slowly and began to walk toward the screened porch thinking that this couldn't be his airplane. It wasn't big enough. It just couldn't be.

His dreams of having a functioning plane drained with every step as he walked toward the house. He had used ten weeks of allowance dimes to collect the box tops, and remorse surged as he took one step after another toward their front door thinking that he could have had something substantial with all that allowance money. Was the plane just a stupid dream? Why didn't he ask more questions about it? What was he going to do with a bunch of balsa wood slats and no motor to drive the propeller?

He knew that Mama would be inside. He would show her the envelope that had finally come, but by the time he reached the door, he was sniffing at the tears.

Martha heard the door close behind her and spun to see who had come in. It was too early for Jason.

"What's wrong?" she asked when she saw Steven's contorted face.

"The airplane came," he said in a low, weak voice as he held up the envelope.

"So. What's wrong?"

Steven hesitated, turning toward the window, then shuffled his feet before looking back. "It's not right, Mama." Steven's head was down; his voice just louder than a whisper.

Martha took a deep breath and put her hands on her hips, staring at her son. She looked at her watch. Jason was working late again.

"What's not right about it, Steven? Surely, the plane will work."

"Noooo," the five-year-old said slowly. "It won't work. It just won't. The picture on the box was of a plane that had a body and wings. It was like a World War II plane that Dad told me about."

Steven tried to swallow the tears. He didn't want to cry; that was for little kids, and crying didn't fit him anymore. It wouldn't be so bad if he hadn't told Lawrence about the plane. Lawrence was okay, of course; he'd understand that the wooden pieces with notches for the wings weren't really a plane like the picture on the box. But Lawrence told Big Henry, and that was trouble.

Steven knew that he was going to cry, even though he didn't want to. He'd waited so long for the plane to come in the mail, and now it was nothing like he'd expected, and he didn't have any money left.

"It's just wrong, Mama. Just wrong." He hung his head again, a Norman Rockwell little boy with his heavy brogans, suspenders, and a red face with tears ebbing.

"I did everything right, Mama. Everything. I met every deadline, and we wrote them the nice letter when we sent the box tops. And they sent this thing that won't fly. Anybody can see that. It doesn't even have wheels for the landing gear, and they were so cheap that they didn't even send a rubber band for the wind-up propeller."

He couldn't let himself cry, not now, but he swallowed hard again trying to choke back the emotion.

"It just isn't fair, Mama. It was supposed to be a real model plane that would fly." Steven breathed rapidly, sniffing up the sobs before they became tears. "I wanted a real plane, Mama. A real plane, not this pile-of-nothing pieces of wood."

"Now, Steven," Martha began, "we need to see if what they sent in the envelope can be made to fly."

"It won't," Steven mumbled, looking down. "It just won't. Hadn't even got a rubber band," he repeated. "It can't."

"I have plenty of rubber bands, Steven. Plenty. Let's get one and go out in the field across the street and see if we can get it to fly."

Martha turned the gas off on her stove, hung her apron on the hook by the cabinet, and took the open envelope from her son.

It took less than a minute to assemble the thin wooden slats into something not much more substantial than a paper airplane. They connected the rubber band and twisted the propeller.

Martha knelt down and handed the plane to Steven. "Now run across the field and release the propeller just as you throw it."

Steven stared at her through the puffed eyelids, holding the wound propeller with his index finger. After a deep breath, the five-year-old turned his head from side to side slowly, then sniffed hard. "I'm not supposed to have to do that, Mama. The picture on the box was of a real plane flying through the air." Steven stared through watery eyes. "They tricked me, Mama. That's all there is to it. They tricked me. I spent my money on something that I don't like, and I didn't get anything for it. I let them trick me."

"Well…we don't know that, Steven. It might fly. We just don't know that yet, do we?"

"It doesn't look anything like the one in the picture, and I spent all my money. There's nothing left in my Ben Franklin bank."

"Run, Steven. Just try it."

Steven ground his teeth before starting to run. Ten steps out, he heaved the plane with all his strength, and for less than a second he thought it might just fly. It went up a few feet, sallied forward, then nose-dived like a falling duck, landing awkwardly on its side just four feet in front of him.

Steven stood still, his dark brown locks ruffled by the light breeze as he looked at the downed plane. He considered walking off and leaving it right there but couldn't bring himself to do that. Slowly, he bent down and picked up the balsa wood slats that were now disjointed and no longer in the shape of a plane. Without emotion, he turned, clutching the wooden pieces and walked toward Mama who stood in the field, her arms folded across her chest.

"Do you want me to take it and try to glue it together?" Martha asked.

Steven shook his head. "They tricked me. That's all. I should've known better," he said, still thinking about all the money he'd wasted on those stupid boxes of caramel popcorn. "Let's go home, Mama," Steven said, and they began the slow walk back across the field to the asphalt street.

Later that night when she went to Steven's tiny bedroom to tuck him in and say a prayer, Martha saw the plane reassembled and sitting on the window ledge. "Are you sure you don't want me to glue the cracked pieces back together?" she asked.

Steven pressed his lips together and pooched them before he answered. "No, Mama," he said, pausing, "I want it to stay just like it is, sitting there in that window so I can see it and be reminded of how stupid I was. I knew it was too good to be true, and I went for it anyway."

He paused, looking up to his mother, and stared wide-eyed, almost unblinking as his brow furrowed above jaws that were locked. "They won't trick me again, Mama. Not ever."

Martha didn't light the heater the next night either, and by the time he crawled in the single bed against the wall, it was colder still, well below freezing and already deep into winter's inhumanity, even though the solstice was still four weeks away.

She told Steven that she was afraid to leave the heaters on at night and that it seemed like fire was burning someone's house to the ground almost every month and that he just needed to snuggle a little deeper down under the thick patchwork quilts that his grandmother had sewn and given them. Tonight he had three quilts layered on top of him in the single bed. If he didn't have to get up to use the toilet, he might still be warm when Mama lit the heater just before daylight. Steven didn't believe that part about houses burning down. It was the cost of propane, and he knew it.

3

CHAPTER

Steven thought that Christmas would be lean again this year. Dad wasn't getting his full forty hours at the hardware store anymore, and Mama didn't get paid much at the bank, even though she was the president's assistant. He had hoped for a football to go with the oranges, nuts, and snacks that Mama always stuffed in the big red stocking, but after long minutes of fleeting sleep, Steven, clad in the red flannel footie pajamas with big buttons in front snuggled deeper beneath the homemade quilts, bending his knees so that the covers would be long enough for most of his face to also be underneath. Just before closing his eyes and drifting off to sleep, he concluded that the football wouldn't be under the tree this year. Maybe it would just be the stocking this Christmas.

On Christmas Eve, Dad sat in the oversized padded chair with the wide arms made from stained teak. The chair rocked but didn't recline, and it squeaked a little when Dad leaned too far back. It was Dad's chair, his place in the house, and it sat in a tight corner of the little room, almost touching the Christmas tree.

The tree dominated the room, of course, and when it was lit, the large propane heater glowed and warmed them all the way into the adjacent kitchen. This was Steven's favorite room; the family gathered here, a place for laughter and music when they listened to the shows on the shiny cabinet radio that was almost as tall as Steven. He'd learned to tune the dial using the big knobs on the front so he could listen to the cartoons on Saturday mornings. Even when Mama turned the heater off, this room seemed alive—the tree, the radio, Dad sitting in the big chair in the corner reading the newspaper—somehow all of it gave the room a special kind of life that took him beyond the cold and their constant scramble for cash.

Just before dark Steven checked the tree one more time for a football and swallowed hard before starting for the door to go out to the pecan trees that now seemed stark and lonely. Big Henry and his family were gone to his grandmother's house in the country near Waco, and Steven intended to collect more pecan ammunition that he stored in his own five-gallon bucket that sat in the front corner of the car shed. As he opened the door, he looked back at the tree and released a long breath before turning the knob, telling himself that it would be a good Christmas, and he didn't really need that football anyway.

Mama always made Dad's favorite meal on Christmas Eve. She started buying the ingredients days in advance, and on that afternoon the tiny house was awash with fine aromas. Steven had hurried from room to room, chopping the celery for Mama, then sitting with Dad as he read the newspaper, then back to the kitchen to set the table. For this one evening, none of them worried about money; and Doris, Frank, and Bing serenaded with Christmas music from the tall radio.

Dad and Mama didn't give each other presents, but in a good year Steven would get at least one present. Sometimes that didn't come until Christmas morning, but after dinner on Christmas Eve he would be allowed to have his stocking that Mama hung on the wall near the tree. He liked the stocking stuffing and went right at the oranges, nuts, and candy canes. This year he thought he'd seen Mama put chocolate kisses in the stocking, but he wasn't completely certain. The chocolate was his favorite. Mama made some of that herself and put lots of pecans in her mix.

Steven thought that his parents were happier than usual that evening. Dad had come home from work at the hardware store at noon, and on this special night he wore his checked red-and-green bowtie to go with the red suspenders and the starched white shirt.

Mama wore one of her fancy church dresses on Christmas Eve. Steven could tell that, even though she had the long apron on while she was cooking. Sometimes she even wore one of those small velvet hats like he'd seen in magazines at the soda fountain in town. The hat didn't hide her dark hair, and she pinned it in place so it wouldn't be a problem while she was in the kitchen. He'd never thought about Mama being pretty, but he'd overheard Big Henry telling Lawrence that his daddy said Mama was a real *looker*. As he sat on the sofa soaking in the simplistic but unbridled five-year-old joy of Christmas Eve, he thought that Big Henry's daddy was right. Mama was very pretty indeed, maybe even beautiful.

By early evening everything was ready, and they sat at the small table in the corner that was covered with a pressed linen cloth. Dad pulled the chair out for Mama, and he waited until she was comfortable before the men sat themselves.

Mama's clam chowder was the best in town. Everybody knew that. And on Christmas Eve they had those little oyster snacks that he was allowed to put in the bowl. The salad came after the chowder, then the chicken, potatoes, and trimmings. Steven thought it was all just perfect, and his favorite was the custard pie for dessert. They didn't have much money; Steven knew that, but on this one evening they were simply happy.

When they finished dinner and the dishes were done, Mama and Dad would sit beside each other on the small sofa drinking coffee while he unloaded the stocking. Dad smoked his pipe as Bing continued to drone in the background.

Steven looked up from the stocking. "Mama, does every kid get a stocking on Christmas Eve?" he asked.

Martha looked to Jason, then back to Steven. "Not everybody, Steven. But almost all of the people that we know will have a stocking for their kids."

Steven turned back to his goodies. "I bet Big Henry gets five of them," he said without looking back to his parents.

Martha exchanged glances with Jason again, then ran a nervous hand through her hair.

Steven munched a candy cane. There were lots of the chocolate kisses this year and more nuts and oranges than ever before. "I'll tell you what I wish that we could do, Mama," he said, pausing but still not looking back. "I wish we could give some of my stocking to some kid that didn't get one. I can't eat all of this, and we don't want it to go bad or let the mice get into it." Steven twisted toward his parents, extending his arms, with palms up, asking the question with his body language.

Jason stopped puffing on the pipe. "The way that works for us, Steven," he began, searching for the right words, "is that we give money to the church every month, and the church tries to help kids get a stocking and other things that they need all through the year."

Steven didn't think that was a very good idea. "Is that why Big Henry and his family get to sit on the front row every Sunday? They probably give a lot of money," he said as he unwrapped one of the chocolate kisses, not looking back to Dad. "If we can find a way to give some of my stocking away tonight, maybe I can talk Big Henry into giving some his loot away when they get back from his grandmother's house."

"The amount of money that you give doesn't have anything to do with where you sit in church, Steven," Jason said, stopping his son. "We can sit anywhere we like if that part of the pew is available."

"So why don't we just go sit down front where Mr. Watson and Big Henry sit?"

Jason took a breath. "Well... I wouldn't want to take their seats, just like I wouldn't want anyone to sit where we normally sit," he said, omitting that Henry Watson Sr. was the largest shareholder in the bank where Martha worked.

Steven thought that they should just try sitting down front one Sunday, but Mr. Watson was six foot five and weighed at least two hundred seventy pounds. He scared Steven even when he walked down the center aisle of the church. Maybe they should just keep their seats near the back on the left side.

"Who do you think I can give some of my stocking to?" Steven asked.

Jason crossed his legs and leaned back on the sofa. "I'll call the pastor in the morning and ask if he knows anyone who didn't get a stocking."

Steven nodded his approval. That wasn't as good as giving it directly to some kid that didn't get anything, but he was satisfied that it was probably as well as they were going to do for now.

Steven's green eyes stared, unblinking for an intense moment when the thought hit him. He wished there were some way he could take all the stockings away from the kids whose folks managed the Snack Jack company and give them to kids who didn't get anything. He was deep into thought about how that might work when he heard his dad.

"Come sit on the sofa between Mama and me, Steven. You know this is our special time."

Steven didn't really want to do that. He wasn't a baby anymore but agreed that this was one of their traditions. He slowly got up and snuggled down between his parents, still thinking about how to take the stockings from the Snack Jack kids and get them distributed to those who were less fortunate.

*****

It was nineteen degrees just after midnight on that Christmas morning, cold for Texas. Steven had buried deep beneath the triple layer of quilts in his tiny bedroom and was in a deep sleep when he heard the first scream. He surged up, throwing the quilts back as his feet hit the cold floor. Sitting on the edge of the bed, he froze, trying to make sense of the wretched sound. He'd never heard anyone screech like that, and he tensed his body, balling his fists ready to fight an invisible enemy in the dark, cold room. Mama screamed again, and ten thousand spines tingled across his back before he ran barefooted toward his parents' bedroom. He had no idea what he would find when he turned the corner.

As he cut through the door frame, he saw Mama sitting on the corner of the bed clutching the iron footboard sobbing and screaming at the same time.

"Nooooo," she pleaded between the gasps. "No, No, No, No!"

Steven stood in the doorway without understanding, taking it all in, looking from one place to another to find the burglars, thinking that he should have taken the time to get his slingshot from the chest by his bed. He no longer felt the cold. Mama moved to the head of the bed and pushed on Dad's chest over and over before she took him by the shoulders, shaking him and trying to get him to wake up. The small lamp beside the bed was the only light in the house, and it was hard for Steven to see what was happening. Other than Mama's screams, it seemed okay. There weren't any burglars; he could tell that much.

"Jason, you can't. Not now. Not now," she said, leaning down to place her forehead on his. "Please. Not yet! No. No. Nooooo. Not yet!"

Steven felt his stomach churn, and the cold fear of realization swept him as a white-water wave does the sand. They couldn't live without Dad. He did too much. He was their rock, and he lay on the bed stone-still. His eyes were open, but his face seemed gray and his chest wasn't moving. Steven took slow steps as he walked toward Mama, then put his arms around her, hugging her to him.

Martha straightened herself, taking his embrace with arms around his waist, still bursting with uncontrollable sobs. "I... I loved him so much, Steven. He's...he's everything to me. Every...thing. We...we've always been together. Always."

"I know, Mama."

"How...how does this happen? He was just fine. He was happy tonight. When we went to bed, there was nothing wrong. Nothing. My God, he's only thirty-nine. Thirty-nine! This can't be! How does he survive World War II then die in his bed on Christmas morning? How? It's just not fair!" Martha shouted between the sobs. "No. No. No."

Martha sniffed every few seconds, but the sobs didn't stop.

Steven stood still, almost stoic with unblinking dry eyes. He lowered his chin, seeing his dad lying on the bed, wondering why, and paradoxically knowing all the while that there were so very few accidents in a life. His tears wouldn't come, neither did the pain-ladened emotion that built in his throat and made it hard to swallow. He stared ahead, immediately believing that Dad's death was his fault.

He'd been warned that it would be a rough life. Abraham's Council drilled that into him. So did Uncle Melvin and Brother Joseph, the family's barrister in the heavens. Even Laura said as much to him on three different occasions, but he didn't want to believe it. He understood that growth and struggle run in parallels, but he never imagined that others would be hurt to cause him subsequent pain. Dad didn't deserve to have his time cut short. Worse, what did Mama do to deserve this?

Steven stood still, locked in Martha's embrace, feeling his anger building. How could he have been so stupid? It was too late now, but maybe they'd all been right. Maybe he shouldn't have lobbied so hard for life as a human. Maybe he really was being selfish or ambitious like Brother Joseph said. The Level Five barrister always seemed to get things right, and all the family sought him for representation, but Steven knew that he wasn't selfish, much less ambitious. He was barely six years old as he stood still, holding Mama and wondering who else would get hurt because of him.

Gently, Steven broke from Mama's embrace and took a half step back before he moved around her to the very top of the old ironworks bed where Dad lay motionless. Without asking Mama, he extended a finger and put it on Dad's eyelids, pulling them down one at a time before closing his own eyes as he lowered his head, completely convinced that this was all his fault. Dad hadn't done anything wrong.

Martha bent forward, holding her head in her hands. From where she sat, Steven knew she couldn't see him closing Jason's eyes, and her head was still down when he looked to the ceiling, seeing Laura hovering above and pointing.

When his eyes followed her hand, he saw Dad standing before the Review Council. Brother Joseph stood beside him, and Uncle Melvin paced in the back of the room. Steven managed a tight smile before looking back to Laura. She nodded in his direction, then faded. That was the first time he'd seen her since leaving the heavens.

"This can't be," Martha said to no one in particular. "It just can't. We don't own this house. We don't have any savings. How are we going to make it?" she asked, still holding her head in her hands. "How...how are we going to make it?"

"We'll get by, Mama. I promise. We will get by. They won't get to us," he said, his lower lip protruding. "I won't let them, Mama. I promise."

Martha looked up to her son who sounded more like that man from *Dragnet* than her little boy. She shuddered, then hunched her shoulders as she leaned forward again. Long seconds passed before she stood up and began to pace near the lamp.

"Where did you get that voice, Steven?" she asked. "And who are *they*?" She stopped pacing and turned to face him.

Steven dropped his head but eventually looked up again. "The bad guys, Mama. Just the bad guys that you can't see." He closed his eyes, then bit his lower lip, thinking.

"They're always around, Mama. Sometimes they live inside people. Sometimes they swarm like gnats in the spring. You never know where they are, but they don't go away."

Martha stood, hands on hips, staring, almost glaring at Steven. He saw her open her mouth to say something, then close it, turning her head to the side before she shuddered, then sobbed again as she turned back to him.

"Your dad got you the football, Steven. Look under the tree. It's there now, and…this is still Christmas," she said without thinking, instinctively searching for words that would somehow make him her little boy again.

"I won't be needing that now, Mama. We can take it back to the store and save that three dollars."

Martha shook her head and started pacing again, arms across her chest, still wearing her beige flannel nightgown.

Martha Bradford Heard didn't have siblings, and her parents were both dead. Jason's parents had passed ten years prior. Worse, she'd been the prettiest girl in her class, and the other girls despised her for it. She didn't have close girlfriends that would listen or help. Jason and Steven were her only family, her only companions.

She let out a long, slow breath and closed her eyes as she sat back on the bed next to Jason, then lowered her head, covering her face with her hands again, moving only when she had to wipe tears.

"Dad wouldn't want us to quit, Mama," Steven said, still with that strange Joe Friday voice.

Martha didn't raise her head. She began to sob again before she looked up suddenly, brushing the tears back.

"Go in the kitchen, Steven," she said between the gasps. "Get the phone and dial the operator," she managed. "Tell them…tell them to get the sheriff over here as fast as they can."

Steven nodded without speaking and turned for the door but stopped at the kitchen entrance and turned back.

"And light the heater," Martha added. "We're going to have to burn some gas tonight."

Steven stared as she bent at the waist again, burying her face in her hands. "Mama," he said, pausing, "Dad's okay now."

Martha looked up quickly. "Steven… Steven?" She turned her head to the side a little and tried for a tight-lipped smile that didn't come.

"He is, Mama. Dad's okay. I know it," he said, trying to console her, his voice still deep and serious.

Martha stared at him, then simply let her head droop again. "I know, Steven," she finally said. "I know."

"No, Mama. It's really okay. I promise. You can stop crying. Dad's fine. He's with our people now."

Steven looked away, stopping himself. He wanted to tell Mama about Uncle Melvin and Brother Joseph, but he couldn't, thinking that she wouldn't understand. Not tonight.

Martha took a quick breath and looked at Steven again. He was still wearing the worn flannel pajamas. "Steven…" she managed, exhaling. "You're a good son, Steven, a good son. And I'm sure you're right. We'll get by somehow."

Steven started into the kitchen before Martha spoke.

"How do you know that Dad's okay, Steven?" she asked, stopping him.

"I just do, Mama. I don't know how," he said, lying.

Martha stared. Her lips parted as though she wanted to respond but couldn't.

"Just put some clothes on after you make the call and light the heater," she managed, putting her head down again. "There will be people here soon."

Martha looked as though she were lost in a long blank space as she sat on the corner of the bed and stared at the wall.

"What...don't I know? What is happening that I can't...
can't see?" she asked just above a whisper. "Where...will we get the
money?" she added. Instinctively, she brushed her hair back with a
hand, then walked over to her closet. She fidgeted with her flannel
nightgown, staring ahead almost without blinking. Moments later,
she took out one of her better dresses and held it in front of her,
nodding her approval to no one in particular.

4
CHAPTER

Steven went into the kitchen and took the phone from the cradle hanging on the wall. He shivered and hunched his shoulders, seeing the unlit heater across the room. He knew that he needed to hurry.

"Miss Lula," he said in a steady voice after dialing zero for operator, "this is Steven. We need Sheriff Olin over here at our house right now."

"Yes, ma'am," Steven said. "Yes, ma'am, I know it's two fifteen in the morning on Christmas Day, but my dad…has died."

Sheriff Olin Johnson rushed across the screened porch and into Martha's house without knocking. He and Jason had been the ringleaders in *Who's Afraid of the Big Bad Wolf* games on the first grade playground at recess. They played sports together in high school, hunted and fished together, and went through their army physical and basic training together. Olin was initially assigned to North Africa, and Jason went to McArthur's corps of marines in the Pacific. Near the end, Olin was reassigned to the Pacific theater and glimpsed Jason loading his gear into a jeep on Mindanao. Three days later he used his seniority and battle points to get himself transferred to the same platoon so he could be with his friend.

Still sobbing, Martha leaned on Olin, wrapping her arms around him when he walked into the bedroom. It seemed like just yesterday that Jason and Olin had come by her house to accuse her of having cooties for being a girl. That would have been the summer before the fifth grade, but by the sixth grade they were flipping a coin to see who would get to walk her to the school's fall carnival for their first date. That was fifteen years before the war when her life was still simple, even though it often felt like she were managing all of the gears within a Swiss watch simultaneously. Martha knew that she could have married Olin, but by the ninth grade, she'd chosen Jason and planned the remainder of her life around him. Nothing in the plan that she'd written in her diary included the financial struggles that she and Jason endured, nor did it include his passing at age thirty-nine.

Martha sat in the rickety wooden chair by the window and gave Olin space and time to stand over Jason and stare at his friend, now gray and lifeless. Olin took a knee in front of her.

"What happened, Martha?" he asked softly, turning his head to look up to her. "And I know this is hard. I know it is. It's hard for all of us, but just try to...try to tell me everything that you can remember," Olin said.

Martha swallowed and blinked hard at the tears, trying to gather herself. "We'd been in bed and asleep for three or four hours. There was nothing wrong, Olin. Nothing. Jason was sleeping on his back like always. Then I heard a quick gasp, and he sort of shuddered as I sat up."

She paused, leaning forward as she covered her eyes with her hands again. "He tried to turn his head to look at me, but he couldn't do it." She began to sob again and took Olin's handkerchief that he held out to her. "His lips moved and quivered for a few seconds, but no words came out. And then..." she said, swallowing, trying to get control. "And then his head snapped straight in line with his body just like it is right now," she continued, half turning toward the bed. "He was just gone, Olin. Gone. Nothing I did worked," she said, trying to stop the deep breaths and sobs. "I tried to bring him back. I tried. I really did. But nothing worked."

The aw-shucks deputy that arrived just a half-step behind Olin moved to the head of the bed and pulled the sheet up over Jason. That was the last time Martha saw Jason looking like himself. She barely recognized the man in the coffin three days later.

"Marvin, check the house," Steven heard the sheriff say. "Look for anything strange or signs of forced entry."

Marvin stood hands on hips, staring back at his boss, furrowing his brow.

"Just to be sure, Marvin. I know it's unlikely, but just to be sure."

The mercury in the Coca-Cola thermometer by the back door had dropped to sixteen degrees, and it was still Christmas morning. Marvin had dressed hurriedly and didn't take the time to wear his long johns or shave. He scowled at his boss, then turned and started for the back door.

"So, what exactly did you try to do, Martha?" Olin asked, hesitating as he glanced toward Marvin.

Martha looked down but didn't respond.

"I don't like having to ask you questions right now, Martha," Olin said. "I think you probably know that. But I just have to. Take your time. I can only imagine how hard this must be for you."

Martha nodded, still covering her eyes as she periodically brushed the tears back.

"I screamed," she said finally. "I called for Steven, and then I started mouth-to-mouth. I didn't get anywhere with that, so I started pushing on his chest like the man at the bank seminar on safety told us when he gave the presentation."

Martha turned her head, biting her lower lip. "Olin, it just didn't work. I got nothing. I mean, nothing. There was no response at all after his head snapped straight. So…after a little while, I gave up."

She closed a hand into a tight fist and held it to her forehead. "I gave up. I just gave up. I wanted him to come back so bad, but I gave up. I got nowhere at all." She released a heavy breath. "And I gave up," she said again, shaking her head from side to side slowly.

"It's okay, Martha. I promise. You did all the right things," Olin said, obviously trying to help her through the moment. "All the right things."

The sheriff took a quick breath and cut his eyes to the side then back to Martha as she dropped her hands and looked up to him with that distant, blank expression.

"Did I, Olin? What if I had kept pressing on his chest? Would he still be here? Would he have left the other side and come back?"

Martha twisted in the chair and turned toward the window, staring into the night. "Why did this happen, Olin? What did Jason do to deserve this? You were boys together. You went to war together, for God's sake. You knew him as well as anybody. What did he do to deserve this?"

Marvin came back before Olin could answer. "Ms. Martha, I'm going to send Uncle Eugene over here tomorrow to fix the lock on that back door. A baby could get past that thing. Uncle Eugene won't charge anything. It'll be okay. But you and that boy can't stay here very long with that door like it is."

Martha nodded and thanked him, wondering what else could be wrong with the house. What else did she need to deal with? What else did she need to do that she didn't know about? And where was she going to get the money to pay for Jason's funeral?

"Anything outside, Marvin?" Olin asked.

"Nah. It's clean. No sign of anything. Except that back door. Ain't nobody forced their way in here, boss."

Olin stared up at Marvin, still kneeling in front of Martha who huddled within herself, arms crossed over chest and bent forward, now rocking her torso back and forth again.

Marvin rubbed his chin, almost glaring at Olin.

"There weren't no foul play here tonight, boss," he said aloud as he cut a chew of tobacco with his pocket-knife and began to soften it in his mouth.

"What you thinkin' about?" he asked.

"Something...just doesn't seem quite right," Olin said as he released a heavy breath. "This is just strange. Really strange," he added almost in a whisper.

Steven stood across the room leaning on the doorframe that led to the kitchen. He still hadn't shed a tear. He thought that Mama had cried enough for both of them, and he just stood there, watching. That person under the sheet wasn't his dad. Even the skin felt different. Too different.

Olin shifted his weight to his opposite knee. "Now, Martha," Steven heard him say, "are you sure that nobody came into the bedroom while you were sleeping?"

"Olin, I promise...there was no one in here but us," Martha said.

"But you were asleep, you said. Is it possible that someone slipped through that back door and did something to Jason? Poisoned him or strangled him?"

"No, Olin. It's just not possible."

Steven took a half-step forward and sniffed to clear his nose. "Sheriff, I'm a real light sleeper," he began. "They might could've got in here without any of us knowing, but they couldn't have got out. Mama screamed right off, and I came running. If there was somebody in here, I would've run slap into him as he tried to get out of Mama's bedroom."

"Marvin, check outside one more time," Olin said.

"Dang, Olin, ain't nothin' out there tonight except the cold. And it's Christmas," Marvin said in protest.

Olin's square-jawed glare seemed obvious to Steven.

"I suppose I can go look again just to be sure," Marvin managed as he turned to go outside again. "Boy, why don't you come with me? Get your jacket," he added as he motioned with his head toward the back door.

5
CHAPTER

Steven led the way as they walked through the kitchen, past the small wooden table toward the back door, and Marvin went outside first. When they were down the three wooden steps Marvin stopped and turned to face Steven, the tobacco juice ebbing on his lower lip.

"Son, I need you to understand something, and I know you're way too young to have this talk, but your daddy's gone now and somebody's got to explain a few things."

Marvin hesitated, rubbing his beard-stubbled chin. "And... I also know that this is a real bad night for me to have to tell you this." He looked away and spat the tobacco over the handrail into the six-teen-degree night. "But you're just going to have to stand there and listen a minute. I don't care how cold it is."

Steven shivered and shoved his hands down into his blue jean jacket. His ears burned, and he turned the collar up on his coat as he stared up to the deputy.

Marvin rubbed his chin again before turning his head to the side as Steven stood as still as he could, constantly rolling his tongue back and forth across his teeth, trying not to sniff or look scared, telling himself that he needed to bear up and not complain about the cold, just the same as Dad would have done. Marvin shook his head a little and released a heavy breath before he spat tobacco juice again.

"Everybody liked your dad," he said, hesitating. "Everybody that I know of, at least. I think he just died. I don't think anybody killed him, but we're gonna look up under the house and go all the way around again. But that ain't the problem."

Steven saw the tension that made Marvin breathe a little too fast as he wrinkled his brow.

"Here's the problem, boy—"

"It's Mama, isn't it?" Steven blurted, interrupting.

Marvin nodded.

"Your mama is a right pretty woman, son. Right pretty indeed." Marvin sat on the bottom step putting him eye level with Steven. "When a woman, especially a pretty woman, is suddenly a widow, some fellas—not near all, mind you—but some get to thinking that she might…" he hesitated, "she might like their company in the bedroom because she's lonely and in need of a man. They'll convince themselves of that and come to her house and try to get cozy. Doesn't matter if the woman even knows their name. Doesn't matter if they're older or younger than the woman or if anything about their…uhmmmm background…is anything like the lady's. They just convince themselves that the woman is sitting there lonely every night and pining for their company. Sexual company."

Marvin stopped, leaning back on the steps, then let out a fog cloud of hot breath before turning back to Steven who stared somewhere in the distance, not seeing Marvin and, for the moment, not feeling the cold. He knew what "sexual company" meant. Big Henry and Lawrence told him what they heard from their big brothers who were already in high school. He gritted his teeth, not liking the idea of Mama being close to anybody other than Dad.

"Do you understand what I just told you, boy?"

"Yes sir, I do. You want that lock fixed 'cause you think some of the town fellas might come here and try to spark with Mama since Dad's not here anymore."

"That's right, boy. And you got to understand that some fellas will convince themselves that your mama would want them to do things that she ain't got no intention of ever doing, not with them and probably not with anybody else for a long, long time. Maybe even never."

Steven nodded, embarrassed, and let his eyes fall. "So what do you want me to do if somebody gets in and bothers Mama?" he asked.

"Are you a good whittler, boy?"

"Yes sir."

"Okay, then you pick you out a good straight limb that's about as long as I am tall. Make sure it's a green limb, and hickory is always the best."

Steven stood stiff, staring at Deputy Marvin.

"And then you sharpen it to a point. Can you do that, boy?"

Steven's Adam's apple moved as he swallowed. "Yes sir," he said quickly. "Dad gave me an Uncle Henry knife two years ago, and I know how to sharpen it. Most days, it will shave."

"Good. Then if some fella gets in the house and bothers your mama and you're really sure that she doesn't want anything to do with him, then you take that stick and run at him as hard as you can, jamming that point in his leg or in his ass."

Steven visualized a man reaching down to pull the spear out, blood spurting on to the floor and all the ruckus that would be going on. He told himself that he could do that, and at that moment, he believed that he could do that.

"That fella probably won't see you coming with the sharp stick since I suspect he'll be distracted, trying to bother your mama. And you got to be sure...really sure...that the fella is a problem for your mama before you ram him with that stick."

Marvin paused, staring at Steven who was trembling with the cold now. "Are you sure you understand, boy?"

"I am, sir," Steven said, the intensity rising in his voice. "I'm real sure."

"All right, boy. And just one more thing...well, maybe two things," Marvin said, pausing again. "I know it's cold out here, but I got to tell you this, and you got to remember it no matter what."

Steven nodded, fighting his chattering teeth.

"When you ram him with the spear, try not to hit him in the gut. Ain't no use in trying to seriously hurt anybody, especially at your age. But...but you get that point razor-sharp; you hear me? And make it a long point so it'll have a chance to go in good and deep."

"Yes sir, I can do that. I know I can. That stick will be sharp. I'll guarantee that."

"Now…when that green hickory dries out a bit, you take some sandpaper and polish that point all around so it can't help but go into that man when he comes after your mama?" Marvin tilted his head forward and furrowed his brow. "Okay, boy, now this is the hard part."

Steven looked up, not understanding how anything could be harder than ramming a fella in the leg or in the ass with a sharp hickory stick without him seeing it coming.

"After you get the fella with that stick, this fella is going to be yelling and swatting at you; all the while, he's going to be trying to pull that stick out of his leg. Can you see how all this could happen?" Marvin asked, moving his hands in front of him to give emphasis to his question.

Steven nodded, smirking a little.

"Now this is what I want you to remember. After you ram him and you know that you got him good…run."

Steven winced, not liking that idea. He thought that he would need to get that fella away from Mama. Maybe he would sharpen two or three sticks so he could keep ramming the fella.

"Why would I run?" he asked.

"Because you ain't big enough to kill him, and you don't want to do that anyway. And because he's gonna be trying to get that stick out and come after you."

Steven still didn't like the plan, but Marvin seemed serious about it.

"Just run," he heard Marvin insisting. "The fella will be hurtin' bad enough that he'll leave your mama alone, and he's gonna want to break your neck. So you run next door and use Ms. Jackson's phone to call us. I promise that we'll be here lickety-split."

Steven shoved his hands deep in his pockets again. He released a heavy sigh, still not happy with the plan. He just didn't like the idea of leaving Mama to run next door and use the phone.

"You ain't trying to kill the man, son. Remember that," Marvin said. "You're just trying to help your mama and hurt this man enough that he's disabled until we can get here. Don't try to be no hero, boy.

Just help your mama and try to get to Mrs. Jackson's house. Don't matter what time of the day or night."

Steven bobbed his head. Dad kept the Christmas tree saw hanging in the car shed, and he knew where there was a stout hickory sapling. He'd sharpen it the saw first thing in the morning.

"Now I don't want you talking about this plan to nobody else. Do you understand?" Marvin asked.

Steven bobbed his head again.

"Good. Now let's use this long, silver flashlight and check up under the house one more time before we go back inside. There's a nasty cold out here tonight, and my knees were already hurting before the sheriff called me to come over here."

*****

Steven heard the door to the screened porch close behind him before the big man with a black scruff and the off-white suit pushed past, bumping him hard enough that he had to catch the wall to avoid falling. He reminded Steven of an immovable mountain as he stood, feet apart, staring down at Marvin and Sheriff Olin with a sour face.

Marvin spun toward him. "Dillard, what are you doing out this time of night?"

"Just passing by," Dillard Wilson said. "Saw the cars and thought I'd see what's going on."

Marvin cocked his head and squinted. "Jason passed about an hour ago. The coroner's on his way," he said.

"Humph," Dillard muttered. "Thought it might be something like that."

Dillard shoved his hands in his suit pockets, the sweet, sickly smell of spilled whiskey permeating the air around him. Steven saw the bulge of a flask in one of the coat pockets and understood. Dillard had money and two sons, but lived alone after the divorce.

"It happens, I guess," Dillard said as he looked to the ceiling, then let his eyes rove slowly around the room before glancing to the floor. "Need anything?"

"Nahh," Marvin said. "Routine stuff now."

"Okay. Now I remember this house. Decent little rent house when I had it," he added as he strode back through the bedroom door, bumping Steven a second time. "Be seeing you, Marvin," Steven heard him say when he'd passed.

"You driving tonight, Dillard?" Marvin asked.

"Of course. What else would I be doing?"

"How about I drive you home?"

"Ain't no use in that, Marvin. I just had a child's portion. I'm fine."

"It's Christmas, Dillard. I'm coming with you. You can get yourself killed some other day, but not on Christmas. Just sit tight; I'm coming."

"Marvin, you ain't driving me home. That just ain't in the cards."

"Yeah, I am, Dillard. It don't matter what you want. It only matters that you don't have trouble on my watch," Marvin said.

"Marvin, I ain't ready to go home. I just come by here to see what's going on. Now, leave me alone."

"Dillard…you're going right now, and you're going in my squad car. I'm through talking about it," he said, patting the blackjack strapped to his side.

Dillard gave him an eye roll then took a step toward the front door.

Marvin stood and looked to Olin, who nodded his approval.

"Go quick," Olin told him.

"Uncle Eugene will leave you some sandpaper when he comes to fix the lock in the morning," Marvin said to Steven as he started toward the front door to catch up with Dillard.

*****

Standing in the kitchen, Steven saw that the door closed fine, but Marvin was right; it wasn't secure, and he made a mental note to put a chair under the knob when everybody left. When Marvin and Dillard were gone, Steven stumbled into his room and sat on the corner of the bed. The heater blasted warmth in the family room, and for once, it was almost warm in his tiny area, though the small lamp in the corner did little to brighten the room that still had the re-assembled Snack Jack plane sitting in the window sill.

Dad leaving so early was the surprise. Steven believed that they would wait until he was older and worn down with work and struggle before they came after him, but it obviously didn't go that way. He let out a deep sigh as he tightened his lips and pulled them inward. They'd come after him when he was barely six years old. Not even Brother Joseph warned him that it could happen that early, and he wasn't prepared. *Neither was Mama*, he thought as the warmth from the heater sent ten thousand needles pricking the cold numbness away. Slowly. Worse, he hadn't expected that anyone else would get hurt because of him.

Steven stared at the bedroom floor trying to consider what they might do to wear him down more. Would they go come for Mama too and leave him without any family support? Would they disable him and make him soft physically? Would they make him and Mama so poor that they became ineffective beggars? He shook his head hard like a dog trying to dry itself. He needed time to clear the brain fog. He swallowed, then let out a deep sigh. What if they were all right? Uncle Melvin, the Council, Brother Joseph—they all warned him that it would be a hard life. What if he lived his years constantly fighting the bad guys and never got any peace? What if he died alone…and never found Sarah?

Why didn't he listen to them? Why didn't he understand that terrible things could happen to him or any of his friends and family? He grimaced, silently chastising himself for being so stubborn. If he had listened and accepted, maybe Mom and Dad could have had a normal kid and lived together for full lifetime. But now Dad was dead and Deputy Marvin was trying to teach him how to poke a man in the ass with a sharp stick if he came after Mama.

He released a deep breath and leaned forward with his elbows on his knees. His breathing seemed shallow, and he tried to swallow again. Tears were finally ebbing in the corners of his eyes.

"I just didn't understand," he muttered, barely above a whisper as he clenched his fists before catching a glimpse of the broken plane in the window sill.

"Stupid Snack Jack kids," he said, standing to sweep the plane to the floor with a full roundhouse blow. "Bet none of you lost your dad on Christmas morning."

Steven slammed his fist to the bed telling himself that it just wasn't fair, that they had to give him a chance. It was too soon. His two front teeth still hadn't started to come back in. "Why?" he muttered. "Why?"

"Because you wanted to come here just like every other human," he heard Laura say without another audible sound being uttered. "You pled for a human life. Almost begged for it. Argued before Abraham himself that a stone could be used for a weapon or a protecting wall; that it could make you wealthy or it could build a road. But it couldn't give or receive love. That was your argument. You needed a balanced love, like you once had. You were dynamic and convincing with the Council, even though some still cast their votes against you."

Steven nodded. He hadn't remembered all of that until she said it.

"You won't win at life as a human, Steven. It doesn't work that way. Nobody wins at life as a human. You're not here for yourself, and you should know that by now. You have a mission, a purpose, and we hope that you'll come back better equipped to work in the more complicated world of the heavens. Not a better human, but a better person. Do you understand that difference, Steven?" she asked.

Steven was tired of folks asking him if he understood, but nodded. It still hurt. And it still wasn't fair that the powers of the heavens allowed Dad to be taken and start punishing him so soon.

Laura paused, hesitating, and took a deep breath. "But…when you get near the end of this, you'll know what kind of life that you've lived. You'll know that long before you reach your next Council. Everyone who has eyes to see himself understands this about himself."

Steven looked down, seeing the plane in pieces. He pushed his hair back as he turned toward Laura. "How do they know?" he asked just louder than a whisper. "Those that would do me harm. How do they know who I am and where I am? I'm just a snaggle-toothed kid. I'm a nobody here. How do they know…and why would they care about me?"

"They can see who you really are, your soul, even when you can't see the same. It's stamped on you…almost like a license plate. They started tracking you as soon as you and I left Uncle Melvin and Brother Joseph to come here."

Steven bit his lower lip briefly and nodded before he looked down again. "All this trouble just for me?" he asked. "Dad dies early. Mama is in for a bad time. All because of me?"

"A Level Three attracts plenty of attention as a human. They'll work hard. Very hard," she said, pausing. "You should expect that."

Steven looked up. She hovered somewhere above like guardian angels tend to do. He could barely hear her.

"Nobody on our side wants you to struggle, Steven," he heard her say. "Nobody. But everybody on their side wants you to curse God and give up," she said as her image dimmed further. "Do this right, Steven. Don't let them ruin you. You have much to do, both here and in the heavens."

Steven took another deep breath and let it go quickly as he looked down to the floor, still sitting on the corner of the bed.

"Remember what I've said tonight, Steven," he heard her saying. "I won't see you again for a very long time."

"Laura," he said quickly, hoping to catch her.

She stopped somewhere above, but he couldn't see her when he looked up.

"Have you…have you always been with me?" he asked.

Her slight smile tightened as she paused. "Yes," she finally said. "Yes… I have, even though you didn't know it."

Steven barely breathed, hoping that she would tell him more.

"It's not me that you're looking for, Steven. We've been close for a very long time, but I'm not the one…" she added. "Her name now…is Erin, and I understand why she would be important to you."

Steven swallowed hard. At least he had a name. Not that he could do anything about it. It bothered him that he couldn't remember anything about her beyond the absolute joy of their balanced love, and that she'd been taken from him too soon, just like Dad.

41

Steven let his eyes fall to the floor. "Erin," he whispered. "But I'm just a *nothing* kid." He shuddered as though a blast of cold air had swept through.

"Don't let them beat you down, Steven. You have a very difficult mission," he heard her say. "And if you fail, someone else will have to come in your place to do the same."

Steven sat still on the corner of the bed, dumbstruck, paradoxically sad and simultaneously shaking with joy. "Erin," he mumbled as he sat mindlessly staring at the floor. "Erin."

6
CHAPTER

Uncle Eugene came the next day and fixed the back door just as Marvin promised. Steven didn't think that he was really anybody's uncle, but everyone seemed to call him that. Even Karl, the butcher, called him Uncle Eugene. The locks were both strong now, and within a week his three hickory spears stood in the corner of his bedroom. Despite all, he still shoved a chair under both doorknobs every night before they went to bed.

Steven thought that Mama held it together well after the funeral. She went back to work the next day, and for a time all those ladies from the Methodist church came to the house to visit, especially on the weekends. That seemed to cheer her up some, but in time, the visits became less frequent. He knew that she still didn't have any close friends and worried about her.

He didn't like leaving Martha when he went to school every day. Once she was at the bank, it didn't bother him so much. She took her lunch and didn't have to go outside during the day. When the weather was really bad, she would drive their '47 Chevy to work. Mama told him that she had budgeted for a tank of gas once every three months and that they had to watch how much they used the car. Normally, she walked to the bank and seemed to be cheerful about it. Steven wanted to walk with her and take one of the spears along, but Mama would have none of it.

Martha kept a black notebook in the drawer of the little table where their party-line phone now sat. Steven knew that she worked on their money things there and that she made her notes in that little book. He wanted to get it when she wasn't home so he could know where they stood but thought better of it. That was Mama's private notebook, and he was afraid that bad things would happen if he invaded her space.

Karl had pushed Mr. Wilson to let Steven work at the grocery store every evening and all day on Saturday. He took out the trash, then swept the floors before breaking down the boxes out in the alley. After that, he used the water hose to wash all the blood and meat shreds to the sewer grate. It didn't pay much, and it was a nasty job, but he averaged almost three dollars a week, which was enough to pay for gas in the car when they had to use it and the propane that heated the house in winter.

In late November, just after Thanksgiving Steven walked up and down the hills of Richland to get home in the evening. The blistering July heat and the blue cold that arrived with the winter rains broke the sidewalks into odd-shaped pieces. Steven stumbled twice in the dark as he went as fast as he could, still trying to avoid the bad luck that would surely come if he stepped on a crack. He huddled within his jacket and gritted his teeth as the north wind sliced him again and again. Mr. Wilson had kept him at the store late on that Tuesday evening to mop the floors. He didn't mind the extra work and knew that he'd get paid a little extra. Mr. Wilson was always fair about that. As he turned left off of Elm on to their street, he thought that Mama might have the big gas heater blazing when he got home.

"Dinner in twenty minutes," he heard her say when he closed the door behind him and stood in front of the heater to take some of the chill away.

"Okay. I may need to go outside for a few minutes anyway," Steven said.

"Tonight? Again?"

"I won't be long, Mama," he said, grabbing the leather sack from between his mattresses. "Just a few things to check in the car shed."

Martha, standing in front of the gas stove and still dressed in her hunter green suit that she'd worn to the bank, turned quickly as Steven strode through the front door and on to the porch. She stared at the closing door, tensing her jaws. "Why won't he tell me what he's really doing?" she muttered aloud to no one as she continued to stand, hands-on-hips, and stare.

Steven closed his eyes, allowing them to adjust to the dark after he crossed the street and got well beyond the reach of the meager street-lamps. He thought it would be easy tonight; there was a strong wind and it was late in the season. Thinking that he could fill the bag in less than ten minutes, he managed a tight-lipped smile. Big Henry and Mr. Henry Watson would never know he was there. Just to be sure, though, he stood still with his back against the trunk of the first pecan tree for a full minute, watching their house.

Steven imagined them sitting in front of the den fireplace playing dominoes and having a good time, but he was always careful to hug the tree trunk and watch until he was certain that he was the only one in the grove.

The key to gathering pecans without getting caught was to crawl on all fours. He could find them easier in the thick grass like that, and those that he missed with his eyes would often be felt as lumps beneath his hands and knees. Every night he systematically worked a new tree, always avoiding the few trees closest to the house. Mrs. Watson sent the yardman out in the mornings to gather pecans for them. Steven didn't want him to see body trails in the grass and get suspicious. The yardman rarely needed to go beyond those first few trees to fill his five-gallon bucket.

Steven's sack was almost loaded when he saw the flashlight beam shoot from the back door of the Watson house.

"Who's there?" he heard Henry Watson Sr. yell.

Steven flattened on the cold ground and didn't move, thankful that the moon was early in the first quarter and that it was a cloudy night.

"Ain't nobody out here, Papa," Steven heard Big Henry say.

"I'm as sure of it as a man can be. I heard Jake bark, and he don't bark unless there's something going on."

Steven considered crawling on his belly back toward the hill and away from the house like he'd seen the soldiers do in the World War II picture shows. He didn't like the idea of crawling backward, and he was a good fifty yards from the back door where Big Henry and his daddy stood. They couldn't see him with that flashlight beam unless he stood up or they came closer. Steven didn't think that they would come into the trees to look. It was already cold, and they'd have to get out in the icy wind to do that.

"Jake's in front of the house, Papa. He ain't back here," Big Henry said.

"I just got a feeling, boy. Something's going on back here."

"Papa, it's cold out here. Maybe I should go get Jake and bring him around here. You and me don't need to go stumbling around in the dark on a night like this."

Henry Watson Sr. turned his head slowly looking down to his son. "Now that's a good idea, boy. A real good idea," he added as he furrowed his brow.

"You can go back inside by the fire, Papa. I'll go around the house and get Jake."

Henry Sr. let the screen door with the long spring slam and double-locked the wooden door behind him as Big Henry started for the corner of the house.

Steven didn't move. Without warning, Big Henry stopped and turned toward the grove, moving the light from side to side as he stared into the pecan trees.

"I know you're out there," Big Henry said, the anger rising in his voice. "And by God when I catch you, I'm gonna beat your ever lovin' face to a pulp. You don't steal from no Watson and get away with it. Do you hear me? I'm gonna beat your face in the ground! One day. Soon! You just wait."

Steven chuckled to himself as Big Henry headed for the front door, stepping fast. The wind was cold and Jake was nowhere around, having long since returned to his doghouse, nestling in the very back on the old quilts. Big Henry called the pup, then leaned down and shined the light in the oversized structure but still couldn't get Jake to come out. Seconds later, he opened the front door hurrying inside where he lied to Papa, saying that he and Jake searched the pecan trees but didn't find anything.

Steven lay still for another three minutes, then finished filling his sack and sneaked back across the road to the car shed where he kept his stash in a big wooden storage box that he'd made from old apple crate boards. It was a heavy box that he secured with a combination lock, and he was the only one who could open it.

By the time he made it back inside, Mama was taking the baked potatoes out of the oven and unwrapping the aluminum foil. He didn't want her to see the grass stains and wet spots on his jeans. Steven sat on the end of the sofa and tuned the cabinet radio to a rock and roll station that he played softly, hoping not to upset her with the new style of music.

7

CHAPTER

1962

Steven cracked and shelled pecans, then filled small paper sacks with the clean halves on Sunday afternoons when he didn't go to the picture show to see the World War II films. Sheriff Olin sold the bags that Steven provided as a benefit for the deputies' retirement fund. Most people would pay a higher-than-normal price for shelled pecans that they didn't have to crack and clean themselves, and the idea of contributing to deputies who were paid meager wages appealed. Steven was almost certain that Mama didn't know about his pecan sales and even more certain that she didn't know that Olin split the money fifty-fifty between him and the deputies' fund.

Steven cut his eyes to the hollow spot behind the loose baseboard hidden by the edge of his bed and released a slow breath that was a precursor to a faint-but-brief smile. From the years of working for Wilson's Grocery, cleaning up at the Pontiac dealership, and pecan sales, he had a large sum of cash in his hideout. The money gave him a sense of security, the antithesis of fear and condescension that he'd fought since the night Dad died. Big Henry didn't have money like that. He was sure of it. Big Henry didn't have a job, nor was he interested in one. He just went to his dad's insurance office after school and did his homework before riding home with Papa for dinner and television. His schedule was full, and he didn't have time to work. Steven allowed himself a slight smirk when Sheriff Olin told him that Mrs. Watson bought out all of their stock for the pecan pies that she made at Thanksgiving and that Big Henry had carried the quart bags to the car for her. Later, deep in the night before he slept beneath the hand-sewn quilts, he convinced himself that none of the Snack Jack kids would have as much money as he did. They were too much like Big Henry.

*****

Steven kept a special box of pecans in the back corner of the car shed. It was smaller than the wooden box with the combination lock and filled with pecans that had particularly sharp tips. He didn't sell these to the sheriff. Even though they wobbled too much and sometimes missed their targets, these were his slingshot pecans.

As he lay in bed, sleepless and frustrated, Steven saw the reassembled Snack Jack airplane in the windowsill, and the idea came to him like a comet zipping through the heavens. The following afternoon he hustled to finish his assignments at Wilson's Grocery then rushed home, making it to the car shed thirty minutes ahead of his normal. Using a rough file from his dad's rusted toolbox, he shaped the edges of three pecans, making them more aerodynamic like the wings of a plane, but each time the delicate wings broke just from handling.

Hiding behind the old '47 Chevy where no one could see him from the street, he worked deep into the gray minutes of the evening. He'd broken through the shells of five pecans before he had one with wings that remained whole. Steven stood still, rolling the pecan across his fingertips, thinking that it probably wouldn't fly. He didn't like the way the wings extended, and the point where the shell joined the body of the nut was too thin. Briefly, he considered not trying the pecan at all, then changed his mind and put the file back in the toolbox and rushed toward the grove just before the dark swallowed him.

He spread his feet and tightened his leg muscles before taking careful aim at the trunk of the closest tree about twenty-five yards away, then held his breath and released the stretched slingshot smoothly, missing the trunk by three feet to the left. Without hesitation, he took a small rock from his pocket and let it fly. Splat. It hit dead center.

It was completely dark by the time he reached the shallow ditch between the pecan lot and his house, but he was satisfied that he now knew what to do, and at least the slingshot was still accurate. Three afternoons later he had one pecan that he thought might be in just the right configuration.

Again, just before dark when he was certain that Big Henry and Mr. Watson weren't home, he slipped into the orchard, braced himself, and fired again. Splat. Dead center. Same tree. Same distance.

Steven walked slowly toward the tree taking measured steps and counting the paces to be sure of the distance. His eyes tensed and his locked jaws showed no sign of joy nor triumph, just the tight lips and the unmistakable intensity of eyes that narrowed and penetrated. Even though the sharpened edges had broken into shards just as he thought they would, several of them impaled themselves into the tree trunk itself. At that moment, the skinny kid with a buzz haircut knew he no longer needed Marvin's spears. He was beyond that now, and without hurrying he turned and made his way back to the car shed. Four days later, he had a sack with the special pecans and his slingshot under his bed, convinced that he was ready now, not that he knew what he needed to be ready for.

*****

Big Henry's uncle, Dillard Wilson stole his start-up money from his brother when their father died, having falsified the Will, forging the necessary signatures, and pushing it through Probate before any of the other siblings knew what he'd done.

Dillard stood six foot one and weighed almost three hundred pounds. Steven had never seen him without his trademark beige suit and skinny black tie, even in the dead of winter. With thinning, slick-backed black hair, oily skin, and his tan-and-white wing tips, Dillard was an imposing fifty-year-old that made Steven uneasy.

Dillard didn't own any portion of the grocery store. His brother, Sam Wilson built that business and owned it outright, though Dillard sued him and tried to take the business in a three-year legal debacle. Karl told Steven that Mr. Sam Wilson was an okay boss, even though he didn't go to the Methodist church on Sundays and he seemed a little out of touch with the customers that came in daily. A goody-two-shoes numbers type Karl had called him, but still okay.

Steven and Karl sat on the concrete back step that led to the alley taking a break late one October afternoon when Dillard drove by on Richland's main street.

"And there goes a mean man," Karl said, pointing. "One of our truly nasty rich folks."

Karl rubbed his hand on his blood-smeared butcher's apron, then spat a glob of sinus congestion to the side. "I licked him three times when we was boys coming up, and he ain't never forgot that. Hates me to this day."

Steven twisted toward him, probing with his eyes as Karl sat with his elbows on his knees, looking straight ahead. "Why'd you fight with him?" Steven asked.

"The first time, he was messing with this little fella in our class at recess. He rammed him from behind knocking him down, then jumped on top of him and slammed his head into the ground. Broke the little fella's glasses. Messed up the kid's nose." Karl gazed down the alley, looking away from Steven. "The little fella was a nice kid. Smart kid. Lived down the road from us. Minded his own business and didn't bother nobody. Dillard was just a fat-ass town boy with a mean streak. And his daddy had money, so he thought he could do whatever he wanted."

"Did you whip him good?" Steven asked.

"Not good enough, I guess...not that day." Karl rubbed his hand across his three-day beard, then wiped his runny nose on his bare forearm as he continued to stare down the alley and across the street to the Baptist church. "Oh, he was beat-up some. Busted his nose. Knocked one tooth out. Made him eat the dirt where the little fella had left blood behind."

Steven just looked at Karl. He'd heard plenty of Karl stories from the mechanics at the Pontiac shop where he swept up three days a week.

"Dillard came back at me two days later when I was walking down the dirt road to our house. Had a couple of other town boys with him. They was all lard asses that thought they knew something about fighting," he said with a solemn voice, just loud enough for Steven to hear. He paused, looking down again. Steven knew that Karl didn't like to talk about fighting; he'd spent too much time north of the thirty-eighth parallel ten years prior.

"So what happened?" Steven asked when Karl didn't volunteer anything more. "I mean...it was three against one."

Karl nodded, wrinkling the skin on his clefted chin. "Yeah... it was. I shouldn't have done what I did, I guess, but I got mad." He released a deep breath and shook his head. "You know, with them riding up on me from behind on them fancy bicycles..." Karl turned to face Steven. "They worked me over pretty good right at first. Two of them was holding my arms back and pulling on me, trying to jerk my shoulders out of the sockets. Dillard was doing his best to pound me with his fists. It wasn't going very well, and we were a good two miles from the house. I couldn't run, and wasn't nobody coming to help."

Steven's green eyes fixed on Karl. He'd walked down that stretch of dirt road lots of times. One side was lined with pine trees, and the other side ran along a big hayfield that seemed to go on forever. There were only two houses on the road that looped around and eventually came out by the junkyard where everybody from town hauled their trash.

"So what'd you do?" Steven asked as Karl sat there on the step staring.

"Got lucky I guess," he said, taking a deep breath. "Them boys had a pretty good hold on my arms, but before they could pull me down, I landed a good solid kick to Dillard's jaw. I had on my steel-toed boots, so it sounded about like a high-powered rifle going off when his jaw broke. It kinda exploded, I guess. Blood come out of his mouth and nose like a water hose." He looked toward the church, thinking. "Made that white sand turn red. Dillard was out cold; his eyes rolled back. Thought I might have killed him at first, and the world would've probably been better off if I had," he added, "but he was still alive."

"The other two still had you by the arms?"

"Yeah, but Dillard's jaw cracked so loud it scared one of them enough that he let up on his grip and I slung him down in the ditch. Since I had my good arm free then, I reached around and caught that other one by the back of his hair and brought his head down pretty hard just as my knee reared up. That busted his face fairly good, and I flung him down in the ditch on top of the first one."

Steven sat still, almost afraid to talk. Karl went quiet again, and Steven swatted at the flies that swarmed him and the bloody meat boxes in the alley. He thought they were more aggressive than usual for October, and he stood up so he could swat them easier.

"So, was that it? Did you just leave them there and walk on home?" Steven asked.

Karl grimaced and turned his head away without answering. A few seconds passed before he turned back to Steven who was still swatting the flies. "Well... I was still pretty mad. Them boys in the ditch was squalling some, and there was a good bit of blood there too. I could see that Dillard was still breathing, so I stood over him for a bit; then I stomped his right arm and broke it pretty good," Karl said, pausing. "And then... I...uhmmm... I kicked his ribs in some."

"That was bad, Karl. You shouldn't have done that."

The big man shot him a cold stare, then shook his head a little.

"It was a different time back then, boy. We was all young. Your daddy, me, Jack Tatum, and the sheriff...none of us had been to war then. Just a different time, but yeah...that was pretty bad. Not that I regret it much. Anyway...after I busted Dillard's arm, the two in the ditch was scrambling to get away, trying to run on all fours at first. The last time I saw them, they was running toward town as fast as they could. After that, yeah... I just walked on home and told Papa about what happened."

"Did you get a whippin'?"

"Me? Nah. I think Papa was kinda happy that I come out okay when it was three on one like it was."

Steven chuckled under his breath. He had heard parts of that story when Dad and Mr. Tatum sat on the porch years ago, but now he had the whole thing. So Karl broke Dillard Wilson's jaw, arm, and ribs on an August afternoon then left him in the road to bleed out.

"I bet there was talk in town when everybody was sitting around in front of the picture show that night," Steven said.

"I wouldn't know about that. Getting to town was a long walk, and we didn't have no money for the picture shows anyway."

Karl heaved another snot glob on one of the boxes that Steven had cut up and stacked. "Anyway, boy, you stay clear of Dillard Wilson, do you hear me?"

"I will, Karl. I promise," Steven said, lying.

8
CHAPTER

Steven knew that Dillard Wilson held paper on their 1947 Chevy and that Mama was behind on the payments. He also owned the house that they rented. Steven overheard the barbershop fellas say that Dillard loaned money to people that were down on their luck at a high interest rate, then took the property away before they had time to recover and catch up on their notes. He and Mama had to have a car, even if it were old and the cloth seats smelled of rancid mildew. Despite Martha working at the bank, she and Dad couldn't qualify for a loan when they needed a car, and Dad borrowed the money from Dillard. Mama hadn't missed a payment until four months ago.

Big Henry had lunch with Dillard at The Big R Café and later told Steven that they didn't have to pay the bill because Dillard had an account, and that the folks who owned the Big R owed him money. Big Henry had called it an "interest lunch" and told Steven that he had two pieces of lemon meringue pie for dessert because of the interest that Dillard wasn't getting otherwise.

Steven saw Dillard riding through town almost every day in his shiny 1960 Fairlane 500 with the sleek fins on the back and the rolled chrome over the front panels, the emblem square in the middle of the hood up front. Dillard's car was a deep candy apple red with white trim and wide white-walled tires. Steven thought the car looked good, but he took notice when Dillard drove close to him, just as Karl advised, often repeating to himself that Dillard Wilson was a mean man.

*****

The December dark and cold engulfed Steven as he turned the corner and saw the Fairlane 500 parked in their driveway. He stopped cold, staring, hoping somehow that his vision was bad and maybe the car was really parked in the driveway beyond theirs. Steven tinkered within his mind, briefly debating with himself before starting to jog toward Mrs. Jackson's house where he pounded on the back screen door.

The gray-haired lady who always seemed to wear an apron was slow coming to the door. Torn between scrapping his plan and running straight to his house, Steven nearly bounced on the steps as he begged for Mama to hold on until he could get there.

"Why Steven," the squat lady said when she saw him.

"Mrs. Jackson, I need to use your phone right quick. Please. I need to make a call quick."

Mrs. Jackson's eyes widened as she unlocked the door and motioned him toward the phone that hung on the wall. The sheriff's night dispatcher answered his call and caught Marvin at the door as he was leaving at the end of his shift.

Marvin rubbed his jaw and didn't say much as he listened to Steven.

"Deputy Marvin, I don't have time to argue about this. Mama's in there with Dillard, and there ain't no telling what's going on in our house right now. I got to go. Please. Just be there. The corner of Elm and Prosper. Ten minutes, max. Please," Steven said as he hung up the phone and sprinted toward the car shed.

His heart raced as he fumbled with the lock in the dark. What if he were too late? Why didn't he come home sooner? He didn't have to linger, talking to Lawrence on the steps in front of the picture show. "Should've known better," he told himself.

He fumbled with the lock for what seemed like an eternity, finally getting it to open. He reached inside for the small box of tools that he'd inherited from his dad. It was black dark, and the streetlight was a good two hundred yards up the way as he shuffled through the tools hoping to find one small valve wrench that he'd gotten from his mechanic friends at the Pontiac dealership. His first try failed, and he considered turning on the car lights but thought that could foil the whole plan.

Steven ran his hand through the metal box a second time. Nothing.

It was there. He knew it was there. He'd seen it just a few days ago. Steven released a long breath, trying to calm himself before he very slowly fingered every tool until he found it snugged in the back corner of the box.

He slammed the lid down thinking that there was no time to put everything away now. Later, he promised himself as he started to run toward the fancy Fairlane.

The broad white wall tires caught a little light, and he found the first tire stem easily. Unscrewing the cap quickly, feeling his way, he slipped the slotted rod of the three-pronged tool into the top of the valve stem and turned it counterclockwise until he heard the air releasing at a good clip. Then he screwed the valve cap back on for just a couple of threads and repeated the process on the other three tires. Without thinking, he shoved the valve stem wrench in his pocket and raised the hood as quietly as possible. The fellas at the Pontiac shop were spot on. He jerked the coil wire from the Fairlane 500 and silently lowered the hood back in place. Just before beginning to run for the screen door that led to porch and the main sitting room, Steven opened the Fairlane's door and took the keys from the ignition.

Steven saw Dillard Wilson's tan-and-white wingtips under the kitchen table and his hand on the inside of Mama's thigh near the point where her stockings normally connected to the garter belt. It was after work and Steven knew that Mama took the stockings off as soon as she came in every evening. Steven thought his heart would pound out of his chest, and he considered going to his room to get the one spear that he'd kept after perfecting the pecans for the slingshot, then fought with himself over that idea, and walked as slowly as he could toward the kitchen table.

"Oh, Steven," he heard Mama say as Dillard jerked his hand back and turned around. "You're late tonight."

"Yes, ma'am, I'm sorry. I stopped to talk to some fellas down in front of the picture show."

Wilson's hand was on top of the table now. Steven couldn't imagine how the big greaser could think that he wouldn't get caught groping Mama. Catching Dillard in the act made Steven feel better about his plan. Still, deep within, it bothered him.

He walked past the fold-down kitchen table and stood behind Mama, staring at Dillard, wondering which arm Karl had broken.

"Steven, Mr. Wilson is here to talk about the car," he heard Mama say. "You know we're a little behind on the notes, and he came tonight to offer a little arrangement that might get us by."

"What type of arrangement, Mama?"

"Well…we don't have to talk about that right now. You and I can discuss that later."

Steven's eyes cut toward the wall when he saw something shiny beside Mama's leg. He smiled to himself. She had the sixteen-inch butcher knife tucked in the fold of her skirt.

"Okay Mama," he said pausing as he lowered his chin and began to breathe deeper and faster.

Wilson pushed the rickety chair back and leaned on the small table to help him lift his weight. "I guess I should be going now," he said as he wrinkled his brow and looked down on Martha.

"That's probably a good idea," Mama agreed.

Wilson turned without speaking to Steven and started for the door that led to the front porch.

Steven let him take three steps before he spoke. "So… Mr. Wilson, how much money do we owe you on the car?" he asked in a firm, deep voice that got Wilson's attention.

"Well, boy," the big man said as he turned back, "I don't think that's any of your business. That's between your mama and me."

Steven flipped open his Uncle Henry knife and began to fiddle with the blade as Wilson reached for the doorknob. "How much… do we owe on the car?" he asked again in a demanding, even deeper voice that stopped Wilson.

Dillard Wilson heard metal click of the knife blade locking in position, but he couldn't imagine that it would be the skinny kid in overalls. He released a slow breath as his face reddened and turned back to the table once again. Steven flashed his Uncle Henry blade, and Wilson stood still, staring with one hand dangling by his side and the other resting on the back of the sofa.

"Boy, you ain't threatening me with that knife, now are you? That wouldn't be smart on your part 'cause I believe I could snap your neck with one good twist."

Steven didn't flinch and was even further convinced that his plan was justified. "No sir," he said, pausing. "I wouldn't do that. Not at all." Steven looked away from Dillard toward the windows, then turned back with a bland, emotionless stare. "If I'd wanted to kill you, your throat would already be slit, and there'd be blood all over Mama's rug right now," he said in a matter-of-fact tone.

"Humph…" Dillard snorted. "Well, I suppose you are your daddy's boy."

"That I am, sir," Steven snapped. "You can bet your last dollar on that." Steven locked eyes with Dillard. "Now…how much do we owe on that sorry old car?"

"It's not that much, boy, but it's more than your mama's got right now."

"How much…do we owe?" Steven demanded, without blinking, still staring right into the big man's eyes.

Wilson ground his teeth. "Look here, boy, there's no purpose in any further discussion tonight. I'll just have Charlie come with the tow truck in the morning and get the car."

He was about to turn to the door again when he saw Steven reach in his overalls pocket. Wilson cut his eyes back in time to see Steven pull the coil wire out and lay it on the kitchen table.

"Now… Mr. Wilson," Steven said without any waver in his voice, "this coil wire was specked for your 1960 Fairlane 500. It's a specific length and one of a kind. The center carbon wire in the middle of that rubber coating was designed to carry a certain number of electrical pulses every second. If you get a coil wire that's too long, it won't work. Your timing will be off. If you get one that's too short, it won't work either. If you get one that's the right length but has a different diameter, it won't work neither."

Wilson's face went slack as he stared at Steven and the coil wire. "Boy…you mess with my car and I'm gonna beat you in the ground out behind this here house. Do you understand me, boy?"

Steven didn't flinch. "There's not another coil wire exactly like this one in Richland, Texas, sir. If something were to go wrong with this coil wire, your car is going to sit in our driveway for about three days until one can get here on the Greyhound from Dallas," Steven said quietly. "And what would folks say about that pretty car of yours sitting in our driveway all that time? Why it could actually be five or six days if Alf is a little slow ordering the new wire and the bus gets delayed by the holiday season."

Martha slowly turned her head toward Steven, looking up to him as he stood behind her shoulder still holding the knife.

"Now this knife, Mr. Wilson… I want you to know that I work on this knife almost every night. Sir, not only will it shave but it will glide right through the hair on your arm cutting them off perfectly smooth and gathering little bits of skin with every stroke. This knife, sir, will shorten any argument with a very simple flick."

Wilson took in a deep breath. "Boy, this is beyond ridiculous. If you damage my car or try to hold me hostage, I'll have the sheriff put you in jail, even if you are just a kid."

Wilson took a lunging step toward the table, and Steven swooped up the coil wire with his left hand, caught a loop in it and slid the knife blade in place to cut it in half.

At fifty, Dillard Wilson's reaction time was a half-second slow, and he stumbled as he reached for the wire, falling to his knees as his girth drew him down.

Steven stared in silence as Wilson caught himself and looked up to Mama and him, neither of whom had broken their stares. He closed his eyes briefly and looked down to the wooden floor simply shaking his head.

"I can see that you'd now like to have a business discussion about this matter, Mr. Wilson," Steven said, still calm, almost placid in tone and disposition. "If you can manage it, sir, you can return to your chair now, so long as you keep both hands on that tabletop."

"Boy," Wilson shouted, "you'll never work in this county again. Do you hear me, boy? Never!"

Steven stared in silence as Wilson struggled to his feet and pulled the wicker straight-backed chair toward him. "That's really not a very good negotiating position, Mr. Wilson," Steven said, continuing in that monotone.

Strangely, in the midst this critical moment, Steven thought about Karl, standing over a semiconscious Wilson who lay in the red dusty road over thirty years prior. He understood now, almost smiling as he stared at the repulsive human that sat in front of him.

"Not a very good negotiating position, at all, sir."

"Mrs. Heard... Mrs. Heard, can I—I—I have a conversation with you?"

Steven began to slide the knife back and forth against the outer rubber coating of the coil wire.

"Boy! Don't do that. Don't do that. Do you hear me? Boy!"

"Dillard," Mama said in a steady, smooth voice before she paused. "Dillard, you've been taking advantage of folks in this county for a long time now. A very long time. But tonight is your lucky night. Maybe the luckiest night ever for you."

Dillard Wilson looked from Steven to Martha then back to Steven. "Who do you people think you are? You're nothing but renters that owe me money. You can't threaten me!"

Dillard cut his eyes toward Martha again. The shine on his forehead brightened as beads of sweat blended with the oil of his skin. A long strand of greasy dyed black hair dangled from one side of his comb-over.

"You see, Dillard," Mama continued, "if Steven hadn't come home just when he did, you'd likely be facing the Almighty right now," she said, pulling the three-inch-wide-by-sixteen-inch-long butcher knife from the fold of her skirt, holding it by the wooden handle in an overhead stabbing position. "Maybe even worse... maybe you'd be trying to get by Jason Heard before you had an audience with the Almighty. And you just think that it was bad when Karl broke you up when you were boys," she added, letting her last words trail.

Steven saw Dillard shift his bottom in the chair as the red hue of his face deepened. He thought that Karl was right, of course; Dillard was indeed a bad man, but mostly, he was a bully that had become a small-time criminal, skirting the edge of the law with his wealth and influence.

Steven already knew that there were six remaining payments on the car, but he needed Dillard to speak to that.

Martha swallowed hard, then gritted her teeth. "It is your lucky night indeed, Dillard…for now. But it's not like the night you planned it to be. If I were you, I'd try to make a deal with Steven as fast as I could."

Dillard looked from one to the other again, then let his head droop. "This ain't right," he said. "You owe the money." He ground his jaw teeth as he looked up, but Steven cut him off before he could speak.

"One more time, Mr. Wilson," Steven began, letting the anger build in his tone, "how much do we owe?"

"You're six months behind, and it pays out in one month after that," Wilson said, trying to get the words out as fast as he could before he cut his eyes to the big knife that Martha held.

Steven just stared at Wilson, holding his face frozen and emotionless. "How many dollars is that, Mr. Wilson?" he asked. "Dollars."

"It would be ninety dollars, boy, plus fifteen dollars for the pay-out month."

Steven nodded, still staring in silence. The blundering giant had no idea how much money that he actually had to spend, and he who speaks first in a price negotiation almost always loses.

"Is that your best price?" Steven asked, still without emotion as he stroked the coil wire with the dull side of his Uncle Henry blade.

"Well…well if you paid all of it tonight—which I know ain't possible," he added faking a laugh, "maybe then we could consider a little reduction. Maybe a…a…a five-dollar reduction." Dillard rolled his lower lip up and clamped it lightly between his false teeth.

Steven just stood there, saying nothing for over thirty seconds building tension.

"Well... I can see, Mr. Wilson, that you're not really interested in negotiating," Steven said, nodding to himself but never breaking eye contact with the big man. "That's too bad," he added, "not only is your car not going to run for five or six days, but everybody in the county is going to know that you came here tonight to take advantage of my mother...a widow just trying to earn a living and take care of her family."

Steven clinched his jaws and slipped his left hand up on the coil wire, pretending to tighten his grip as he readied to make the cut. "It doesn't look good for you at all, Mr. Wilson. In fact, it looks like you've made serious errors in judgment tonight. Serious errors. Texas folks won't take kindly to the way you've conducted yourself here tonight, and it seems to me that you're in a bad spot. I suspect that the consequences of your decisions are gonna be pretty bad either way you go with this thing."

Steven flipped the knife blade effortlessly and shoved it through the loop, ready to cut.

"Just...just...just a minute, boy. Just a minute now." Wilson cocked his head to the side and shot Steven a sideways look. "I could take seventy dollars and be happy. I guess I would take seventy. Tonight," he said looking away. "But I know you ain't got that kind of money."

Steven let his eyes drift to the ceiling, wrinkling his chin. He let at least fifteen seconds pass in silence.

"How 'bout it, boy? You got the seventy dollars? Here? Right now? Tonight?" Wilson asked in a guttural, slobbering voice, running the questions all together. "We can settle this thing right now if you got the money."

Steven turned on him suddenly. He now knew how Karl felt when he decided to crush Dillard's arm...just because he could...and because Dillard deserved it.

"Mr. Dillard, you've sure disappointed us here tonight. You're supposed to be smarter than this, and you're just not putting all your cards on the table. I've about had enough of you, and you might as well start walking back toward town right now."

Steven knew Marvin would have had enough time to get in position at the corner of Elm and Prosper by then. "I suspect that Sheriff Olin will give you a ride on to the county jail after we give him a call. He'll likely want to talk about your behavior with Mama tonight. Threatening a widow like that. It don't look good for you, Mr. Dillard."

"Boy! Puke on you, boy! Who do you think you are? You ain't nothin' to me. Nothin'." The sweat was heavier on Wilson's big head now, especially where his hair had receded.

Steven turned to the side, almost ignoring Wilson's tirade.

"What do you want, boy? I made you a helluva good price and you know it."

Steven spun around so quickly that Wilson lurched backward in the chair stopping himself from falling at the last moment. Confused, Wilson froze, wide-eyed as Steven grabbed his right ear and stretched it away from his head. Slowly, Wilson turned his eyes to Steven who stood over him with the Uncle Henry in his right hand and holding his ear in the middle of a fisted left hand.

Steven stared down on the suited predator for long seconds, then nodded his head ever so slightly. "Less than a second," he said barely above a whisper as he cinched on the ear even tighter.

Wilson's brow furrowed, and he began to stutter.

"That's how long it will take me to slice this ear off. Less than a second."

Wilson tried to pull away, but Steven had a tight grip, and Dillard settled himself.

"Pay me fifty dollars, boy. Tonight. Now and let's be done with this. I'll still make a little money on the deal, and you and your mama will have your car all clear. All clear," he repeated, without ever having the intention of letting that happen.

"I'll hold out another five dollars for the trouble I'm gonna have re-installing that coil wire that I found on the ground outside," Steven said, still holding the ear. "I'll pay you forty-five dollars tonight."

Wilson nodded his agreement as best he could with Steven still gripping his ear.

"Now, you sit up straight, sir, and put your hands back on the table, just like you started out."

Wilson complied, looking again from Martha back to Steven.

"Mama," Steven said, "take that big knife with both hands and hold the tip about a half inch over Mr. Wilson's knuckles. If he moves at all when I go to get his money, even if it's just one little fraction of an inch, you slam that knife down as hard as you can and nail that hand to the table."

"I can do that," Martha said. "I can do that very well."

Less than a minute later, Steven returned with forty-five dollars, two sheets of paper, and a pencil.

"Mr. Wilson, sir, before I give you any money, you take this pencil in your right hand and write out a receipt made to Mrs. Martha Heard for having received it. And make sure that you date it and sign it. I'll witness it a little later on."

Wilson swallowed hard and let out a disgusted breath as he took the pencil and began to write, stopping to glance at Martha still holding the butcher knife over his left hand.

Steven gritted his teeth as he watched Wilson write, thinking that Marvin would definitely be in place now and the tires ought to be about right.

"There! Now leave me alone," Wilson said, shoving the paper over to Steven who didn't budge.

"Mama, don't let that hand move, you hear me?"

"I've got it, Steven. You shouldn't worry about that at all."

Steven glanced at the receipt, then shoved the second piece of paper toward Wilson.

"What's that for, boy? You got your bloody receipt."

Steven half rolled his eyes. "Now write out a full Bill of Sale for the car. Date it and sign it."

Wilson turned his head up to glare at Steven, hate brimming in his eyes as he moistened his lips lightly, then turned his head to the side, then began to write again.

Steven took the Bill of Sale and handed it to Martha, then gave Wilson his forty-five dollars.

"You can draw that butcher knife back now, Mama," she heard Steven saying. "Mr. Wilson and I are going to walk outside. He'll be leaving us alone now."

The screen door slammed behind them, and Steven felt the rush of the December cold at the same time he smelled the smut that spouted from the paper mill fifteen miles to the south. He had never been so happy to be out in the night air that smelled of sulfur or rotten eggs.

"Just sit in the driver's seat and wait a few minutes. There's not a key in the ignition," Steven said. "I found that on the ground too," he added, lying. "Not that your Fairlane is going to start without this coil wire anyway."

That was more than Wilson could stand, and he lunged at Steven, swinging his massive arm around to hit him on the left side of Steven's head. Steven didn't weigh a hundred pounds and was lean from his work and sports activities. He sidestepped the intended roundhouse blow and raised the hood just in time for the beefy hand to catch the front metal edge with full force. Steven heard bones crunching before Wilson jerked it back trying not to yell.

"I wish you hadn't done that, sir," he said. "Really do wish you hadn't done that. We made a deal fair and square. There wasn't any cause for violence."

Wilson grimaced showing his teeth as he tucked the left hand inside his suit coat, putting pressure on it under his right arm.

"No cause for violence at all, sir," Steven repeated without emotion.

Wilson just stood there gritting his teeth.

"Now you go sit in the car like I asked, and I'll install this coil wire that I found when I came in tonight," he said.

"Who are you, boy?" Wilson asked, suddenly somber.

Steven stared at him for a brief second before turning away. "Well, I work for your brother down at the grocery. And I sweep up the shop and offices for Mr. Earl down at the Pontiac place."

"Nah...no, no, no," Wilson protested. "That ain't what I mean and you know it."

Steven stared him down in the darkness. "Just a boy, I guess, sir. Thirteen years old now, but still just a boy."

"You ain't no boy, and we both know it. And your daddy wouldn't be proud of you at all right now. That is, if he had lived. Are you a Satan, boy? Is that it?"

Steven smiled, even though he knew that Wilson couldn't quite see him through his thick, sweated glasses. "Just go sit in the car like I asked, sir. When you're in there and the door is closed, I'll go under this hood and put your coil wire back in. I wouldn't want you to be tempted to slam that hood on my head when I was leaning in, so just sit inside and you can go home soon."

"You're just a Satan; that's all you are, boy. Just a pond scum Satan that needs killin'."

When Steven slammed the hood shut, he walked to the driver's side door where Wilson sat inside with the window down and his good hand extended, palm up. Steven dropped the button key chain with two keys in the beefy hand.

"This ain't over, boy. Do you understand me? This ain't near over. You can count on that."

As Dillard Wilson rammed the car in gear and lurched backward, Steven saw the tires. There couldn't have been more than five pounds of air in any of those wide white walls that now looked to have the thickness of bicycle tires.

"No sir," he said just above a whisper, "that's one thing you are right about. It's not nearly over. You shouldn't have messed with my mama. Now I'm about to get your ribs…just like Karl did, just like David did a long time ago."

9
CHAPTER

Steven didn't wait for the Fairlane to back out of the driveway before running toward the screened porch. By the time Dillard Wilson put the car in Drive, he was already inside, striding toward his bedroom.

"Steven," he heard Mama call as she came toward his bedroom door. "Steven, we need to talk. Now! I mean *right now!*"

Steven couldn't let the moment pass, telling himself that he had to crush the ribs...just because he could and because Dillard deserved it.

"Not now, Mama," he said, reaching under the bed for the slingshot sack with the twenty sharpened pecans. "I'm in a hurry. A real hurry."

"Steven! Now," Martha said, undeterred and demanding. "Where did you get all that money? Have you been stealing from Mr. Wilson's cash register?"

Steven could see Martha's face getting redder as she speculated, the intensity in her tone ratcheting up.

"Mama. Try to be calm, Mama. I know it's been a bad night, but just be calm. I haven't been stealing money from Mr. Wilson or anyone else. I promise you that."

Martha started to protest, but Steven hurried past her, rushing through the kitchen to get to the back door.

"Mama, I need fifteen minutes. That's all. Give me fifteen minutes and I'll be back and explain it all to you."

Martha let out a frustrated breath and lowered her eyes. "No more than that, Steven. You be back here in fifteen minutes."

Steven saw her standing in the kitchen as he lunged through the door and out into the cold.

"Mama, lock both doors and put chairs under both knobs," he said, turning back to her.

"Steven, where are you going this time of night? It's black dark out there. And cold!"

Steven didn't answer as he ran down the steps and started through Mrs. Jackson's backyard. He was almost out of time. Dillard should be there by now.

*****

Dillard stopped the Fairlane at the corner and sat still long enough to massage his hand and take stock of what had just happened. His windshield began to fog up, and he flipped on the defrost, then reached under the seat for a cloth and wiped the white layer away in his impatience. Seconds later, he reached down and took the silver flask from beneath the seat and guzzled Kentucky whiskey. As the thick liquid burned its way through him, he let his eyes close for a brief moment before he turned right on to Elm Street and headed for the heart of town. Three blocks further down, Dillard heard the screech of metal on concrete.

"Well, spit in the wind," he said aloud, shifting the car to neutral and pulling the brake handle. "I ain't never had a flat going through here."

He opened the Fairlane's door and swung his feet to the pavement but didn't stand. His back faced Steven, whose lungs still heaved as he hid just twenty yards away behind what was left of Mrs. Robertson's giant daylilies.

Marvin sat in the driver's seat of his squad car, parked halfway up the block on Prosper Street. There weren't any street lights on that section of Elm, and the sliver of a moon that still ambled in the clear night sky didn't provide enough light to expose Steven. Only the Fairlane's interior dome light shined, and it was no threat.

Dillard took out the metal flask and turned it straight up, taking big gulps as he sat sideways with his feet on the pavement.

"That little cuss!" Dillard yelled as he stood and put one foot in front of the other, starting to ease around the car with a flashlight to check the flat tires.

Without thinking, he slammed his knotted left fist on the roof of the Fairlane, then screamed in pain.

"Rot!" he shouted, wincing as he tucked the beefy hand back inside the armpit and bent forward, moaning. "Rot! Rot! Rot!"

Two steps later, he paused at the back of the car, holding on with his good hand that still held the flashlight.

"He ain't got no right to let the air out of them tires. No right at all," Dillard said to no one at all.

Dillard took two more steps down the passenger side before he stopped again.

Steven allowed himself a slight smile as he slipped the slingshot and a sharpened pecan from the canvas bag. He hardly breathed as he waited for Dillard to move toward the front tire. One step. Two steps. Then finally, three steps, just to be sure. Steven held his breath and pulled the slingshot back in a smooth motion just as he'd done hundreds of times before, and without a moment's regret, he let the pecan fly and froze, waiting.

The smack of the sharpened pecan on Dillard's right cheek sounded even louder than it had when he'd shot the pecan tree trunk, and Dillard involuntarily reached toward the side of his face with his damaged hand as he began to fall, all the while flailing for something to grab that might keep him upright.

Steven slipped a second pecan from the sack as Dillard came down and lay in a heap near the passenger side front door. Blood oozed from the lacerated cheek and began to seep toward the pavement. The big man sat still, not moving at all.

Marvin's squad car lights came on, and the red flashing lights began seconds later as he moved down toward the corner where he turned left and pulled the squad car nose to nose with the Fairlane, leaving the engine running and the lights on.

Steven, still hunkered down in the daylily jungle, let out a slow, grateful breath when Dillard rolled on his side. He wasn't dead, and that's all he needed to know as he started to belly-crawl back toward the deeper, dark space between Mrs. Robertson's house and Ned Monroe's shed. He pushed himself to go faster, thinking that he didn't want Marvin to see him so he wouldn't have to lie under oath, if it came to that.

Marvin walked toward the Fairlane and knelt beside Dillard as Steven stood still, staring, almost invisible against an oak's trunk on the moonless night.

He hadn't imagined all this happening tonight, but he'd visualized the scenario hundreds of times. Karl was wrong about one thing, Steven told himself. Dillard Wilson wasn't as tough as he seemed. At least, not on this night.

*****

Marvin shined his silver flashlight on Dillard as the drunken blob began to squirm. The deputy took his handkerchief out and pressed it against the gash on Dillard's face, before a beefy arm swatted it away.

"It was the boy. I know it was!"

"What boy are you talkin' about, Dillard? Looked to me like you just fell in the dark while you were checking them flat tires," Marvin said as he scooped up the pecan remnants and stuffed them in his pocket.

"That boy of Jason Heard's. He was over there hiding in the bushes, waiting to ambush me," Dillard said, waving an arm in the direction of the flower bed. "The little sucker set me up and then ambushed me."

Marvin cut his flashlight in that direction. "Ain't nobody around here but you and me, Dillard. How did you get all them flat tires?"

"The devil with you, Marvin. You know it was that boy, and you just don't want to help me," Dillard said as he pushed himself up and leaned his back against the Fairlane's passenger side rear door.

"I'm telling you, Dillard, I've shined this flashlight all over this area, and there ain't nobody here but you and me."

"Little Satan was here, Marvin. I swear it," Dillard said as he reached for Marvin's handkerchief to wipe the blood and sweat away. "It's way too hot for December," he uttered without thinking.

Dillard spat in the handkerchief, then pressed the moistened cloth to the cut on the side of his head. The wound had begun to sting as the sweat ebbed.

"You look a mess, Dillard. What's this about a boy? And why would any boy be after you this time of night?"

Dillard's antennae went up. He couldn't let the word get around that he'd put his hand on the inside of Martha Heard's bare thigh.

"They owed me money on that old car that I sold to Jason," he managed. "I went by there tonight to collect, and that boy of Jason's came in while I was there."

"And I suppose they couldn't pay you, and there were hard feelings about that?"

"Nawh...that sorry kid came in and paid cash for what they was behind, then paid off everything else that was left on the note. Probably stole all of it..." Dillard paused for several seconds before he pulled the handkerchief away from the nasty laceration that still oozed blood. "Yeow!" he shouted as the handkerchief caught a piece of pecan shell and raked it through the middle of the cut. "I'm gonna have to kill that boy. What in the devil did he shoot me with?"

Marvin let out a long sigh as he sat on his haunches holding the metal flashlight that lit the area. "Dillard, you're getting too old now to be talking about killing anybody. You just fell down. That's all. Nobody shot you, and there wasn't any boy over in them bushes. That's all there is to it, Dillard."

Dillard cut his eyes up to Marvin. Convinced that the crusty deputy was up to something, instinct drove a hot flash of fear through him. He cut his eyes away wondering if Marvin already knew what happened at Martha Heard's house. Why was he protecting the boy and how did he get here so quick? Dillard looked down, clamping his jaws tight for a long minute as he dabbed his cut, hoping with each touch of the handkerchief that the blood would stop oozing.

"Dillard, is that aftershave that I smell on you, or is it some fancy liquor that I heard you'd been ordering from the catalog?"

Dillard didn't answer right away as he wondered how many others knew he'd been to the Martha Heard's house. Was it all a set up? Was Olin in on it too? His eyes darted from one side of Mrs.

Robertson's house to the other, searching for Steven. Something was wrong. This wasn't supposed to happen like it had. Martha had that monster butcher knife ready, and that boy showed up at just the right time with the coil wire in his pocket. A boy…a thirteen-year-old boy can't know about a coil wire.

"I regret to say that it wasn't no liquor in me tonight, Marvin," Dillard said. "Maybe just a little aftershave," he added, lying.

Marvin stood straight, towering above Dillard as he stared in the distance.

"Even the air stinks tonight," Dillard said. "Rot! Ain't nothin' going right."

"Augh…it's just the wind coming out of the south and catching the smoke from the paper mill. Probably rain in a few days, and we need that," Marvin said.

"Dillard," Marvin began again after pausing, "when you gonna quit?"

Dillard knew that his girth wouldn't let him get up easily, and he shot a quizzical look toward Marvin. "Quit what? What do you mean?"

"When you gonna quit trying to be somebody big?"

"Well, I ain't trying to be somebody big, Marvin. I'm just me. You know that."

"Dillard, you been trying to prove something since we was boys, and you can't lie about that. You know that's right. Deep down where you really live, you know it," Marvin said.

Marvin crossed his arms over his chest, still staring down on Dillard. "You ain't got nothing to prove anymore, Dillard. You got money. You got property. You got a nice car. And everybody knows that the mansion you live in is all paid off. So why do you keep trying to steal from folks that don't have much in this world? Folks say that you're no better than a thief. They come to Olin and me, wantin' us to lock you in the jail." Marvin rubbed his chin for a brief second. "They call you a thief, Dillard. A thief."

"Thief!" Dillard shouted in protest. "I'm no thief, and you know it, Marvin. You've known that since we was boys."

Dillard looked down, shaking his head a little. It was a dark night with strange energy exuding from the stars that weren't visible in the heavens. He blinked hard and shook himself a little, wondering what he'd done to deserve the beating that he'd just taken from a kid. He should have been home by now, sitting in his chair.

Marvin cleared his throat. "Dillard, do you understand what a predatory loan is?"

"Nawwww, but it don't sound good."

"It's not good, Dillard. Not good at all. But that's what you do."

Dillard cut his eyes up to Marvin but didn't argue.

"You just sit back and wait until you know some poor soul is in trouble for money; then you go loan them a little at an unfair interest rate that you know they can't pay. And when time goes by and they don't pay, you go and take their things…their land, their house, or just maybe their old car. Then you sell *their stuff* for a profit."

"Ain't nothin' wrong with that, Marvin. That's just good business, and you know it."

Marvin ran his fingers through his hair, letting his eyes close briefly as he shook his head from side to side slowly. "Do you even know what a predator is, Dillard?"

"'Course I do, Marvin. I ain't stupid. I'm one of the richest men in the county. I wouldn't be rich if I was stupid."

Marvin leaned on the Fairlane's front fender, silent for a moment. The December wind blew harder now, and he pulled his crossed arms tighter to his chest.

"You know that little jerk also broke my left hand," Dillard said. "I can sue him for that. I know I can," Dillard said.

Marvin continued to stare at Dillard without speaking. Dillard slurred his words badly now.

"He did! I swear he did," Dillard said, holding his black-and-blue swollen hand up for Marvin to see.

"Did he hit your hand with a hammer or something heavy?" the deputy asked.

"Nawhhh… I missed him when I swung at him, and he dropped that there hood just at the right time so he could use my own car to break my hand. I ain't never seen anything like it, the timing of it and all. That boy's a Satan. Got to be. Ain't no normal human could have planned that just right."

"Dillard, you're drunk and you're out of your mind. How in the world could a boy do all that just right so that a grown man three times his size would end up with his hand broken and sitting in the street soaking in his own blood? There ain't no judge nor jury in this county that would believe that crock." Marvin paused. "And besides, the boy is a minor. You can't sue a minor. Even if you could, he ain't got no money. So why would you want to do something like that?"

"That boy's got more money than I do. I swear it. I saw a roll of hundred dollar bills that was four of five inches thick," Dillard said, lying. "Ain't never seen anything like it on a boy like him. He must've been stealing from everybody in town for years to have that much money."

"Dillard," Marvin said slowly, "before I take you home, you're gonna have to tell me what happened at Martha Heard's house."

"Marvin, I done told you that. I went there to collect what was owed to me, and that boy worked me over."

"I thought you told me that the boy paid you off."

"Not all of it," Dillard said, grinding his teeth. "He had this knife that he said would shave, and…and he had the coil wire for my car that he was threatening to cut in two with that knife. He told me that he wasn't gonna pay the full amount that they owed. I swear he did. It was blackmail, Marvin. That's it! Blackmail. Maybe even extortion. He made me sign that Bill of Sale for about half of what I shoulda got out of them."

Marvin still leaned on the Fairlane, listening. The night air settling now, heavier with moisture. The forecast was cold enough for frost in the early morning. He looked at his watch, then shook his head.

"And Martha…she had this butcher knife," Dillard said. "I'm a telling you, Marvin, it was a trap. A trap, that's what it was. I'm just lucky to be alive."

Marvin released a deep sigh and shook his head again.

"One…more…time," Marvin said. "What happened in that house tonight? Martha Heard is one of the kindest, gentlest humans alive, and that boy is too young to do what you just described. Last time, Dillard. If we have to get the truth out of Martha in a court-room, it'll be worse for you. You know that the sheriff and Jason Heard served in the same outfit in the Pacific."

Dillard cut his eyes up to Marvin, then turned away quickly. He didn't remember that, and his mind strayed again to the image he had of Martha as he idled the Fairlane through town late that after-noon and saw her walking home when she got off work at the bank. She wore that smart navy suit, and her shape was the same as it was when she was in high school. Right then he knew that going to her house would be a bad idea, but he couldn't help himself.

"Yep," Dillard said. "I do know that, Marvin."

"Jason jammed his fingers in Olin's carotid artery for over two hours one night when a Jap bullet grazed the sheriff's neck." Marvin shifted his weight. "Two hours. Bullets flying over their foxhole all the time. A man don't forget that kind of thing."

"I swear, Marvin. Nothin' happened in there tonight. Nothin'. I promise. Not that I didn't want it to. But she had a butcher knife. A razor-sharp butcher knife as long as my arm."

"Did you lay a hand on her, Dillard?"

"Not much of one," Dillard said with a sheepish tone, his head drooping.

"Dillard, you're nothing but a predator, in every sense of the word."

"Why hell, Marvin. She didn't have no stockings on, and I just touched the inside of her leg by accident once. That's all. It weren't nothin' to it. Nothin' at all. She probably didn't even notice."

Dillard's chin slumped further toward his chest, almost lost in the jowls and rolls. Without warning, the eastbound train whistle split the night air, and Dillard lurched, thinking every bone in his body was broken.

"I guess I might have made a little move right before the boy came in," he said without lifting his head from his chest when the whistle had stopped its screeching. "Nothin' serious. Nothin' at all really. It's just a blur now anyway. I don't really remember, and it don't matter none. I didn't really do nothin'."

Marvin's face reddened, and his jaws flexed constantly in the silence beyond the rumbling train's dominance. He released a long breath, seeing a condensation fog as he turned toward the dome light that was slowly dimming. "Dillard," he said, pausing, "this is a godawful mess, and I'll just tell you, I don't know where it's gonna end up. You opened the ball when you went to Ms. Martha's house and did what you did. Now look at you. You're drunk. You got a busted hand, and you're covered in blood. This ain't good, Dillard. You got a bad problem with this thing, and there ain't no two ways about it. Touching Ms. Martha like you did just ain't right. I don't care if you were owed money."

Dillard turned his head toward Marvin and cut his eyes up to him before he twisted himself to be more comfortable, still sitting on the ground waiting for the roar of the train cars to subside. He pulled the silver flask from his coat pocket and took a long swig before he looked up to Marvin, bolstered by the liquid that burned its way down.

"Drink?" he asked, waving the silver flask in Marvin's direction.

"Nawh," Marvin said, scowling. "Nawh. And I thought you weren't drinking tonight."

"Maybe just a little," Dillard said. "Nothin' to write home about."

Dillard looked away and turned the flask up again, his back still leaning on the passenger side rear door.

"Ain't nobody been by here, you know," Dillard said, looking down the street away from Marvin. "If you'd drive me home and get Sonny to come air up them tires, why, nobody would ever know what happened tonight."

Marvin chuckled to himself as he shook his head a little. "Got to give it you, Dillard, you're a piece of work." He paused, then shook his head again. "How are you going to explain that broken hand and that cut that Doc Raley's gonna have to sew up in the morning? Folks will notice those and start to talk."

"Awww, to the dickens with them good church folks, Marvin. Don't you worry none. I can handle all that. I got enough influence in this town to make all that right. You just get me home and call Sonny to take care of this car."

Neither man spoke as the night's silence blanketed them. Marvin shifted his feet, rolling his lips, then crossing his arms over his chest as he stared down. Finally, he stood straight as he stepped away from the Fairlane and faced Dillard.

"What we gonna do here, Marvin?" Dillard asked. "I'm gonna git that boy. You know that now, don't you, Marvin? Cain't let no boy do this type of thing to a man like me. No sirree. That ain't gonna happen. Not to me, it ain't. I'll get Big Henry to whoop his ass good, just for starters."

Marvin closed his eyes for a brief second as he let his head droop. "Can you stand up, Dillard?" he asked as he raised his head.

"Not just yet," Dillard said before he used his good hand to turn the flask up and empty the last of it, rolling the smooth liquid on his tongue and into his jowls.

Dillard looked back to Marvin and offered a tight-lipped silly smile before he flung the silver flask into Mrs. Robertson's thick St. Augustine sod.

"Now, Marvin," he managed as he pushed himself to his knees, "get me up and let's go home."

Marvin stretched his burly arm and caught him by the back of his coat at the neck and helped pull him to his feet.

"Why don't you get Sonny on that there radio of yours? If he'll just get over here and air up them tires, I could be on my way by myself. You wouldn't even need to drive me home."

"You're not going any further than the front seat of my car," Marvin said as he put his arm around Dillard's back and started him walking.

"What we doin' here, Marvin? You gonna take me home, then go arrest that boy? What about my car? You gonna get Sonny or not? One of my boys can come get it, you know, or Big Henry, if need be."

"Try not to get any blood on my car seat, Dillard," Marvin said as he eased the drunk with long strands of dyed hair into the seat. "I don't want to have to do any more cleanup behind you than I already need to," he added.

Marvin got in and started the car, driving slowly toward the sheriff's office that stood on the side of a hill across town. Dillard slumped in the seat, closing his eyes until the squad car stopped in the side parking lot of the courthouse and sheriff's office. He pushed the hair strands that dangled across his face back as he sat up. His eyes opened wide as he realized where Marvin had taken him.

"What's going on here, Marvin?" he asked, pushing himself up in the seat. "You were supposed to take me home and get Sonny and the boys to take care of the car."

Marvin turned to face him and stared but didn't answer.

"Talk to me, Marvin! What am I doing over here at the jail? Man, you were supposed to take me home and go arrest that boy. That boy is a devil; that's who he is. And he needs to be in jail. Not me."

Marvin didn't budge.

The dim light in the parking lot made it difficult to see who was coming and going in the December night. Olin worked a twelve-hour day, six days a week, and had another hour to go on his routine.

"Marvin, you ain't gonna arrest me. You can just get ready, 'cause that ain't gonna happen. I'll get William Henry over here in a New York second, and he'll have *you* in that jail if you try to arrest me."

Marvin let him talk, sitting still, staring.

"You ain't got no solid case against me, Marvin. You ain't got no witnesses that are going to be willing to talk, and I'll swear that I fell down while I was checking my tires and busted my hand and cut my face at the same time."

Dillard spat saliva with every word as he turned his head from one side to another. He knew that Martha wouldn't talk about what happened. She'd be too embarrassed for that, but that boy of hers, Steven, worried him some. Still, nobody was going to believe a thirteen-year-old boy over him. The situation might make a lot of noise, but he thought William Henry should win this one easy if it went to trial. If he could get her on the stand, William Henry might even make it look like it was Martha's fault...somehow. He turned toward Marvin and took a deep breath.

"What you gonna do here, Marvin? You know that you and the sheriff are up for re-election this year. Those folks down in the south part of the county don't much like you anyway. I'd guess if they had a big campaign fund, we might have a new sheriff and a new bunch of deputies."

Finally, Marvin cinched his jaws and released a sigh as he turned away from Dillard.

"Now look here, Marvin," Dillard said, "I ain't going in that there jail. A man like me don't do that. Not here. Not in this town. Why... I'm respected here, and you know I can get you fired. You know that, even if Olin is re-elected. If you take me in there and arrest me, you won't never be able to get another job in this county. You'll lose your family land. Your boy will be run out of school, and you ain't never going to own your house 'cause I'll buy your note and raise the interest so high that you'll lose everything. Two months. That's all I'll need to put you in the poor house!"

Marvin pulled the metal handle on the squad car and walked around to the passenger side. "Get out, Dillard," he ordered after opening the door. "We're going to see the sheriff."

Dillard sat like a stone and glared at Marvin.

"Get out, Dillard," Marvin repeated. "Don't make this any worse than it already is. If I have to add Resisting Arrest to your situation, it won't look good for you in the newspaper."

Dillard still sat stark still, staring straight ahead, grinding his teeth. Finally, he released a deep breath. "Marvin...you do know that I'm a prominent and respected man in this community?"

Marvin didn't respond as he stood straight, holding the door open for Dillard.

Dillard turned to face Marvin. "Prominent and respected," he repeated. "You got that?"

"Dillard," Marvin said, "you've got money and property. And everybody in this town knows how you got it. 'Prominent and respected' ain't nowhere in anybody's description of you. That's what you can count on. Now let's go. Right now," he added as he reached inside, catching Dillard by the neck of his suit coat again to lift him out of the car.

Dillard's face turned beet red as he stood. "Marvin, you hear me well on this. And don't you mistake this for no whiskey talk," he said staring at the deputy with locked eyes. "My boys and Big Henry are gonna beat the ever-living tar out that Heard kid. You can bet your last dollar on that. If it takes us fifty years, we're gonna get even with that boy. That… I will absolutely guarantee!" he added as he leaned forward, nodding his wrinkled brow.

Marvin brushed a hand across his beard-stubbled jaw, pausing. "Dillard," he said, "when you get inside, go to the restroom and get a good look at yourself. There's still blood running down the side of your face. After that, think about that fine car of yours out there on the road with four flat tires. Maybe by now, somebody has come by and put it on blocks to steal the wheels."

Dillard stared up at Marvin in the dim light, still grinding his teeth. "It better not be nobody stealing my wheels. This here is a small town, and I'll find out and beat the crap out of them too."

"Ain't nobody gonna help you around here, Dillard. Nobody," Marvin said. "And as for that Heard boy… I really don't think he'll need much help to handle you or your boys."

It took a solid hour for Olin and Marvin to question Dillard and write their report. They didn't allow him to contact William Henry, calling their work just a "preliminary report." To add emphasis to their process, Olin had the county photographer make Dillard's picture. The side of his face was still matted with blood, and his stranded black hair dangled down over the forehead again, accurately depicting him for who he was.

By the time the interview completed and Dillard was back in Marvin's squad car, Sonny had aired the tires, and another deputy took the car to Marvin's house, leaving the keys in the ignition. Marvin drove Dillard home in icy silence. Even though Olin didn't arrest him, Dillard didn't say a word on the ride, nor did he speak before he slammed the car door behind him and hurriedly waddled toward the front door.

Olin told Marvin before they began the interview that the full disclosure of the night's troubles would likely cause a mix of pressure and publicity that the bank wouldn't be able to stand, and that

Martha couldn't afford to lose her job. Marvin watched in silence as Dillard went inside and slammed the door behind him.

"Doesn't seem fair," he muttered as he put the car in reverse. "Should've hit him when I had the chance," he added as he tightened a hand into a fist.

10
CHAPTER

Steven's chest still heaved as he closed the door gently behind him and locked it, trying not to make noise. He needed time to think, but he knew that Mama was primed for a serious discussion. The house was too small for him to avoid her. It was going to happen, he understood that, but thought she might go easier on him if he didn't slam the door and rush in. He tiptoed through the kitchen and had taken a step toward his small bedroom when Martha saw him.

"Steven," she said, stopping him.

It was her tone that got him. She didn't shout. There was no panic her voice, just that deep monotone that he hadn't heard many times in his thirteen years. He released a sigh and swallowed. "Hi Mama."

"Where have you been tonight, Steven? And where did you get all that money?"

Be casual, he told himself. *Try to relax. She can't be that mad.*

"Your face is red. You've been running in the night," she added, her voice gaining intensity.

"Uhmmm, it's just the cold, Mama. I think we might have frost by morning," he said, knowing all the while that she wouldn't buy his answer.

Martha stared at him without blinking. "I need you to tell me what's going on, Steven. You've been acting strange lately. I think it started the night that your father died, but it's much worse now. Sometimes, I'm just not sure what you're doing, and I'm a little worried...to tell the truth," she added.

Steven's shoulders drooped as the tension ebbed. He walked over to Jason's padded chair with the wide mahogany arms and sat on the front edge, his elbows resting on his knees, looking at Martha sitting on the sofa with her legs crossed, still wearing the dress she'd worn to work, now with an apron covering most of it.

"I know things, Mama. Sometimes. But not all of the time. Things that most folks don't know. And I don't know how I know them. I knew Dillard Wilson would come here to cause trouble," he said, looking down to the faded green rug on the floor. "I started planning what to do about it a long time ago. I can't explain how I know these things, but I just do. And… I don't forget much. I can remember almost everything I've ever done or seen since I was a little boy."

Martha took a deep breath, nodding her head just a little.

"You're still a little boy, Steven. I hope you won't forget that. But I do think you're awfully driven for someone your age."

She looked toward the windows and the cabinet radio, then ran a hand through her hair, tucking it behind her ear. "Maybe it's because Jason passed when you were so young; I don't know. I don't live in your mind. But sometimes you don't seem much like a thirteen-year-old…child." She paused, a tear coming to her eye as she swallowed. "I didn't want that, Steven. I knew it could happen when Jason died, but I didn't want that at all. I tried. I want you to know that I tried really hard to do everything right so you could have a decent childhood."

Steven grimaced and shifted his weight in the chair. He couldn't tell her that Dad's death was his fault. She'd never understand that, and she would argue about it. He didn't dare mention Brother Joseph and Uncle Melvin. Not tonight. That would frighten her even more. But he did agree that he was *driven*. There wasn't any use arguing about that.

"You couldn't help the way things happened, Mama," he said, taking a different tact. "I know you tried hard, but you didn't really have much of a chance," he added, smirking a little. "Mama, I want you to know that I'm still mad at all those Snack Jack kids about that airplane that wouldn't fly."

Martha laughed aloud and couldn't hold back the tears. She stretched her arms out to Steven who took two giant steps to meet her with a bear hug. "It's been so hard, Steven. So hard. And there's nobody to help. Just nobody." She paused, closing her eyes for a brief second. "All my folks are dead, and your dad's people live too far away, not that they care much about us anyway. They've got their own problems.

"You've got to go to college," she said, "and that's only four or five years away. I don't know how we're going to do that, but Jason would never forgive me if you don't get to go. Banks just don't pay much. I've got a good job, and Mr. Durrett is nice to me, but it's just not enough money."

Steven stood there with his arms wrapped around Martha, staring without blinking. Big Henry didn't have this type of problem, neither did Lawrence. They were both planning to play on the eighth-grade football team next year. Lawrence might even get to play quarterback. Steven swallowed hard, telling himself that he didn't need that stuff anymore. Those things were for kids.

"The Snack Jack kids," he heard Mama saying. "What would I do without you? But... I do wish that you didn't need an enemy so much, Steven. You seem to be at your best, or maybe it's your worst when you're in a squabble, and that does bother me. If you don't listen to anything else I tell you, hear me on this," she said, holding him at arms' length. "It's really hard to find any peace in this life if you're always fighting with someone."

Martha pulled him to her, hugging him again. "Oh, what would I do without you?" she asked, lowering her eyes for a brief second as the tears began to well again. "You're wonderful. You try to take care of me. You do things for me, and I understand all that... I think. But I do miss your dad, probably more than you will ever know. We were kids together, but in the fourth grade, he wouldn't have anything to do with me because I was a girl and he told me that girls had cooties. But by the seventh grade, we were sweethearts.

"As much as I love you, no one else lived those same years with me. No one else did what we did together, and that's the worst of it..." she said, letting the words trail away. "I was just a girl in love with my best friend. We were so naïve. We saw some bad things happen to others, but I never imagined they would ever happen to us. And never in my wildest dreams was it possible that someone like Dillard Wilson would come into my house and threaten me or touch me like he did. Never. So long as your dad was around, something like that just wasn't possible. But now I have to be careful every day." She paused to gather herself. "I've tried so very hard, Steven, but I do miss your dad. I'm sorry. I just can't help it."

Martha collapsed on the sofa, leaning back with her head resting on the top of the upright cushion. "I was so stupid. I never thought my life would go like this. I'm almost forty years old, and my life is misery, pure misery.

"I want you to know something else," she began, "something important."

Steven nodded without speaking.

"I know there are things that you have to do. Like it or not, you're a boy, and boys sometimes need more *room* to grow up. You won't understand this right now, but it sometimes takes boys longer to grow up than it does girls."

Steven wondered where she was going with this. What was she really trying to say to him?

Martha sat up, letting her eyes fall for a brief second, then blinked hard. "I'm going to try really hard to give you the space you need to grow up, but there are a few things that I need you to tell me. I think you owe me that."

Steven continued to stare before he pursed his lips and glanced down, nodding his agreement.

"First…where exactly *did* you get the money?"

"I worked for it, and I saved it. Every penny of it. For a long time."

"You didn't steal any of that money?" Martha asked, giving him a look of askance.

Steven hesitated, looking away from her toward the door. "Mama, you know that I've worked for Mr. Wilson for almost five years, and now with sweeping up at Mr. Earl's' Pontiac dealership too, I do okay for a kid."

Martha was having none of it. "Steven," she said with firmness in her voice, "don't put me in a bad position. This is a small town in Texas."

Steven shoved his hands deep in his pockets. That second sharpened pecan was still there.

"Did you steal any of that money?" Martha asked, one word at a time. "I'm still your mother, and I need to know that. Please."

Steven rolled the saliva in his mouth before swallowing. "No… but some of the money was paid to me by Sheriff Olin."

Martha's mouth draped open as her jaw dropped.

"Olin? What…why would Olin pay you money? You don't work for him too, do you?"

Steven pushed his long brown hair back, then let it fall into place again. He knew Mama wasn't going to be happy about this part. "You know about his Retired Deputy Program where he pays the power and water bills for some of his older deputies that didn't get much money before they retired?"

Martha nodded.

"And do you know that he sells pecans as one way to raise money for the fund?"

Martha gritted her teeth and took a deep breath, then nodded again.

"Well… I provide all of the pecans, and Sheriff Olin gives me half of whatever cash he gets."

"And where exactly do you get these pecans, Steven?"

"Oh…just around town. Lots of folks don't want to take the time to pick them up or crack and clean them. I don't mind that, so I pick up the pecans, and the retired deputies get some of their bills paid. When you add what the sheriff pays me to what I earn working, I had enough to pay off old Dillard when he came here up to no good."

"But Steven, that's stealing. You just can't do that."

"No, no, Mama. Most folks don't care if I get the pecans, and for some of them, I pick up on *shares*."

"But not all the folks…"

Steven shrugged his shoulders and looked toward the door. She was right, but he didn't want to admit it. Not to Mama.

"What about…the folks across the street, Steven? Did some of the pecans come from all those trees behind their house?"

Steven bobbed his head up and down, tightening his lips simultaneously.

"And do you pick up on *shares* there?"

Steven shook his head and looked down.

"So you just steal them there?" she asked, frowning.

"Uhmmmmm… I wouldn't exactly call it—"

"Do they call you the Robin Hood kid?" Martha asked, cutting him off. "Are you stealing from the rich to give to the poor and getting the sheriff to go along with you for cover? Is that what's going on here, Steven? Are you stealing from folks to make a profit for us and the deputies?"

Steven looked up to Martha, sheepish and silent, cutting his eyes from side to side, scrambling for a defense that made sense. He didn't see anything terribly wrong with taking a few of Big Henry's pecans and selling them to help the sheriff. And, it was a way for him and Mama to make up just a little of the money that Dad would have brought in. He spun that story to himself, still knowing that it was a weak argument, and that she wouldn't accept that. "They don't know, Mama. All the pecans I take to the sheriff are really good, and I couldn't tell you which ones come from where. But only the sheriff and Marvin know that I bring in the packages of shelled and cleaned pecans."

Martha cut her head to the side and bit her lower lip. "Ms. Nancy Estes bragged to me about Olin's pecans. She roasted some in butter and salt for last Saturday's bridge club meeting. Nancy went on for some time about Olin and how considerate he was to help those elderly deputies that served for so many years."

Martha released a short sigh and shook her head before turning back to Steven. "You know that I need to punish you for all this, don't you?" Martha said as she looked back to Steven.

"Well… I know you probably need to do that, Mama. I do," Steven said as he cut his eyes toward the kitchen. "You could do that.

Sure could. You could whip me with Dad's leather belt. It would hurt for a little while. Yep," Steven added as he nodded, agreeing with himself. "But you know what, Mama…it would all be worth it. Worth every lick of Dad's belt…if you chose to do that. Because Dillard Wilson is just an overgrown bully with money that he stole from lots of good folks. Karl whipped him once when they were just boys, but he's been getting away with things like he did tonight his whole life. He lost tonight, Mama, and I'm proud of that. Even if you need to whip me, I'd still be proud of what I did. That greasy old man with money lost to a thirteen-year-old kid living in a rent house. That's worse for him than a big man like Karl breaking his arm and kicking his ribs in."

Martha stopped in mid-thought. "Karl told you that story, did he?"

Steven nodded, not thinking Mama would have known about all that.

Martha stood and began to pace slowly. "We all thought Dillard was going to die," she began, speaking slowly in a hushed voice. "Kinda hoped he would die, actually," she said just loud enough for him to hear. "But he obviously didn't, even though Karl made a mess of him." She put a hand to her chin, looking down. "I'm not going to punish you, Steven. There are lots of folks in this little town who would've liked to have done what you did tonight. Plenty of them, actually. Dillard has done a lot of bad things in his life," she said, shaking her head a little with a slight shudder to her shoulders. "Lots of bad things that hurt too many folks."

Steven didn't like what was happening in front of him. Mama was too quiet and subdued. He wondered what she wasn't telling him.

"Mama…nobody but you and Deputy Marvin know what I did tonight. After he left our driveway, Dillard didn't see me. I'm pretty sure of that."

Martha's brow wrinkled. "Uhmmm…you haven't told me what actually happened yet," she said with her chin tilted down and the wrinkles in her forehead even deeper than before.

"I'm hungry, Mama. We didn't get dinner because of old Dillard."

Martha stood, offered a tight-lipped, fake smile and turned toward the kitchen. "I'll get the pie from the safe," she said. "You get the milk. But…you're going to have to tell me what you did."

*****

That first bite of apple pie always got him. Nobody in town made a better apple pie than Mama. The crust flaked from the top strips like old crepe paper caught in a wind. It was crisp and paradoxically juicy sweet when those dried apples from the spring picking were just right in the sweet sauce that she made.

Steven took a second bite and reached for the milk to wash it down.

"Steven, where exactly did you go tonight?" Mama asked.

Steven paused, licking the crumbs from his lips, afraid that she would be really angry with him. He took a deep breath. "I… uhhmm… I needed to finish settling things with Mr. Dillard Wilson."

"Settling things?" Martha asked, glaring.

"Yes ma'am. *Settling*. He came here and did some things that he shouldn't have done. I needed to even the score. And I did, Mama."

Steven watched as the air seemed to go out of her. Martha looked down and swallowed hard before glancing again to Steven.

"So, what happened? We might as well get it over with. I don't want any surprises when I walk into the bank tomorrow."

Steven rolled his tongue inside of his mouth, clearing the pie remnants. "Well… I guess the first thing is that Mr. Dillard Wilson now has a broken hand."

"What!?"

"Yes ma'am. It's broken, pretty bad," Steven said almost matter-of-factly. "He tried to hit me when I was putting that coil wire back in his Fairlane, and I dropped the hood when I moved back to dodge his punch."

"He tried to hit you? Really! I'm sure it was just a friendly tap to thank you for putting the coil wire back in his car."

"No ma'am. He was mad. Maybe worse than mad. It was a serious roundhouse swing that would've broken my jaw and knocked me out. No question about it."

Steven looked up at Mama just in time to see her swallow hard and ball her fists at her waist. "I was lucky that he was too slow and missed. Just barely. But there ain't no doubt that he intended to hurt me some. I don't suppose he'll be hitting anybody with that broken hand for a good while. That hood caught him just right. You could hear the bones crunching when that fist caught the edge of the Fairlane's hood. There was probably some blood too, 'cause that hood had to have cut his fingers when he hit it that hard."

"Steven! You broke Dillard Wilson's hand?"

"It wasn't me, Mama. It was just something that happened when he tried to hurt me," he said, shrugging his shoulders. "It happened too fast. I couldn't have planned something like that on my best day."

Steven paused and took a deep breath, thinking that he had to tell her about the tires even though he didn't want to do that. And the slingshot pecan to the side of his face would be the worst of it. He still felt guilty about that; it was overkill, and instinctively he knew it. If he'd been an inch or two off with his aim, he could have hurt Dillard pretty bad or put his eye out. It had scared him when the big man didn't move much after he made the shot. Still, he tried to convince himself that he was right to scar Dillard, so maybe he wouldn't be so quick to take advantage of folks who were in trouble. That logic didn't work, and he knew it, but he couldn't think of anything else. He didn't want to admit that he just got really mad and was determined to hurt Dillard. He lowered his chin for a second before looking back to Mama. "But I might as well go on and admit that I did plan the four flat tires that Dillard had after he left here," Steven said, sneaking in just a hint of a smile.

Martha walked across the room and sat down abruptly on the sofa, then leaned forward, resting her face in her hands the same way she'd sat on the night that Dad died. "Steven, do you understand the term 'collateral damage'?"

Steven shook his head. He knew what "damage" meant, of course, but "collateral" was a big word that he'd not heard before.

"Let me try to explain this. It's a little complicated, so listen carefully."

Steven nodded.

"Let's say you're cutting grass, and you work really hard to get up close to the edge of the yard and cut that grass just right, but while you're doing such a good job with that, you hit a rock or a stick, and it flies up and hits Ms. Jackson's window, breaking it."

"Oh, I wouldn't do that Mama. I'd always turn the mower away from Ms. Jackson's house so it couldn't throw anything out in her yard."

Martha raised a hand as she pursed her lips, closing her eyes for a second. "No, Steven," she said, protesting. "That's not what I meant. Just pretend that the rock hit Ms. Jackson's window."

"Okay."

"You didn't mean to break Ms. Jackson's window. You were just trying to cut the grass just right...which you did. But Ms. Jackson's window is still broken, even though you didn't intend to do that. That's called 'collateral damage.'"

Steven sat at the kitchen table, looking across to Mama on the sofa, trying to understand how Dillard's hand and four flat tires had anything to do with anyone other than him and Dillard. Even the slingshot pecan didn't involve anyone else, except Deputy Marvin who had to put up with Dillard for a while.

"Mama, there wasn't anybody else around tonight. It was just me and Dillard, and I didn't get hurt at all. So how is that gonna create any collateral damage?"

Martha took a deep breath before cutting her eyes toward the front porch then back to Steven.

"Dillard Wilson," she said, pausing for composure, "owns almost eight percent of the stock in the bank where I work. He has a great deal of influence on the Board of Directors for the bank, even though he's not a member of the Board. And...he has the second largest amount of cash on deposit with the bank. His brother-in-law, Henry Watson Sr., the man that you've been stealing pecans from, he has the largest amount of cash in the bank."

Steven felt the blood rushing to his head as he began to rub his teeth against one another. He didn't know any of the things that Mama had just told him.

"I know... I know that you were just trying to protect me tonight, but now you know why I sat so still when that filthy, nasty man had his hand on the inside of my thigh before you came in," she said, staring at him. "I didn't sit there because we were late on the payments. I sat there and gritted my teeth because I didn't want to lose my job in the morning."

Martha sniffed up her emotion, still sitting on the sofa with her hands covering her face. "If I lose my job, we won't have a place to live, and I can't imagine that anyone one else will hire me."

Steven walked across the room and sat beside her, looking down. It hurt him to hear her sob, and he understood that it was his fault. This wasn't the way he visualized his return from the war with the evil old man. He didn't know what to say to make it better and clamped his lower lip between his teeth, almost afraid to take a breath.

"Steven, you have to understand that everybody isn't like us. Lots of people don't tell the truth very often. They tell others things that aren't true, lies that will benefit them, and they don't care who their words might hurt. When Dillard Wilson finishes telling his story in the morning, everyone will think I invited him to come over this evening, then scorned him. He's going to lie, Steven, and the rumors will spread all around town in an hour's time," she said, standing and beginning to pace. "People will think I'm a floozy. They'll think that I wanted to get close to Dillard to get some of his money. It won't matter what the truth is. People will believe Dillard's story just because it's exciting, and they'll tell it over and over."

Steven kept his eyes on the floor, thinking. He would have to do something about this. Mama was right. She needed to keep that job, and it wouldn't be fair for her to lose it just because Dillard came to the house and tried to take advantage of Mama...and because he chose to fight back.

"Where is Jason when I need him?" Steven heard Martha mumble between the sobs.

"He's playing dominoes with Uncle Melvin right now," Steven blurted in a low, monotone voice without thinking or looking up.

Martha stopped sobbing and twisted toward Steven, staring. "Steven! What did you just say? Say it again, every word just like you just said them. Every word, Steven. Do you hear me? Every word."

Steven rolled his tongue over his front teeth. He'd never intended to say those things to Mama. It just came out. Now she would figure out that everything that had happened tonight was his fault, that Dad's death was his fault, that all her pain and anxiety was his fault. None of this would have happened to Dad and Mama if he hadn't pled to Father Abraham's Council for a life. Steven took a deep breath and repeated his statement slowly, word for word, but he couldn't look up at her. He just sat there, gazing at the floor.

Martha sat on the sofa again and turned away from Steven, letting her head rest in her hands as she closed her eyes. A long and awkward moment of silence passed before she spoke. "Who... Steven... is Uncle Melvin?"

Steven tensed himself, drawing his shoulders in as he clinched his fists. Why did he slip up and tell her? She wasn't ready for that and would probably think he was just looney. If Dillard Wilson hadn't come tonight, none of this would have happened. He released a short breath.

"Head of all the Heard family...everywhere." He swallowed hard. "Really. Everywhere," he said almost without expression in his voice. "And he's actually a very nice guy. Too nice really. I should have been more like him, I think. And I should have paid more attention to what he had to say. Maybe we wouldn't be in this mess if I had," he added.

Martha stared at her son, her lips parted just slightly, but she didn't speak. After a long and confused fifteen seconds, she eased herself down into the padded rocker with the wide arms and crossed her legs, leaning back, allowing her eyes to close.

Static rattled from the cabinet radio with the dial on the front. Steven stood and went over to the radio to tune it to the right frequency. It was the Perry Como Hour, and Mama always liked that program.

"I'm sorry, Mama," he said, his face reddening as he turned and stood in front of her, staring down to the floor. "I shouldn't have said that," he added as he sat back on the sofa.

Martha locked her jaws and didn't answer at first. "Is it true, Steven?" she finally asked in a meek voice. "The thing you said about your dad and Uncle Melvin playing dominoes, is it true?"

Steven nodded.

"How do you know this? How could you possibly know this?"

Steven dropped his head. He'd made too many mistakes tonight, and none of this was necessary. Why did he have to say anything about Dad and Uncle Melvin? He knew better.

"Because I can see them, Mama. Not always. Just every now and then. Mostly when things are a little rough. But they can see us all of the time."

"They can? Are you sure of that?"

"They have to, Mama. If they couldn't see us, how could they do their jobs?"

"Jobs? What kind of jobs, Steven?" Martha asked before she laid her head on the back of the chair cushion again, closing her eyes.

Steven studied her, still regretting that he'd ever mentioned Uncle Melvin and Dad.

"Mama," he began, pausing, "we all have to help God when we're there. He needs us to do things. There are warring angels, armies, and guardian angels, all kinds of folks."

"Steven. Steven. Steven," Martha said, "you have such a vivid imagination." She paused again, and Steven saw the muscles in her face begin to relax. "Steven, you're just imagining all of this. All of it," she said, pausing. "Listen to me on this. You have to listen to me now and believe me," she said, cutting her eyes away then back to him. "You can't see your dad, and God only knows who this Uncle Melvin character is that you've invented. You're imagining it all. You're a boy without a father who has too much time to think because you spend far too much time alone. That's all this is. There is nothing in your dad's family history or mine that would make me believe that you're some kind of prodigy."

Steven sat perfectly still as Martha paused, looking down. He thought she was still angry…at herself, at their situation, and at him. He decided to stay silent and sit back on the sofa.

She looked up quickly. "Steven, I'm going to get fired tomorrow…because of what happened here tonight. Because Dillard Wilson has a broken hand and will be embarrassed." She paused, biting her lower lip for a brief second. "It's not fair. Not at all. I do very good work as Mr. Durrett's assistant, and I've been in that job for eleven years. But none of that will matter. I will get fired, and there's nothing that I can do to stop it."

Steven wanted to interrupt but decided against it. He fidgeted while sitting on the sofa, kicking off his worn-out Converses that she'd gotten him at a Thrift store, then lowered his head, seeing the cracks in the hardwood flooring. Mama started to cry again, low at first, and her voice cracked some.

"And I don't know what we'll do for money when I get fired. That's the problem," she said, spreading her hands in front of her. "And I don't want to hear any more of your weird stories about those who are dead and now watching us…and having jobs. That's senseless. Absolutely senseless. If that were true, somebody would have been talking and writing about it for thousands of years. No more. Do you understand?"

Steven nodded and let his eyes fall to the floor again.

"Now, one more thing, only because I have to know before morning… What…" Martha began, "what did you do to Dillard's tires?"

This was one of the questions that he didn't want to answer… this one, and the pecan to the cheek slingshot attack. If he just hadn't hit Dillard with the slingshot pecan, he'd be in a much better position with Mama. He made a quick decision not to tell her about the cut on the side of Dillard's face.

"Well… I…uhmmmm… I let just a little bit of air out of them."

"How? How did you do that? I don't know how to do that. Did you put a nail in his tires?"

"No, Mama. The guys at the Pontiac shop have to let air out sometimes. It's not hard to do."

"It's not hard to do?" Martha asked. "You don't put a nail in a tire, but you let the air out slowly so they all go flat at one time? That's not hard to do?"

"Everybody knows that Fairlane of his, Mama." Steven took a breath and shook his head just a little. "I knew who was here when I walked up to the house, and I figured he was going to cause trouble. Bad trouble."

Steven stopped and shrugged his shoulders, looking up to Martha, waiting for her to acknowledge his point.

"Okay, okay. So you were right about that. But you just don't go around letting the air out of people's tires because you're suspicious about them. How *did* you do that anyway?"

"I got an old valve core wrench from the Pontiac shop about a month ago."

"Borrowed? Got? You mean you stole it, just like you stole the pecans?"

"No. No. I didn't steal it. The edge of this one got crushed when Mr. Johnny got it stuck up under a floor jack. He threw it in the trash can and ordered a new one. They don't cost much, and I got the old one out of the trash and fixed it with a pair of needle-nose pliers and a file. Didn't take long."

"Okay, so you didn't steal it…this time. Thank God!"

Steven stared at her. She was in no mood for his explanations, and he knew that it was all about the job. He was still beating himself up mentally because he didn't think about that until she explained it.

"So anyway, when I got home and figured what was going on, I decided that the main thing was to get him out of here but to make sure that he got caught. I didn't want him to get away clean like he has with almost everybody else. I got the valve-core wrench from the car shed and loosened all four valves where the air would come out slowly. I wanted him to have to leave that fancy car here overnight or maybe get stranded in the road before he got home. He's a bad man, Mama. I couldn't let him get away with bothering us like that."

"And you also took that wire thing out of his car? The thing that you almost cut in two with your knife."

Steven looked straight at her. "I did. And that saved us a lot of money, Mama. A lot."

Martha inhaled deeply and let it out as she considered what he said. "But it cost me my job."

"Maybe. But maybe not. I've got an idea about that."

"I don't want to hear any more of your ideas. And don't you meddle with this tomorrow morning. Do you hear me on that?"

"Yes ma'am. I do," he said without hesitation, knowing all the while that he was going to make his move in the night, not tomorrow morning, and therefore, he wasn't lying to her. Dillard wasn't going to win this one, he told himself.

Martha stood in front of the padded rocker for fifteen long seconds before she stopped grinding her teeth. "I think I'm going to bed now, Steven. It's been a really bad day, and I don't need anything more right now."

"Yes ma'am," he said without looking up. "It has been a rough day...for everybody."

Martha turned and took her first few steps toward her room, but in a flash of logic debate, Steven made the decision that he had to finish telling her about Dillard, even though he surely didn't want to do that.

"And... I don't suppose that Dillard Wilson will be in the bank very early in the morning."

Martha stopped, turned, and glared at him once again. "Oh..." she managed.

"Yes ma'am, I do suspect that he'll need to visit with Doc Raley for a while before he goes to the bank. He might need a few stitches and some special attention to that hand. That's assuming that he's sobered up by then. I'd guess that could delay him a little bit too."

"S-t-e-v-e-n! What in God's name did you do? If you've done something else, we'll have to leave this house and move to another town. Do you know how many problems that would cause? I—don't—have—any—money! Do you understand that? Nothing. Not a single dollar. I couldn't even go to the grocery on the way home tonight. We have nothing!"

"Mama..." he said, raising an open palm in her direction. "Just...just don't get upset. It'll be okay. I promise you that it'll be okay. I've got more money if we need it. There's no way I was going to show all my cards to the likes of Dillard Wilson."

Martha stood over him, staring down, speechless. She was about to turn and go to her bedroom when Steven cleared his throat.

"And I guess Old Dillard could also be going to see Mr. Henry Watson at the cleaners to see if he can get all that blood out of that fancy suit and white shirt that he's so fond of wearing."

Martha let out an exasperated sigh and closed her eyes for a brief second before rubbing her hand across her forehead. "Are you going to jail, Steven? That's all I really need to know right now. Because if you are, I need to know where you hide your money so I can use some of it to come and get you out of jail."

"No, Mama, they aren't going put a thirteen-year-old like me in jail," he said, pausing. "You know they won't do that. And besides, Deputy Marvin helped me some tonight already."

"I should've known that, Steven. I don't know how it would escape me that you wouldn't have enlisted the authorities in attacking an unarmed man."

"Dillard was armed, Mama. There wasn't no question about that. I saw that big Colt up under the edge of his front seat when I first took his keys out of the ignition."

"And you...you did all of this anyway?"

"It wasn't a problem, Mama. I had my slingshot and some of those special pecans that I showed you once."

"Ohh...oh, great. That's brilliant, Steven. Just brilliant. He had a Colt and you had a slingshot and pecans, but it wasn't a problem. Right!"

Steven hesitated just for a second but wished later that he'd let her win the point.

"Well... I guess it wasn't a problem in the end. Dillard ended up lying in the street for a good while, soaked in his own blood, before Marvin got him up and hauled him to the sheriff's office."

"So...did Dillard get arrested after you...shot him?" Martha asked, standing, hands on hips, glaring.

Steven put a hand to his chin as he stood between the sofa and Dad's rocker. Mama's face was beet red now. She wasn't merely tolerating him, and he knew it. "Well, I don't know about that, Mama. I was back in the shadows when Marvin put him in his car. They might have turned him loose. I don't know."

Steven saw her stiffen, pulling her shoulders in as she refused to look at him, before she started for the bedroom one more time.

"All I know is that Dillard Wilson is going to still have a good-sized scar on the side of his face on the day they bury him. I do know that, Mama. And he deserves it."

Martha didn't look back as she strode toward the bedroom and flung the wooden door closed behind her.

Steven had started toward his small bedroom when he heard her door open again.

"Why? That's what I want to know, Steven. Why?"

Steven turned back, shoving his hands in his pockets as he looked down. Seconds passed before he looked up to Martha. "Because I could, Mama. Because I could. That's all. He insulted us. He insulted you, and it felt like he was spitting on Dad's grave. I didn't like it, and I knew what I could do about it. That's all. I got mad, and I got even."

Martha ground her teeth, still glaring. "This night will haunt you for the rest of your life, Steven. It's not over, and you may never get even. It doesn't work like that. Never, never, never," she added, shaking her head like a distraught old master before she marched back to her bedroom.

11

CHAPTER

Steven sat on the corner of his single quilt-covered bed, thinking. Mama needed that job, and it wasn't just the money. She didn't have family other than him, and the folks at the bank had been good to her since Dad died. He knew that she needed those people, that routine, and he couldn't let her lose that job. He had to fix the damage, and he had to do it tonight. Tomorrow morning would be too late.

Martha's bedroom had been quiet for over an hour when Steven stood up. It was only eight thirty, still not too late.

The blue December air grabbed him as he eased the back door closed and toe-walked down the steps in silence. If Mama were asleep, he was certain that he hadn't waked her getting out of the house.

John Walden's Esso station didn't close until ten o'clock, and he knew that Sonny, the night clerk would let him use the phone. He walked down Elm Street toward Main as fast as he could. He shivered, then hunched his shoulders, tensing himself against the cold. It was well below freezing, and the incessant northwest wind cut through his sweatshirt and jacket, blowing at thirty miles an hour. He hadn't expected this much cold. It wasn't like this a few hours earlier.

Steven went through the side door of the office between the first bay and the cash register. Sonny had one of Mr. John's museum cars up on the rack and was underneath changing the oil when Steven let the door close behind him, a little louder than usual to let Sonny know he was there. It was almost nine o'clock.

"Steven…hey. Good timing. Hand me that funnel over there, if you don't mind," Sonny said, his hands and forearms covered in black greasy crud as he struggled to get the filter out. "What are you doing out here this late? It's bad cold tonight."

"Uhmmm... I had a little problem tonight and wanted to see if I could use the phone for a minute. Local call. Definitely not long distance."

Sonny was ten years older than Steven, wiry and already losing his coarse sandy locks. "You're a little young to be calling the girls this time of night, aren't you?"

Steven shrugged and tried to be casual, telling Sonny that he just didn't want Mama to know what he was doing. Steven thought Sonny would understand that; the culture among them demanded circular support, even if it were pretty Martha Heard that he was avoiding.

Steven went back in the office and lifted the earpiece of the big black phone and pulled a scrap of paper from his pocket. He'd carried the number since the night Dad died but never had to use it before that moment. He dialed slowly, making sure that he got the number right. A deep, serious voice answered after two rings.

"Sheriff Olin, this is Steven. I'm calling from the Esso station phone since I didn't want Mama to know anything."

"You've had a busy night, haven't you, son?"

"Yes sir. We had trouble tonight. But I figure you already know all about that."

Steven hesitated before continuing, and the phone went quiet for a second. "Well...well, Sheriff, I...uhmmm... I've got two things on my mind, and I'm sorry to bother you so late. I've never had to use the number that you gave me until just now, but we got a bad problem coming in the morning, Sheriff Olin." Steven paused, struggling for courage. "And a lot of it is my fault. There were some things I didn't think about before all the ruckus started tonight."

Olin let out a deep breath as he stood beside his bed listening to Steven apologize for shooting Dillard with the slingshot, then told him about Mama getting fired tomorrow morning. Olin was ready for bed when the phone rang and stopped Steven when he'd heard enough. "I know your mama's upset," Olin said. "Anybody would be upset with a situation like this. I actually thought about coming by tonight to check on your mama but decided that I should wait until tomorrow for that. From the story I got from Dillard and Marvin, it seemed like the two of you came out okay when he was at your house."

"Yes sir. We did all right, I guess," Steven said. "He left Mama alone and got paid, and I got a Bill of Sale."

"And as far as your mama's job goes, she shouldn't worry about that too much. I'll call Hubert early tomorrow morning. Unless his Board does something strange, your mom will be fine."

"I sure hope so, Sheriff Olin. She's really mad at me right now, and I didn't see that one coming," Steven said, hesitating, not wanting to ask for anything else. He looked around the green-and-tan plastered wall in the old gas station as he curled his toes, shuffling his feet.

"Uhmmm…you know, Sheriff, I know… I know it's not your problem, but we don't have much money, and Mama worries about that an awful lot. I used some of my savings from our pecan sales to pay off Mr. Dillard. If…if you've got any extra work, sweeping floors, mopping jail cells, anything at all… Mama doesn't get paid much and if I could work—"

Olin released a deep breath and cut him off again. The wrinkles on his brow deepened, and he stared down to the floor in his bedroom. "I know, son. And, that's been bothering me some too," Olin said, stopping again to think. "Give me a couple of days to work on something and then come by the office when you get off at the grocery store. We'll find something for you to do," he said before they ended the call.

*****

Olin slipped off his house shoes and sat on the side of the turned-down bed. Mary's glasses rode the end of her nose as she read her book.

Olin winced as he put the phone back on the cradle and sat on the side of the bed, leaning forward with his hands on his knees.

"What is it?" she asked in a monotone voice.

"Martha's having a hard time," he said in that gravelly voice, shaking his head a little. "Dillard Wilson was over there tonight bothering her."

Mary turned a page but didn't take her gaze away from the book. "Fix it, Olin. You owe her that. Worse, you owe Jason that. Do what you should have done a long time ago," she said, still not turning her gaze away from the book she was reading.

"I'm up for re-election this fall, Mary. It won't look good."

Mary still didn't move. "That boy has to eat. He has to go to school. It's going to be cold this winter, and propane is expensive." Then she put the book down and rolled on her side. "Look at me," she demanded.

Olin twisted toward her.

"Martha and Steven could just as easily be Junior and me," she said, looking over her glasses. "It could've been you that died when Jason did," she said, looking over her glasses. "Fix it now, Olin. I'll go see Martha tomorrow evening and make sure she's okay. That greasy fool didn't lay a hand on her, did he?"

"Not much of one," Olin said sheepishly, dropping his chin.

Mary let out a disgusted sigh. "And what exactly does that mean?"

"Dammit, Mary. Why do you always have to be such a hard ass?"

"Olin! What happened?"

Olin shook his head and grimaced, thinking that he got far more respect at the office than he did at home. "He put his hand on the inside of her leg right before Steven came in."

Mary bolted up in the bed, dropping her book to the floor. "So is the fat buzzard in jail right now or not?"

Olin twisted away from her glare, turning to face the wall. "Mary, Dillard Wilson can cause a lot of trouble if he wants to. Trouble for me. Trouble for Martha and Steven. Even trouble at the church. He has money, and he has a deep hatred that comes up fast. I have to keep the peace! Before anything else, I have to keep the peace!"

Mary glared at him, her face reddening as she began to clinch her teeth. "You know, Olin, it's 1962, and there are protests and marches and people dying for their causes all over this country. The kids are going nuts using drugs, listening to strange music, and having some sort of sexual revolution that I don't pretend to understand. It's a stupid, crazy time. Just crazy," she added, pausing as she glared at her husband, who was perhaps the most powerful man in the county. "You can say that about keeping the peace, and that sounds really nice. Yeah. Nice. But this is still Texas, and you have to do what's right every single day here. Not just every now and then. Not just when it's convenient for getting re-elected. Every…single…day," she said as she stalked toward the restroom. "That man ought to be in jail right now, and you know that he should. I don't care about reelection. No self-respecting woman should have to put up with that type of thing…especially in her own home," she added as she slammed the door behind her.

Olin turned back around, leaning forward, mentally absorbing the blows. She was right. He knew that, but he didn't know how to fix it. Every scenario that he considered was flawed. No matter what he did, somebody was going to get upset with him.

Mary came back to bed, turned off her bedside lamp, and didn't bother to say *good night*. He turned from side to side fluffing and positioning his pillow, visualizing Jason Heard hovering over him in that foxhole with fingers stuffed in his carotid artery, keeping him alive.

12
CHAPTER

Hubert Durrett stood six foot four inches tall and wore a three-piece suit and a solid colored tie every day. He used horn-rimmed spectacles full-time now and had combed his hair the same way every day for forty-seven years. He arrived at the bank promptly at nine o'clock every morning and left at 5:01 in the evening, with one exception. At noon on Friday, he had lunch at the club and followed that with a round of golf. And if there were rain, snow, or extreme cold, he would simply have lunch, then go home, and settle in his favorite chair for a nap, the same as his father and his grandfather would have done.

Hubert insisted on using number 2 yellow pencils for everything that he recorded during the day, and Martha had six of them sharpened and on his desk before he arrived each morning. She also made sure that the fountain pen that he used to sign documents was fully loaded and that the blotter was fresh and placed beside the pen.

Hubert slammed his newspaper to the table when the housekeeper interrupted his breakfast and called him to the phone at seven thirty on Friday morning.

"It's the sheriff," she said as she handed him the phone and left the room.

"Olin? It's early. Do we have a problem?" Hubert asked, skipping the small talk.

"We do, Hubert. We do indeed," Olin said. "Can you come to my office before you go to the bank this morning?"

Hubert thought for a moment. He had an investment report for the Board in-work and planned to leave at noon. If he wasted time with Olin, he wouldn't be able to finish the report.

"I'm pretty busy this morning, Olin," he said, knowing that the weather was beginning to get cooler, and those crystal clear afternoons with temps in the sixties weren't going to happen for much longer, even in South Texas. "Can we deal with your problem next week?" Hubert asked. "I really do have to finish—"

"Hubert," Olin said, interrupting with his sternest tone, "this morning. My office. Eight thirty. Don't be late. It's important."

Hubert had never heard that decided tone from his friend, the former lieutenant colonel. He swallowed hard, staring at the black phone after it clicked in his ear.

*****

Olin's assistant opened his door and ushered Hubert into the sheriff's office at eight thirty on the dot. Both men wore their respective uniforms, Hubert in a gray three-piece suit and a burgundy tie with a sliver of a white handkerchief in the coat pocket and just a hint of English Leather cologne, and Olin's tan sheriff's uniform was both fresh and pressed, his starched white shirt gleaming.

"What's this all about, Olin? This is most unusual, and I really do have to be at the bank at nine o'clock."

Olin stood eye to eye with Hubert when he walked to the front side of his desk, crossing his arms across his chest. Hubert's dad sent him to one of the East Coast's best schools, but Olin had won the last three elections easily and had the bulk of the county in his corner. Hubert knew that he couldn't ignore whatever it was that Olin wanted to discuss, but on this particular morning, he stood a little too close and seemed far more aggressive than he'd seen Olin be in the past.

"Have a seat, Hubert," he said. "This could take a few minutes."

Hubert stood ramrod stiff for a good ten seconds, then snorted a bit, and slowly turned, lowering himself into one of the ribbed wooden chairs with a padded bottom that sat in front of Olin's desk.

Hubert touched his gold watch in the sliver of a pocket in his trousers, thinking that this better not take too long. The bank could always put money in the campaign fund of Olin's next challenger, but deep down, he knew that wouldn't do any good. Still, it bothered him that Olin was being so abrupt and demanding.

Olin briefly described Dillard's visit to Martha and Steven's house, purposefully failing to mention his late-night call from Steven or the shattered, bloody pecan shell that Marvin had given him. When he came to Dillard's assault on Martha, Olin spared no details.

Hubert paled, then turned an ashen gray. "You do know," Hubert said, interrupting, "that Mr. Wilson is the second largest shareholder in our bank."

Olin cut his eyes to the side then back. "I knew he was going to be a problem for you, but no, I didn't know that he was your second largest shareholder."

Hubert ran his fingers through his oiled dark hair, then rolled his lips inward as he considered the perceived issues that would arise. He had to protect the bank at all costs. The bank, the school, and the church were the triple hearts of the town, plus every discretionary nickel that he'd earned through all the years was tied up in bank stock. Dillard Wilson could devastate him personally if he refused to fire Martha. In that initial panicked flare of thought, it didn't cross his mind that being without a job would also doom Martha.

"I don't think... I just don't think we can do it," he muttered in a quiet lull, almost talking to himself. "No. There's just not enough cash right now," he said, mumbling aloud, letting the thought trail.

"Enough cash for what, Hubert? What are you talking about?"

Hubert squirmed in his chair, re-crossing his legs.

"Well... I was just toying with an idea and thought maybe two or three of our shareholders might get together and buy Dillard out, and then I wouldn't have to deal with him. But no...no, that won't work. I'll have to think about this for a bit. We shouldn't do anything too quickly, you know."

Hubert gathered his overcoat and reached for his briefcase. It was already eight fifty.

Olin raised a hand when he got to his feet and Hubert froze. "We're nowhere near done, Hubert, and you might as well slow down. You're going to have a bad day. A really bad day. Actually..." he said, releasing a tired breath, "we're both going to have a bad day."

Hubert dropped his briefcase back to the floor and flopped in the chair, continuing to hold the overcoat.

"You don't have time to think about it, Hubert. And yes, this is going to interrupt your Friday lunch and afternoon of golf."

Hubert simply sat and rendered an expressionless stare. No one should be able to talk with him like that. If it were anyone other than Olin, he would have left right then. "No...no, it can't," Hubert said, looking off into the distance. "It just can't. Everything is all set. We're going to play this afternoon while the weather is still good," he said.

Olin stood up, interlocking his hands at the small of his back as he began to take slow steps, small steps out into the open space behind Hubert, beyond the desk chairs. "Hubert... Dillard Wilson will be out of Doc Raley's office any minute now, and he's going to be blood-red in the face and in your office as soon as he can get there." Olin turned to face the banker and furrowed his brow. "This is Martha's last day as your assistant," Olin said with a defiant tone.

"I beg your pardon?"

"This is her last day. I'm telling you that, and I haven't discussed it with her."

"No. No. No. You may be a war hero, buddy, and you may be the most popular sheriff that this county has ever had, but nobody... not even you...is going to take Martha Heard out of our bank. That's completely out of the question!"

"Then you're going to have to pay her a decent wage and be willing to go to war with Dillard Wilson."

Hubert glanced to the side and swallowed hard. The bank was privately held. Why did the folks in this small town think they could dictate policy? His policies. They had no idea how many nights he'd spent pouring over the books at home to manage cash flow during his fifteen years as president. His turnover rate with key employees was next to none, and they'd showed steady dividend growth every year. No one could have done a better job. And no one had the right to challenge him. Not even Olin.

"I have worked her up the pay scale for eleven years, Olin. I've done everything right; nobody can contest that. It's all documented in her personnel file. We have our rate scales and job categories; it's all contained in a formula with several elements—years of service, a key rating evaluation score—all of that type of thing, and I've missed nothing at all. Nothing!"

Olin stared at his junior friend without speaking. "Hubert," he said finally, "you may have gone to Harvard. You may have done everything just right within your policies. You may have worked every detail of every bank employee's career and their individual cost impact on your dividend schedule, but you don't pay people in this town enough to live on…especially a single mother."

"That's not my fault, Olin. I did follow every policy to the letter of the law. I couldn't help it that Jason died suddenly. Does that mean that I'm supposed to break policy and raise her salary? I didn't cause her loss, and if I'd raised her salary then, I would've had a mutiny on my hands from everyone else on the staff. You…you of all people should understand that. You have far more employees than I do."

Olin bristled at the mention of Jason and turned around to begin pacing again. "Do you want to keep her at the bank or not? It's a yes-or-no question. No double-talk, Hubert. None."

"Why, yes, of course, I do. She's perfect. She never misses a day of work. She keeps me right on schedule and controls who comes and goes to my office. She has a very nice image which is good for the bank, of course."

"Why don't you just say that she's a pretty woman?"

Hubert squirmed in his chair, obviously rattled with the idea that Martha might not be there when he needed her. Eleven years was a long time, and she'd been completely loyal to him. He draped the overcoat over the arm of his chair, then shuddered ever so slightly.

"Yes. Yes, of course she's a pretty woman. I see the fellas come over to her desk all the time when they're in the bank. And that's very good for business. You know that, of course."

"So are you going to pay her a decent wage or not?"

"Well… I just don't know what I can do. She's been at the top of her scale for over ten years, and I have to think about the other ladies in the bank."

Olin crossed his arms over his chest again, staring down on Hubert. "Okay, Hubert, I'm about done here. Either you're going to pay her a livable wage starting today or I'm going to put her in a dispatch job that I've had open for four months. If she'd had enough money coming in, she wouldn't have been behind on her car payments to Dillard Wilson, and obviously, he wouldn't have had a reason to go to her house last night."

"No, Olin! You can't do that. You just can't! A woman giving instructions to your deputies? That won't do."

"She manages all of your business without missing a beat and basically gives you instructions on all sorts of things, doesn't she?"

"Well...that's, that's different."

"My job is almost double the salary that you pay her right now. Are you willing to match that?"

He's bluffing, Hubert thought. *And how can he know what I pay Martha?* "That's preposterous. I can't do that, and you know it. That would upset too many people. And how do you know what I pay her? That's confidential information. Has she complained to you?"

Olin's expression didn't change. The round Coca-Cola electric clock mounted high on the wall of his office showed nine o'clock straight up.

"No. No. Definitely not. She's not complained to me or anyone on my staff, but it's my business to know that type of thing, Hubert, for almost everyone in the county. You may have to protect your bank, but I have to protect the people, which means that I have to have information. You can't control her or anyone else, Hubert, and I am now done here. If she'll take my job, she can start on Monday morning."

"I have to go," Hubert said. "It's after nine o'clock. The staff will be worried."

Hubert stood in front of the worn wooden chair with his overcoat draped over his arm, looking down, thinking, wondering if he'd reacted too quickly and was now in an untenable position. He pushed the rimless glasses up on his nose, turning quickly for the door. He could feel the natural red hue in his face burning now. Nobody had challenged him like this since he was at Harvard.

Hubert was almost to the door before Olin spoke again. "So what are you going to do, Hubert?" he asked. "I need to know."

Hubert stopped and turned slowly. He took his spectacles off, then used his coat sleeve to wipe the sweat and oil from his forehead. When Hubert Durrett stood erect, he was an imposing figure of power and multi-generational Texas prominence, and he looked every bit of the part as he stared down on Olin from across the room.

"Why are you doing this, Olin? You're forcing me into a corner, and there's no logical reason for doing that. What's driving you to upset my family of employees at our bank?"

"Is it the family of employees or the Board that will be most upset if dividends are just a touch lower because you paid your folks better? Or is it that none of you have the backbone to stand up to Dillard Wilson? As nasty of a human as he is, at least I know what he's made of."

Hubert brought a hand to his chin and let his gaze fall to the floor for just a second before lifting his head and glaring at Olin. "Olin, I'm not an evil human. Neither are the Board members. You know that. You know every one of them, and they're all friends of yours. They also don't have any ill will toward Martha or any other employee, but we have to make a profit on very slim margins. It's not an easy thing to do."

Olin propped on the edge of the desk but didn't break his stare. "Hubert, you're a smart guy, so I ask is it the bank's role to take care of its employees, or is it the employees' role to take care of the bank… and the Board?" Olin let the question hang in the air as he stared.

Hubert put his glasses back on, then looked down at the original board floor below. He didn't answer but simply nodded his understanding.

"I'll give you 'til noon, Hubert," Olin said. "Either you're going to take care of Martha and your other employees or you're going to lose them. The county will lose them. They'll go off to big cities like Houston and Dallas where they can make a decent living, even though they'd rather stay here at home. It's not 1950 anymore, Hubert. And it's clearly not 1930. People have options. Folks like the two of us have to do whatever it takes to preserve our town, even if there's short-term pain. If we don't do our jobs and the good folks leave, there won't be a need for a bank or a country club or ladies' shops or a men's apparel shop. Maybe there'll be a farm equipment store or a hardware store, a gas station, and some type of grocery store. The people who work the land will need a few services, I guess, but that's about all."

Hubert didn't look up but swallowed hard. Olin was dead right, and he'd argued that same point with himself many times.

Olin stood up in front of the desk where he'd been sitting on its corner. "I know I hit you pretty hard this morning. And… I recognize that you didn't see any of this coming," he said, putting his hands on the back of the bare wood chair that creaked with every movement. "If it makes you feel any better, I didn't see any of this coming either, but there was a small matter of my getting an ass chewing in my bedroom last night. And I guess that I richly deserved it."

"Humph…" Hubert said, looking up with a tiny smile breaking.

"Felt like a schoolboy when she finished and walked out," Olin said. "I didn't intend to lecture you, and I'm sorry for that. Just let me know what you decide to do."

Hubert took a breath and almost broke his demeanor but stopped himself. He eased his head around to stare at the office's bulletin board on the side wall, then looked back to Olin and nodded before he started for the door. He hadn't answered Olin's fundamental question, of course, and he had no clue what he would do next.

The drizzle from the deep gray sky speckled his suit coat as Hubert walked to the '62 Chevy that sat in Olin's parking lot. He sat in the driver's seat and glanced to the forgotten umbrella under his feet, then grasped the big vinyl-covered steering wheel with both hands before resting his forehead on its upper rim, lamenting his situation.

Martha was his idea of the perfect woman, and since Jason died, he'd repeatedly visualized the two of them in a passionate and caring marriage. He dreamed about her, not so much in a romantic way, but in his mind, Martha filled a void in his life that was larger than the Palo Duro canyon. She understood him, took care of him every day; most importantly, she worked successfully in his world. She was pretty with that dark hair flowing behind her and just the right blend of perfume and powder to create a gentle, but not overpowering aroma when she was close by.

In eleven years he'd never seen her lose her temper or raise her voice. She just didn't blink in the toughest of times, and all of the tellers came to her for guidance on both personal and business issues.

She came to work right on time just two days after Jason's funeral, didn't ask for any special time off to take care of family business, and never mentioned her loss. She was tough-minded and loyal, a woman who could function in his world, a woman that would manage everything perfectly if something happened to him; and he knew beyond a shadow of a doubt that he could not let her leave the bank and go to work for Olin.

Worst of all, Hubert Durrett, the East Coast educated ice man didn't know how he could go on with life if he didn't get to see Martha Heard every day. She was his raison d'être.

Hubert removed his glasses and leaned back in the Chevy's seat letting his head settle on the burlap-covered headrest before he closed his eyes. Another five minutes passed before he sat up and reached for the key to start the ignition. He still had no idea what to do about Martha. And he definitely didn't know what he was going to do about Dillard Wilson, who was now finished at Doc Raley's clinic and also en route to the bank.

13
CHAPTER

Wearing his black high-top Converses and cuffed jeans, Steven almost strutted into Earl Langdon's Pontiac dealership at eight thirty on that same Friday morning and headed straight for the mechanic's shop. He felt good, really good, not chest-out, proud-of-what-he'd-done-the-night-before good...but at least *do-a-little-dance* good. Steven thought that he and Mama had finally come out ahead, even though she burned the toast and was still mad at him, not saying much at breakfast. He wouldn't be certain how they stood until old stuffy Hubert Durrett got to the bank, but for now, he believed that they would be okay.

Steven wanted no part of the backslapping male banter that went on up in the showroom area of the dealership, especially not on the morning after Dillard Wilson came to call and ended up with a broken hand and covered in his own blood. The stitches on the right side of Dillard's face that were in clear view as he left Doc Raley's clinic confirmed that the stories that had run rampant on the party lines late in the night were accurate. Mama was angry and hadn't joined any of those conversations. He knew that. Even if she hadn't been angry, she would never discuss money or personal problems with anyone. Richland was a small town. She knew better, but somehow the word had gotten out.

Steven didn't like leaving her alone, even for the single hour that she had before starting her walk to the bank, but he had business to do. Serious business. And he wasn't sure how it would go as he walked down the steep concrete ramp that opened out into the cavernous building that was the mechanics' shop.

He liked the shop. It smelled like a man's place to him; the combination of grease and dirt, used motor oil, and a hint of body odor on stale uniforms somehow put him in his comfort zone. This was the real world where guys worked hard to make machines run in those sweat-laden summer days and the shivering winter months. They didn't complain about the cold or the heat or the dirt and grease on their hands. They shared their mechanic fixes and got advice from one another on the problems. They earned far less money but seemed happier than those hollow three-piece suits with dangling gold watch chains glad-handing in the showroom above.

And, Steven found the conversation in the mechanics' shop much more to his liking. They talked about all the girls and the town's women, even though some of the guys were too old to be thinking about schoolgirls. Sonny's brother, Robert Earl, also kept a page taped to the inside of his locker door from one of those slick paper magazines. Marilyn Monroe was in full view with that pleated skirt sailing and most of her bottom on display. Robert Earl didn't actually lock his locker, and Steven managed to flip the catch and study her physique for just a few seconds as he passed by. The other guys did the same almost every day, but on this Friday morning when Steven had not the slightest intention of going to school, none of the mechanics were in the change area adjacent to the shop, and he flipped the catch, caught a quick glimpse, then walked on toward Robert Earl's bay.

The big rolling toolbox with its multiple layers and over a hundred little drawers was already open, and Robert Earl was deep inside the hood of a blue Pontiac Catalina.

Steven's shoulders tightened, and he cleared his throat when he got close enough to see the pack of Winstons rolled up in Robert Earl's shirtsleeve, which exposed his biceps. Steven didn't know why he did that. The shop was a guy's place. No self-respecting woman would ever set foot down here, and Robert Earl had nobody to impress in the shop.

Robert Earl backed out of the Catalina's engine compartment and sat on the narrow bench in front of his bay before looking up to watch Steven come his way. "Figured you'd be down here this morning," he said as Steven sat on the bench beside him.

"Yeah…how's that?" Steven asked.

Robert Earl chuckled, twisting away, exposing the long comb that protruded from his back pocket when he turned. Steven got a whiff of the Brylcreem and Butch Wax combination that Robert Earl used to keep his long black tresses in place.

"Sonny was at the house this morning before I left. He… uhhhmm…mentioned that you'd *dropped by* the Esso station late last night to make a phone call."

Steven didn't flinch and simply stared straight ahead. "So?" he said after the creepy silence began to bother him.

"Well," Robert Earl began, "and then he told me about a service run that he'd had earlier where a certain Fairlane 500 had all four tires go flat at the same time." Robert Earl's brow wrinkled as he stared down at Steven, letting the comment soak.

"Yeah…" Steven said, shrugging. "How about that? Wonder how something like that could happen. Seems awfully strange," he added.

"I think we both know how something like that might happen," Robert Earl said, smirking as he looked around for some of the other mechanics.

Steven didn't want the other mechanics to come over there and tried to keep the Catalina in their line of sight so they wouldn't know that he was sitting on the bench. They all knew that he'd dug that valve core wrench out of the trash six months back. And by now they also knew that there weren't any nails in Dillard Wilson's tires. It didn't take the guys long to connect those dots.

Somehow the story of a thirteen-year-old bringing down Emperor Dillard with a repaired valve core wrench and a slingshot was a yarn that stoked them with pleasure, maybe even justice. All the guys had talked about it in the change area before the starting buzzer sounded, chuckling to themselves at the thought of Dillard on the ground with a broken hand and covered in blood. There was talk among them that they too could have done the same things that Steven had, but they couldn't…or wouldn't because they had jobs and families or girlfriends and needed money, or lacked the confidence to take a risk and strike a blow against the systemic conventions that held them hostage.

"I… I wouldn't know anything about that," Steven said, lying.

"Dillard was at your house last night hitting on your mama, and now he's all busted up and over at Doc's getting stitches, and you don't know anything about that? Come on, boy. You know everything about that! There ain't a man down here in this hole that wouldn't give his left arm to be you right now. You got to talk! We got to know how you did it."

Steven twisted toward Robert Earl, cutting his green eyes up to the Richland Fonz before he looked down to the dirty concrete floor, squirming just a little, curling his toes in the Converses. He didn't want to talk about it. That wasn't why he came. "I need you to do something," Steven said without looking up.

"Boy… I'm not doing nothin' for you until you spill your guts about last night. You hear me now? Nothin'. That was big stuff. Big stuff! And I'm not doing nothin' until you talk."

Steven exhausted a deep sigh without looking up. "Robert Earl, I got serious stuff for you to do, and I hadn't got any time to be spreading rumors and getting people excited. What happened…happened. I can't do nothin' about that. I can't go back and change it. I can't fix it or pretend that it didn't happen. It just happened."

Steven twisted toward the thin mechanic again. "It's serious now, Robert Earl. Really serious," Steven added as he ground his teeth.

"Not one thing until you talk, boy," Robert Earl repeated. "Look at you. Not a single mark on you, and that greedy sucker has a broken hand and a two-inch cut down the side of his face that he won't ever outlive."

Steven didn't budge as he returned his gaze to the floor.

"Boy…you don't understand. You cain't understand 'cause you ain't lived long enough yet." Robert Earl paused, taking a deep breath. "Steven, now come on. We're all your friends. You know that. And you're going to need us. Hell, you already need us. None of them Dillard Wilson boys are gonna mess with you if they have to go through us first. And they know that. But you got to come clean. We deserve to know."

Steven rolled his lips. This wasn't going like he'd planned. He just needed to prepare for what he believed was coming next. He didn't need Robert Earl and the guys to pour any gasoline on the small-town fire that he'd lit last night.

"Boy?" he heard Robert Earl saying, but he still didn't look up.

It wouldn't do any good to get Robert Earl sworn to secrecy, and Steven knew that. He couldn't help re-telling the story. It was who he was, and believing that the situation was about to get serious, Steven had laid in bed after sneaking back in the house from the Esso station and convinced himself that he had to have some help. Robert Earl and the guys were his friends, not because he did things to help them but because he fit in with them, despite his age. They could be an army for him. Dillard Wilson would never expect guys like them to support him. He turned to Robert Earl again, then let his eyes drift back down.

"He put his fat hand on the inside of Mama's leg just above the knee. I saw him do it when I stood at the door and looked through the glass. Mama sat there frozen for a second. He jerked his hand back when I came through the door, but I saw enough to know what he did."

Steven gritted his teeth as he grimaced. "Mama is a tough woman. She's had to be since Dad died, even though she wasn't like that before he left. It did something to her that night. Changed her right then," he added.

He paused, craning his neck to look around the Catalina again, making sure the other guys weren't coming over. "I guess she didn't have anything to be afraid of when Dad was around. But now we don't have much money, and we've got the likes of Dillard Wilson thinking he can come into the house and take advantage of Mama just because he thinks he should be able to do that."

Steven frowned again, turned his head to the side, and shook himself a little. "Dillard didn't know it, but he wouldn't have gotten anywhere last night. Mama had a butcher knife most as long as your forearm hidden in the fold of her skirt on the right side. He couldn't see it," Steven said, pausing again. "She would have killed him if she had to."

Steven looked away visualizing Mama running the butcher knife through Dillard's throat and out the back of his neck, thinking that it was best that it didn't go that way, of course. That would have been a nasty mess in the house, and it could have ruined Mama for life. He shook his head almost imperceptibly. Mama would have never gotten over having to do that. Still, he thought Dillard deserved something like that. He turned back to Robert Earl. "Anyway, I already had my Uncle Henry open in the front pocket of my overalls when I went through the door," he said.

"What'd you do?" Robert Earl asked. "He's three times your size and you come walking in like you did. Why didn't he reach and grab you right then?"

Steven's chuckle was low but steady, building in its force like a small wave barely white capping that murmurs as it skips along the top of the ocean then fades, melting into another current just before the shore. "Well… I knew he wasn't going to fight. His type never fights. They always get somebody else to do their dirty work for them. Plus, Karl whipped him like a dawg when they were just boys, and he probably knows that Karl is my friend." Steven paused, nodded his head a little, then allowed himself a split-second tight-lipped smile. "Then there was this small matter of me holding the coil wire of that fancy car of his in my left hand and my razor-sharp Uncle Henry in my right hand."

Robert Earl sat up straight, raising his eyebrows. "You took the coil wire out before you went in the house?"

"Didn't want the old goat to get away. I knew what he was there for. Mama's a pretty woman, and he's a money-stealing slob. My only worry was the time it took to loosen those valve stems and take the coil wire out before getting in the house," Steven said as he swallowed. "I promise you, Mama would have killed him if she had to," he added, nodding his head visibly.

Steven told Robert Earl about the deal on the outstanding balance and getting a Bill of Sale for the car and the Fairlane's hood dropping at just the right time when Dillard tried to hit him. He didn't really like telling the story. It was almost embarrassing to him, and he worried that Robert Earl would embellish everything when he retold it. He skipped the part about the slingshot and the sharpened pecan. He still wasn't proud of that and wouldn't have told any of the story if he didn't need Robert Earl to help him.

"I want to pay you ten dollars," Steven said abruptly as he stared at the mechanic.

"Ten dollars? Why? That's almost a half a day's pay for me. And what are you doing paying me money? You're just a kid, and kids don't have money to hire folks."

Robert Earl took a quick breath and looked away. "Besides… what do you want me to do for ten dollars? I can't go against them Wilsons by myself. They got too much money, and I got to keep this job. Melanie's got a baby coming before long, and we got to get married. This ain't no time for me to get fired."

"You won't get fired for teaching a kid a couple of things," Steven said in that flat, are-you-kidding-me tone.

"Then what's worth that much money to a kid? Teach you what?" Robert Earl asked.

"I need to know how to drive our car. It's a standard shift," Steven said as Robert Earl tilted his head, grimacing. "And… I need you to teach me how to shoot Dad's Colt pistol."

"Boy, you're about to get yourself in real trouble if you think you're gonna shoot it out with them Wilson boys. I'm almost fifteen years older than them, and those boys worry the dickens out of me. I don't want no fight with them. You know… I got to be more careful now with a family coming on."

"You don't have to do a thing but teach me what to do. I saw you at the county fair last year shooting those ducks like it was the easiest thing in the world, and you're also a mechanic. You got to know how to drive just about anything."

Steven looked into Robert Earl's eyes. He was still hesitating, and he couldn't afford more than ten dollars for this. "Maybe we can go out to Mr. Jack Tatum's bottomland pasture. I've heard that it's a big place and there's nobody else for two or three miles around.

Shouldn't take more than a couple of hours for me to get the hang of driving and shooting both."

Robert Earl swallowed, then briefly sneered. "Why didn't you go see Marvin or Karl?" he asked, not understanding why Steven had come to him.

"Marvin probably wouldn't do it. I'm a little over two years away from being old enough to get a driver's license…and a good bit more than that before I can buy a pistol. Plus, Marvin tries to look out for me a little too much sometimes. Driving, shooting a pistol at thirteen…nah, not much chance there. And Karl works for a Wilson brother, the good one. He'd probably be a little nervous if anything went wrong and I actually had to shoot somebody."

"You're being a little aggressive about this thing, aren't you, boy? I know you had a big night last night, but driving a car and shooting a pistol is big stuff. I don't know about all that."

Steven looked up to him sitting on the wooden bench. Ten dollars for a couple of hours on a Saturday morning was good money, even if Robert Earl were hesitant.

"I'm not planning to go shoot it out with the Wilsons or anybody else," Steven said, annoyed that he was having to lobby, "but what would I do if someone came in the night to hurt Mama? If they had a gun and I didn't have nothin' but a knife and Dad's gun that I don't know how to load or shoot, I couldn't do anything but sit there and watch them do whatever they wanted." Steven looked up to Robert Earl with deep furrows across his brow and a reddening face. "That ain't gonna happen, Robert Earl. I'm gonna promise you that right here and now. You can help me, or I'll go figure it out by myself."

Steven watched Robert Earl fidget then take his knife out to clean grease from beneath his fingernails through the awkward silence that followed. Finally, he nodded just a little and agreed to be at Steven's house at eight o'clock the next morning.

"There won't be anybody around. The Tatum place is too far out of town and down all those dirt roads. Quit worrying so much," Steven said as he counted out five one-dollar bills as good faith money.

14
CHAPTER

Hubert parked his Chevy behind the bank in his reserved spot and went in through the back hall that allowed him to get to his office without seeing anyone. It was almost ten o'clock, and he still didn't know what to do about Martha or Dillard Wilson.

The high-ceilinged office seemed cold and impersonal to Hubert, even though he'd hung a number of large pastoral paintings and unique farm scenes on the brick walls and put a nice rug down that covered much of the wooden floor. For security, the only windows were sealed rectangles up high near the ceiling on the wall behind his large mahogany desk, which backed up to the alley where his car was parked. Hubert stood at the back door long enough to clear the brain fog, letting his eyes rove around the room. He'd tried hard not to embarrass his father and his grandfather, but that had come with great pain. He wondered if they'd ever wanted to give up the office and go away to a softer life that allowed for deep emotion, maybe even a little joy…maybe even love and passion.

Hubert knew that he'd have to face them in a few years and tell them what happened on his watch. He dreaded that, believing that he'd never be the man that his grandfather was. And the desk would never really be his. It was his grandfather's desk, his father's desk. Hubert closed his eyes for a few seconds after he saw the six sharpened yellow pencils on the desk in just the right place. Why had he doubted that she would be here? In eleven years, she'd only missed three days of work, two of those being the days surrounding her husband's funeral and the other when she'd been in the hospital after a miscarriage, though he wasn't supposed to know the specifics of that.

Hubert put his briefcase on the small table behind his desk, then shuffled to the standing coatrack and hung the black overcoat just as he'd done hundreds of times before. He took a quick breath, hoping that the pounding in his chest would slow a bit and the tension he'd felt since leaving Olin's office would all be for naught.

"Break the ice," he told himself. He knew, beyond a doubt, that she didn't know how he felt. No one knew of his dreams, his deep feelings, his ardent passions. They couldn't. He was Hubert Durrett III, the banker. That's all that he'd allowed them to know, a cold and hollow man who had shepherded Richland's primary bank for over fifteen years. Hubert walked toward Martha's office, which was between his and the main lobby of the bank. She was wearing that hunter green suit with a bright white blouse and the flared collar. His favorite.

"Ah, Mr. Durrett. It's good to see you this morning, sir. We were all a bit concerned," Martha said.

"Uhmmmm…yes," he managed, clearing his voice. "Yes, just an early morning meeting across town. A personal matter that I didn't put on the calendar."

"Yes sir. Of course, sir," she said, nodding slightly.

"Can you call George Williams for me, please. It's a little too cool for golf today, and I don't think I'm going to make it."

Martha wrinkled her brow. She'd never heard him say that it was too cool for golf. They'd played when it was well below freezing and with snow looming. "Yes sir. Of course, sir. I'll phone him right away."

Hubert took two steps toward his office before turning to catch one last selfish glimpse of Martha when he stopped dead still. Dillard Wilson was halfway down the tellers' lobby and headed for his office, walking as fast as he could. He glanced at Martha, then stood still watching. Dillard's face was red. His fists were clinched. Strangely, Hubert felt ice calm, relaxed, maybe even confident. He finally knew what he was going to do. The tension, the worries, and all the what-ifs that he'd considered since Olin had called that morning gushed toward the sewers.

"Close your door," he said in a hushed voice where only Martha could hear. She half turned, startled by Hubert's voice, his tone, frozen in surprise until her eyes caught motion through the half-glass wall of her office. Even before her eyes connected with her mind and she consciously knew it was Dillard, her instincts flared at the insufferable sight, almost breathless in his waddled strides, rushing toward Hubert who somehow slid past Martha's office door, stepping forward to meet the rotund brute before he could reach her door which was now closing behind him.

Hubert stood in his practiced ramrod-stiff best with arms crossed over his chest. He saw that Dillard's right hand was now adorned with a soft cast, and that his face—stubbled, haggard—had white tape covering some of the stitches on the right cheek. He almost smiled. So it was true. And Olin had left out some of the good parts.

"Good morning, Mr. Wilson. It's always a pleasure to see you in the bank," Hubert said loud enough for the loan officers who sat near Martha's area to hear.

Dillard looked up, snarled, and didn't break stride as he hustled toward Hubert. "It ain't no good morning, and you know it," he said, brushing by Hubert, almost rolling toward the conference room table that stood at the end of the heartless office, opposite Hubert's desk.

Dillard turned to get a look at Martha as he passed her door, but Hubert had purposefully stepped toward his office with his back to Martha's door so Dillard couldn't see her.

"Humph…" Dillard snarled as he passed her area and glared at Hubert over his thick black glasses. "I suppose you know why I'm here," Dillard said as he slid the straight-backed wooden chair out and sat down. "Everybody in town seems to know what happened, so I guess you do too."

"I'm not sure that I know to what you're referring," Hubert said, still standing, towering over Dillard, three-piece suit, a full head of thick hair perfectly coiffed, the faultless image of an iced banker.

"That boy of hers!" he shouted, pointing toward Martha's office with the cast-bound hand. "It was him. I know it. Ain't no question. I know it was him, and you're going to fire her before I walk out of this bank. Do you hear me? You're going to fire her right now! Right now! She's going to leave here this morning before I do," he said, pausing to take a handkerchief and wipe the slobber from his lips.

"Are we clear on that, Hubie? Do you understand what I'm telling you to do?" he asked, jabbing a finger in the air.

Hubert didn't flinch, still standing straight and stiff, staring. Locking eyes with Dillard, he rolled his lips inward and swallowed, getting ready to answer.

"Do you hear me, boy?" Dillard thundered again. "You are going to fire her right now, and I'm going to press charges against that boy for what he did to me."

Dillard shouted so loud that Martha could hear him through the closed wooden door. "That Satan-kid held a knife to my throat and made me put my hand under the hood of my car so he could slam it down and break every bone in it. I'll never have the use of that hand again, and he's going to jail for that. And when I was trying to get back in my car and go home, he grabbed me and slashed the side of my face with that knife of his. Said he wanted to mark me so I'd always remember him."

"You don't say," Hubert wedged in between breaths when Dillard paused.

"I'm telling you that boy is a Satan, as pure a Satan as there is on this earth, and he's got to be brought in and made to pay for what he's done. It's just got to be," he added, shaking his head and slamming his good hand on the table. "Got to be. Do you hear me?"

Hubert shuffled his feet, then leaned on the chair in front of him. "Mr. Wilson, you do realize that Mrs. Heard has done nothing for which I should terminate her employment here at the bank? She's a near-perfect employee. Her annual reviews are exemplary, and she's seasoned in her job, having been with the bank for over eleven years," Hubert said, waiting for the explosion of saliva that would surely come with every word Dillard said.

"To the devil with you, boy! Don't you start with all them fancy East Coast words. Your daddy and your granddaddy would never have put up with anybody like her having access to the bank's investment strategy or everybody's checking accounts. That just ain't right, and you know it!"

Hubert's expression didn't change as he locked eyes with Dillard again.

"Now look here, boy. You can see what her and that boy of hers did to me. And I know beyond a shadow of doubt that I am one of your largest shareholders. And…" he said emphatically, "I've also got more money in your bank than anybody else in the county. You need to show me some respect, boy. And you better fire her right now. If you don't, I'm going to call for a meeting of the Board and take over the running of this bank myself. If you don't fire her, I will sit in your chair as president before the sun sets today. That… I can promise you."

Hubert still stood over Dillard, studying him, allowing him to fume before he spoke. "Uhmmmm… I really don't think that's going to happen, sir," he said in that innocent, almost matter-of-fact tone that acknowledged nothing.

Without thinking, Dillard pushed the broken hand down on the table to stand and protest, then jerked it back before collapsing in the chair, moaning and cursing.

"You see, Mr. Wilson, you're not a member of the Board," Hubert continued, "and you can't call for a meeting, not that it would do you any good, even if you were a member of the Board. As Chairman, CEO, and president, I'm the only person that can call a meeting of the board, and I have neither reason nor inclination to do that. And, I must correct your misrepresentation, sir. Your account with us is certainly significant and very much appreciated, but it's the second largest account that the bank has, not the largest."

Dillard somehow launched himself out of the wooden arm-chair and began to pace the area between the table and the wall, his reddened jowls now glowing through the stubble. "I'm calling your note. Right now. Either fire that woman or I'll own your family's land before quitting time this evening! William Henry will have the papers drawn, signed, and filed by three o'clock."

Hubert gave Dillard a smug look as he eyed him over the rimless glasses. He thought briefly, weighing the risks before he spoke. "You might tell William Henry to give George a call before he wastes time drawing up papers or filing anything," Hubert said. "Being the thorough attorney that he is, I'm almost certain that William Henry will recognize that the note you mention is problematic as I never *signed* that particular document. Of course, that's just a small matter of interest but certainly one that William Henry will find important."

Dillard took a half step forward as though he were going to bull-rush Hubert, then stopped. "Don't mess with me now, boy," he said, shaking his index figure at Hubert. "I own you, and you know it. I want that woman gone from here right now. Get it done, and I'll leave you alone. If she stays, there's nothing old George can do to stop William Henry. That... I can guarantee!"

"I believe that you've mentioned that point already, sir, but I've certainly not agreed to that concept."

Dillard's chest heaved great gulps as his face turned a deeper red. For a brief second, Hubert thought he might have a heart attack or a stroke, but his breathing eventually slowed, and he flopped in the chair again, a great heap of seething animalistic anger.

Hubert shoved the furor of the fight to a back corner of his mind and forced himself to remain placid, giving away nothing as he considered Dillard's options. He knew that Dillard wouldn't back down and that he couldn't lose his family's property. Even if he'd done the deal to help his in-laws, losing family property would never pass muster with his grandfather.

And, he recognized that the lack of a signature wouldn't affect the intent or absolute validity of the contract, against which he'd already been making payments. His argument was thin there, and he considered the manufactured point as merely a plant to give away later.

Seconds later, he concluded that William Henry would try to persuade Dillard to back down. Hubert shuffled his feet, still looking down as Dillard shifted from side to side, almost rumbling in the old conference room chair.

"That don't matter none, boy. This is Texas. A man's word is still as good as a written contract here. It ain't like New York down here."

"Maybe," Hubert said after a lapse. "Or, maybe not."

"Just get rid of her and you won't have any more problems with me," Dillard said as he stood and made a beeline for the heavy wooden door that led to the walkway beside Martha's office and out to the remainder of the bank. Instinctively, he reached for the door handle with the broken hand, cursed profusely at his ineptitude, then took the handle in his right hand.

Hubert patiently waited until the good hand touched the handle before he spoke. "Well, Mr. Wilson, I certainly agree that William Henry is a fine attorney who is most capable of getting the necessary documents in order this afternoon. But...after what you did last night, William Henry might not be inclined to represent you at all...after he gets a copy of today's tape from George."

Dillard kept his hand on the door handle but twisted to face Hubert who had resumed his well-practiced stance with his arms folded across his chest.

"Before you depart, I need to remind you, as I have on three previous occasions, that everything said in this office is retained on tape that's recorded by a voice-activated recorder. This is 1962, Mr. Wilson. We must all be very careful with our comments."

Dillard cut his eyes to the corner shelf. The small red light glowed, and he shot his stare back to Hubert, glaring like a raging bull ready to charge, but Hubert struck first, just as Dillard released the door handle.

"Mr. Wilson," Hubert continued, "are you familiar with the term 'predatory lender'?" he asked.

Dillard's lower lip protruded beyond the upper as he clamped his upper lip between his teeth and stared at Hubert. "That garbage is hard to prove, Hubie," Dillard said, frowning as he looked over his glasses. "And you clearly know that! Besides, I'm fed up with being called that when I'm not."

Hubert took a step to his right, purposefully turning away, then twisted back to Dillard, offering a false tight-lipped smile. "No sir, it's not hard to prove at all in civil court...especially if every word said in a meeting like ours today is on tape. And, as William Henry will likely explain to you, sir, the damages awarded for the plaintiff by civil court can sometimes be more than double the fees charged... sometimes even more than the total value of the original loan."

Dillard looked up, gaping as he breathed through an open mouth.

"With your stellar reputation in the county," Hubert said with a snarky twist, "I would expect a jury to be quite generous with the plaintiff, any plaintiff—that is, of course, if you were sued in Civil court, maybe even by multiple plaintiffs in a class action suit," he added, twisting the dagger that he'd already jabbed to the hilt. "You have demonstrated predatory practices repeatedly over many years."

Dillard pulled his good hand from his trousers' pocket and touched his coat on the side. The silver flask was still there, and the Fairlane was parked on a side street, well out of sight of the bank's front door.

"You just stand by, boy. William Henry will be ringing up that phone of yours in just a few minutes. Then we'll see who wins the field today. And it ain't gonna be you!" he added as he flung the door open and stomped out.

15

CHAPTER

Hubert leaned on the edge of the conference table, rubbing his chin as he looked down, staring over the top of his glasses, simply thinking after Dillard left. He'd trapped Dillard, then run a bluff that might just work, but Dillard was right; it would be hard to win, even in civil court. Still, the story of him harassing Martha, a member of the Methodist church and a loyal widow of a veteran was big news. Even William Henry would have trouble winning that one. The court of public opinion would convict Dillard, no matter how hard William Henry argued. And he now had it on tape that Dillard had been told in advance that everything said in that room would be recorded. "Game, set, match," he mouthed, trying not to feel too confident.

For a long five minutes, he sat on the corner of the table with his hand over his eyes, thinking, running multiple levels of a logic diagram in his silence. Hubert didn't have to fire Martha to save his family property or his job as president of the bank, but he intended to do that anyway. His logic was as pristine as muddy frozen ice that had been crushed over and over when a tire hit that pothole, only to increase the ice's thickness when the new layer of dirty water that splashed from below froze up above once again.

Paradoxically, he loathed the idea of firing Martha and was simultaneously delirious with excitement about the future that it might enable. She was his confidante, his friend, the one person with whom he could discuss bank issues without risk of exposure or leaks. She was also the one person that would both understand and care when he needed to bare his soul. Neither his mother nor his father had the character to understand or care about his most delicate thoughts, but Martha did. He knew it, even though they were yet to have a personal discussion.

Perhaps worst of all, he simply craved her presence, stealing a glimpse of her working at her desk or making up some fool excuse to go to her office and ask a question. If it were simply that he would miss her deeply, he might be able to tolerate her absence, but it was more than that. The bond built over eleven years of close work together was both unbreakable and mutual. No one else would watch his back and discreetly tell him when he was making a mistake with a decision. No one else could be a sounding board that blended candor with tact. He could tell her his deepest thoughts and never fear a condescending response.

He lowered his hand to his chin and opened his eyes, still leaning on the corner of the conference table, then released a deep sigh, wondering why his life was so hard. He wasn't certain that he could stand the loneliness and the isolation of sitting in that office doing that job without Martha just outside. She didn't have to say a word to make him feel better or give him that little burst of confidence. Just the thought of her in that glassed office could sometimes rescue him from the morbid drudgery of numerical profiteering. Firing her would be a huge risk, and simultaneously a selfish and unselfish act in parallel. Hubert studied the pattern in the rug beneath the conference table without realizing he was actually seeing it. It was time. He couldn't put it off any longer, and he opened the wooden door that led toward her office.

*****

"Martha, could I visit with you for a few minutes?" he asked, standing in her doorway.

She turned to him, every muscle in her body taut. She'd heard most of his discussion with Dillard Wilson, and the dastardly boar left in such a huff that she was almost certain that Mr. Durrett had found a way to cut off his revenge. She'd smiled just a little when Dillard huffed out, doing a little mental dance with joy itself. But now it seemed that Hubert was too serious, too intense for having won such a battle. And then it hit her. He'd called her "Martha." In all their years together, she'd always been "Mrs. Heard." The red lights flared, and sirens screeched in her mind. Her shoulders slumped as the wind went out of her chest, assuming that eleven years of her life had just been sold down the river to save his grandfather's property. Unconsciously, she bit her lower lip and nodded before she pushed her chair back and stood. Hubert closed his office door behind them, and she sat opposite him at the conference table…in the same wooden armchair where Dillard had been just a few minutes before.

Hubert caught himself just before beginning the conversation and held up his forefinger signaling that she should hold her thoughts. He pushed his chair back and walked to the corner shelf, flipping a switch on the metallic electrical box. The red light on the recorder dimmed, then went out altogether.

"Now," he said, smiling just a little as he sat down, "we can talk freely."

Martha was now certain that he was about to terminate her employment. Panic about a subsistence for her and Steven leapt from a slow seep to a raging storm. The lump in her throat grew. Her eyes were already moist. Now he had the audacity to turn the recorder off so no one would ever know what was really said. She sniffed just once, then gritted her teeth.

"I need to get your opinion on something," she heard him saying.

Opinion? That one word didn't compute well, and she was confused once again. She sat up in her chair.

Hubert released a deep sigh before continuing. "First, let me tell you that I've been appraised of the situation that occurred at your home last night, and I thought you and Steven handled that well… quite well actually, not that it matters what I think of that, I suppose," Hubert said as he paused, first pursing his lips then tightening his shoulders in a strange shrug before he let them fall.

"Anyway, you should know that Olin and I met and had a rather intense discussion early this morning about that, and that the two of us have come up with an idea that I think you might want to consider."

Consider, she thought. *There must be options.*

"You know, of course, that Mr. Wilson is one of our largest shareholders and also that he has a very large sum of cash in our bank."

Martha nodded.

"You should also know that he has demanded that I fire you and threatened my job as well as my family property if I fail to do so right away…as in, today. Right now," he said, looking away, turning his head to the side before taking off his glasses and looking back to Martha. "And that I have absolutely no intention of doing that."

Martha tried to remain composed but felt a tear ebbing in the corner of her eye. She wasn't going to be fired. The words reverberated over and over. She wanted to believe that, maybe even say something clever, something appreciative, but she'd been so certain that she would be let go that her emotions were on a roller coaster that ran so high and so fast that her mind went flying off the seat much the same as her bottom had done at the county fair when she was just a girl. She couldn't process what was playing out before her, this ungodly thing that was sprung upon her in the December night by a gutter-dweller. Her mouth barely gaped, then closed as she nodded her understanding.

"But there is something that I want you to consider," Hubert said. "Seriously consider. It's something that's good for you and also bad for you. It's something that I'd like to see happen, and it's something that I absolutely detest." Hubert paused, standing, then turning away from her. He shook his head when he turned back, standing, hands on his hips as he began to pace. Finally, he walked back to the table and leaned forward, putting his hands down to support himself. "I want you to consider resigning," he said.

"But, but, but I can't. You know that. You have to know that. I have to keep this job no matter what it takes. Steven and I can't live without my income. And what's the difference in that and firing me? None! Everybody will know that you just soft-pedaled the situation and I was the sacrificial goat. And I didn't do anything wrong! Not one single thing. You said so yourself just a second ago."

Hubert raised both of his hands, palms out, trying for calm. "I didn't approach that well, did I?" he asked, standing straight and taking a deep breath.

"No. You didn't," Martha said in that terse, deeper tone that she reserved for matters that were really serious.

"Let me try again," he said, shuffling the chair beside him. "Olin has a job opening for a daytime dispatcher, and the salary is almost double that of your salary here at the bank."

Martha turned her head, then cut her eyes back to Hubert, searing him. "This isn't all about money, and you know that. The busybodies in this town have to know that I didn't get fired and that you didn't give in to Dillard Wilson. I didn't create this situation, Hubert. You have to believe—"

"I know you didn't," he said, interrupting. "I know. I know. I know. If anyone created the situation, it was me."

Martha pushed back in the chair, still seething but curious.

"If...if I had found a way to change your job description and put you in a higher salary classification, I could have paid you more money, and Dillard Wilson wouldn't have had any reason to come to your home last night." He paused, looking to the ceiling just briefly, almost afraid to meet her eyes again. "But I didn't do that. I thought about it, and just didn't do it. I should have. I could have. But I was too concerned with the political problems that would have been created here in the bank. So I just let things rock along...because I could. I could. So...it's my fault, perhaps even more so than Dillard. He's just an old fool that can't control his ignorant human impulses."

Hubert cut his eyes to the corner of the room where the recording equipment sat, then rolled his lips inward as he turned back.

"All my fault. Everything that's just happened," he said, letting his voice trail. "Everything. My fault. I had the power to prevent it, and I didn't do that. I do hope that one day you can forgive me."

Martha swallowed hard, looked down to the table, knowing that he was sincere. She'd known that for all of her eleven years at the bank. "What now, Hubert? Why do you want me to take this job, whatever it is that Olin has available? The bank...the bank is my second family. Why would I quit just because it's more money?"

Hubert gritted his teeth. He interlaced his fingers on the table, then looked up to Martha with soft, watery eyes that pled for understanding. "There are three good reasons, and none of them relate to Dillard. Well...almost none of them. The first reason is the money. You need the income, and if I shift your job classification here, most of the folks that you've worked with all this time will resent you. They may even start rumors about you and imply that I did that because you were a personal favorite, not because the job was any harder all of a sudden, but because I... I...uhmmm...was trying to get you to like me or something." He turned his head to the side, breaking their stare. "That didn't come out very well, did it?"

"I've seen you do much better," she said, "but okay, I understand your logic with that...and mostly, I agree, but that's not good enough to leave my second family. Number two reason?"

"Oh...that's the easy one," he said, smiling without showing teeth. "Olin is clearly the most powerful man in the county, maybe even in all of South Texas, and he can look out for you better than I can right now. You may not want anyone to *look out for you*, but if you need help, he can protect you from the likes of Dillard Wilson. And I do understand that 'protect' is probably a bad choice of words," he said before he paused, hesitating. "And I'm now zero for two, even on the easy one."

They both chuckled, looking away, almost afraid of what was happening between them, embarrassed by the moment that was silently welding them together and yet afraid to lock eyes.

"Clearly, you are now zero for two. As for 'protect', Olin—or you—would have to fight Steven for that privilege. And from what I saw of Dillard just now, I don't think either one of you should entertain the idea of fighting with my thirteen-year-old son. Well, he's just barely thirteen." She raised her eyebrows. "Reason number three?"

Hubert took in a deep breath and let it out slowly. "This is the hard one. Maybe not for you, but definitely for me."

Martha saw him fidgeting with the chair, tense now, and clearly nervous. She wanted to help him somehow, but couldn't, and the muscles that ran over her shoulders tightened with intensity as she waited.

"Reason number three. Big problem. Big, big problem. Maybe the worst that I've had in my life." He looked up, staring deep into her eyes, his face graying. "I'm… I'm too fond of you…fond of you in ways that I shouldn't be. Ways that just aren't allowed for a married man who is the president of the bank where you work. I know it's silly of me to feel this way, but I've fought this for…for years, and I don't seem to be able to change my sentiments. You're a wonderful human…just a wonderful woman, and I *need*—yes, *need*—to spend as much time with you as I can, for as long as I'm allowed to live on this earth."

He paused, swallowing hard. "God only knows the trauma that you've endured and the anxiety that you've been through since Jason died…and you just keep on going, probably spending more time being concerned for me than you've spent taking care of yourself. And still, after all the stress and pain…you're just perfect…beautiful in every way. You are…without a doubt…the sunshine of my life, and I don't know what I'll do if I can't see you every day."

He paused again, pursed his lips for a second, his eyes ebbing. "It sounds a little corny, I guess, but I…can visualize spending the rest of my life with you, not that I deserve the chance to do that."

Hubert hung his head, then slumped in the chair beside him. "I didn't plan this," he said, looking up toward the windows then back to her. "None of it. And I'm succinctly aware that I probably just made an absolute fool of myself in front of the one person that means more to me than life itself."

Martha swallowed hard but remained expressionless, save the one tear that began to stream down the right side of her face. For the first time in all of the years that she'd known Hubert Durrett, he'd thrown out caution and said something that was both genuine and important at the right time to…her. No amount of money, prestige, or outwitting of Dillard Wilson could equal that.

"Now do you understand why I'd like you to work with Olin?" he asked. "Some things in life are more important than we'd like to admit, I guess."

"Well," Martha said as she looked up, beginning to sniff, her eyes clearly watering, "you're now one for three. And that's the only

one that counted, literally," she added, sniffing more now. "I...
uhmmm... I never thought I would hear a man...a real man...say
something like that to me again, not in this lifetime," she said, leaning back in the chair, running her fingers through her flowing dark
hair and fighting the tears. "Shall I call Olin now or give you my
letter of resignation first?"

Hubert shrugged. The sequence didn't matter, and he said as
much.

"Okay..." she managed, still stalling. "Ohhh...oh, I did not
see this coming. Not at all. And right now I don't know whether to
thank Dillard Wilson or to curse him. Things like this don't usually
happen. Not to me, they don't."

She sat up in her chair, tightening her jaw and staring at him
through the tears. "Hubert, I need you to listen to me on one point.
One important point, and that's all I ask," she said. "I want you to
make it to that golf match this afternoon, cold or not, just make it
there like you always have. I didn't call George Williams and cancel
for you."

Her brow wrinkled. "We're both big kids now, Hubert, and I've
been through too much over these last few years to add high school
pain to the list. You have to appear to be the same person that you've
always been. You don't miss golf matches on Friday afternoon, no
matter what. So I want you to go today."

He nodded his agreement.

"Now, my one request. *If...if* you can't do anything about your
marriage, both of us still have to live here...in this little town. And
we don't need rumors flying around," she said, swallowing the lump
in her throat in time to brush a tear aside. "We *are* very much alike in
too many ways, and I agree that...uhhm... I agree that's a problem.
But... I also recognize that there's a very realistic possibility that you
won't be able to change the status of your ring finger, no matter how
much you might want that...or how much I might want you to do
that," she said, pausing. "I don't have a lot of runway left, Hubert,
and it's been really hard for me since I was a little girl." She looked
away, then turned back. "I know you can't understand that. You just
can't, because you weren't there. We both grew up in this same little

town, but your world was so far beyond mine that…that you'll never be able to understand. Just promise me this one thing," she said, pausing to sniff. "Promise me that you'll never hurt me. No matter what happens, you have to promise me that. I've had too much pain already, and I just don't think I can stand anymore," she said, dropping her head, then covering her eyes with her hands.

"Oh, Martha," Hubert said with his voice cracking. "You have my word. If you'll let me, I will love and protect you to my last moment on earth, no matter what happens. I promise you that."

Hubert took a deep breath and walked around the table and hugged her as she sat hunched forward in the chair, sniffling. It was the first time that he'd actually touched her in all of their years of working together.

16
CHAPTER

The thick Bermuda in Jack Tatum's pasture stood stiff but had begun to smell like fresh cut hay as the Saturday morning frost melted. By the time he and Robert Earl drove through the gate and found a clear path to the pecan trees along the creek, the white morning was simply heavy moisture on the grass that had begun to stumble toward winter's death.

Steven sat up straight in the passenger side seat when they cleared the heavy pipe gate that dragged the ground. Slowly, they made their way over the smooth ground toward the creek, the old Chevy bumping and creaking when they crossed the terraces that led to the flatter bottom-land. He couldn't take his eyes off of the grass, still standing tall, though burned by the frost. It was clearly dying, the smell told him that, but it stood there magically swaying in the gentle wind, defying its death for the season. Silently, he felt ashamed that the car would leave its tracks in passing, though he knew that it wouldn't do any real damage. A deep, serious hush came over him as they eased along, and he gawked at the property, cutting his eyes from one side to the other, trying not to miss any details. He felt the roof of his mouth begin to burn, and he swallowed hard, pushing back a deep sadness that swarmed him.

"Look at all them fine pecan trees that line the creek," he heard Robert Earl say.

"All nine hundred and sixty of them," Steven said in a nonchalant voice, without looking up.

Robert Earl cut his eyes to Steven, sizing up his thirteen-year-old friend sitting on the cloth seat that always smelled of mold, even though it was spotless on the surface.

"What makes you think you know exactly how many of 'em there are? I thought you said you'd never been out here before."

"Hadn't," Steven said, lying, ducking the question, hoping that Robert Earl would let him get away with it. "I just heard that somewhere. Those pecans must be worth a fortune now. Does Mr. Tatum have a grading shed somewhere, maybe a packing house? This is the right time of year for pecans. Maybe we'll get to see them shaking a tree this morning."

"Humph…boy, you're always thinking, aren't you? Always thinking. Maybe I should just start counting those trees to see if you're right."

Steven didn't answer as the car slowed and stopped. He didn't want to get out of the car. He didn't want to look at the panorama of the wide-open property with the special grass and pecan trees that lined the creek, three deep on each side, one hundred and sixty rows with six trees on each row. The rich land near the creek always seemed to have moisture, even in the August heat that blistered their part of Texas. The old trees seemed massive, both in diameter and height.

"I wonder how many acres are in this place," Robert Earl said when they were out of the car and standing near the hood looking at the trees that were now almost free of their leaves. "Must be a bunch," he added. "A man could make a fine living with a place like this. Hereford cattle, butterball fat, some of the finest hay in Texas, and pecans," he said, crossing his arms over his chest and staring into the distance. "And it'd be a fine way to make that living. A lot better than living in town and working in a garage, even though I do make first-class money there. First class!" he repeated. "Still…this is special."

"Two sections, twelve hundred and eighty acres," Steven said.

"You sure you've never been here before?" Robert Earl asked, turning quickly to Steven. "Seems like you know too much."

"I forgot that I used to come out here a long time ago...with my dad before he passed away. I heard him and Mr. Tatum talking about things. That's all."

Robert Earl turned away, shaking his head. "You know, kid, folks are still talking about what you did to Dillard Wilson. Everybody knows it was you. It wasn't me that said anything, mind you, but everybody knows. I'd bet even Big Henry will tiptoe around you now."

Robert Earl shoved his hands deep in his pockets and began to take slow steps away from the 1947 Chevy.

"You know, you just ain't a normal kid," he said, twisting to look back at Steven who still stood beside the front fender leaning on the corner panel. "Not normal at all. I don't know of a single grown man in town that would've done what you did Thursday night." He stopped walking and chuckled to himself, shaking his head a little. "Who thinks of pulling the coil wire out to hold somebody else hostage? And the valve wrench for the tires. Who thinks about that kind of stuff?" he asked to no one in particular as he squinted in the morning light.

Robert Earl took out one of the targets that he'd bought at the Five and Dime store and started walking through the thick grass toward one of the massive pecan trees.

"What are you doing?" Steven asked.

"I'm gonna tack this target to that tree over there and teach you to shoot," Robert Earl said as he walked straight ahead without turning around. "Got to earn my other five dollars."

"Uhmmm...we don't want to do that," Steven said.

"Why? Won't hurt nothin'. You ain't gonna hit it much, no way."

"Nawh. Nawh," Steven said, feeling his heart quicken, "those aren't our trees, and I don't want to go to jail for trespassing and killing somebody else's tree."

"I'm telling you, it ain't gonna hurt nothin'. I do it all the time when I need to sight my rifle. And besides, there ain't nobody around here no more. The old man died about five years ago. Didn't have any boys. The place is going down pretty quick now."

"What about nephews or cousins?" Steven asked before thinking.

"You're really curious about this place, aren't you, boy?" Robert Earl asked as he tacked the first target to the tree.

Steven didn't answer. He'd said too much already, but he couldn't put any lead in that pecan tree. That was senseless. They were huge trees now, and that seemed so very strange to him. Uncle Melvin told him about the trees before his final Council session. They'd used handhole diggers and shovels to make the box holes in the ground to plant them. Every sapling got a quarter-barrel of water carried from the wagon in buckets as it was planted. They'd filled three pieces of dried bamboo with store-bought fertilizer, burying each about eighteen inches from the trunk. It had taken four years to plant the trees and another eight years before they brought in the first decent crop. He couldn't let them be hit with lead.

"Robert Earl," Steven almost shouted, "you need to take that target down. Let's go about six hundred yards to the east on the other side of the creek. There's a sixty-foot bluff that rises out of the creek bottom there with a big iron ore rock on the right side. We can put the target there. That rock is soft, and the lead won't ricochet."

Robert Earl turned quickly and stared. "Kid…what's going on here? You don't sound right. You sound like an old man all of a sudden, and how in the devil do you know so much about this place if you hadn't been here since your dad passed? You been lying to me about something, kid?"

Robert Earl spat on the ground, then rubbed the back of his neck as he stared up toward Steven. "Come on now. How do you know this stuff, boy? It just don't make no sense. You say you ain't been out here in a long time, but you know where everything is… stuff I ain't seen before, and I been out here plenty of times. Don't lie to me now. You better not lie," he said, walking back to Steven with the target in hand. "How?"

"My dad came out here bird hunting pretty often. I tagged along with him once. We didn't get many birds that day. Wind was up. The dogs wouldn't hold a point, and the birds kept running on the ground," Steven said, lying.

Robert Earl continued to stare at him. Steven knew that he didn't believe him, but it was a good line, and he had no real reason to doubt him. It was actually a perfectly plausible answer, but still, they both knew it wasn't true.

"Why don't you just get in the car," Robert Earl said. "We're gonna ride down there and see if this bluff is really there. I ain't never seen this bluff that rises sixty feet almost straight up from that bottom." He paused, thinking. "But if you're right, that'd be a fine place to put a deer stand. Yes sir. A fine place."

They bumped through the pasture without speaking. It was all coming back to Steven now. Every detail. And it frightened him.

The car jolted him as it hit a hole where a hog had wallowed.

"It's right over there," Steven said, pointing. "A log footbridge… if it hadn't fallen in since I was out here with Dad," he added, trying for credibility. "If I remember right, you can't drive across the creek unless you go all the way to the south edge and hit that dozer cut-out at just the right time of year when the water's not too high."

Robert Earl cut his eyes to Steven again but didn't say anything.

The bluff was only a hundred yards across the flat grassland beyond the footbridge, which didn't show any deterioration at all. The hickory logs that made the bridge were peeled and seasoned before they were assembled with nails that were so long that they looked like spikes. Holes were drilled in the hickory with a brace and bit before the hammer could pound the twelve-inch nail spikes into place. Robert Earl walked ahead and put his target up on a bush near the edge of the bluff.

For twenty minutes, Steven slowly aimed the old Colt pistol and fired at the target. The first seven shots missed completely, but by the end of the shooting session he could at least hit the circle, and one shot struck close to a bull's-eye.

The clutch-accelerator coordination of the standard shift drove Steven nuts as they stopped and jerked all across the pasture for a full ten minutes before he found rhythm. He never learned to hit the gears without grinding them, but by the end of the session, he could drive, if the only thing he had to dodge were immobile pecan trees in an otherwise wide-open field. The north wind velocity increased by the time they finished the driving lesson. Though the frost was long gone, the ominous sky cast a pall over the nearly abandoned farm, and the cold hurt Steven when he pulled out a five-dollar bill and handed it to Robert Earl.

"Easy money. A lot easier than mechanic work," Robert Earl said, smiling a little as he slipped the bill into his money clip. "You sure seem to know a lot about this place. That don't make much sense to me."

"Guess I heard Dad talking about coming here and remembered more than I thought."

"Humph..." Robert Earl managed as he opened the driver's side door. "Still don't make much sense, but I don't see any other way you'd have found out."

At the gate, Steven put his hand on the dash and turned to face Robert Earl. "I know it's some trouble," he said, "but could you take me back to that footbridge?"

Robert Earl squinted and wrinkled his brow. Steven understood the expression and didn't wait for the question.

"I want to walk over some of this place and see if I can find where Dad and I bird hunted when I was a little kid," he said, knowing that he and Dad had never hunted on the property.

Robert Earl turned his head to the side and took a deep breath.

"Sumpthin's wrong with you, boy. You ain't right. That's all. You just ain't right."

"I'll pay you another five dollars if you'll come back and get me about one o'clock."

Robert Earl let out a deep sigh and nodded before he turned the car around and started back toward the footbridge. "What you gonna do if a wolf comes along or some bum that would kill you for the boots you're wearing, much less for the money you've got in your pocket?"

"I've got my Colt, and I can shoot now," Steven said.

"Yeah. Yeah. I suppose you might can," he said, stopping at the footbridge. "Just remember this, boy. If sumpthin' comes along, you shoot quick, and you shoot straight. And don't hesitate none at all. You shoot to kill if you shoot at all. I've been seeing some wolves that were way too thin down this way, and it bothers me some to let you out here by yourself. I got to go meet Melanie at the drugstore Sundae Bar, but I'll be back here right after that. I don't like this none at all."

"Robert Earl, I'm thirteen now. I'm stout, and I'm quick-minded," Steven said, almost glaring. "You take your time with Melanie."

17
CHAPTER

Steven made his way to the base of the bluff and started to climb the rocky crag covered with bushes and vines, arriving beneath the big trees that shaded the shelf of land high above where the original house stood. Once on top, he stood still, staring at a thick mass of weeds, briars, and scrub trees that had once been the clean and orderly heart of a working farm. Steven let his head droop, briefly closing his eyes, thinking about the hours and years of work put in on the bluff, the times that the family fought off critters and marauders, the grand social events that they hosted. He looked up again, letting his eyes move slowly across the eight-acre hilltop, then shook his head a little before turning away, unable to accept what had happened to a lifestyle gone from peaceful fruition to an unimaginable jungle, void of prosperity.

He turned back slowly, releasing a disgusted breath as he searched for the spot where the house had stood. Nothing. He dropped his hand to the Colt in his waistband just to be sure it was still there and took a step toward the house site, pushing the brush and briars down with his feet.

He found the water well first. It had been filled with dirt, but the sunken ground was thirty-six inches in diameter and in a near-perfect circle. Located on the porch of the house, the well had been a luxury feature with its hand pump, rather than a bucket on a rope used to draw the water.

Steven swatted at the late-season mosquitoes that buzzed him, then bent a willowy sweet gum sapling about head high, and used his Uncle Henry knife to cut it off, making him a staff to use against the dense underbrush.

A chill ran between his shoulders when he glimpsed the first of the massive iron-ore rocks that once supported the floor beams and still marked the house's location, though some were nearly buried with underbrush and debris now.

From there, he knew exactly where the cemetery lay, some fifty yards behind the house on the south side of the bluff. Despite the sweet gum staff, the scrub brush grabbed him, pricking him with thorns as he worked his way there where the seventeen graves lay marked by cut iron-ore rocks, some of which were three-foot squares hewn a full twelve inches thick. Faded by weather and dulled by rotted leaves and mold, the inscription on the rock that marked the center grave was barely legible. Steven used his feet to kick the brush away and his hand to sweep debris from the rock until he could read the inscription that read simply, "Sarah—Died March 10, 1832."

Steven didn't hurry, thinking that Robert Earl could wait if need be. He recognized that he might not recall any of this by morning. His memory of things beyond the present came and went. Sometimes he could remember all, and sometimes he remembered nothing.

Five minutes later, Steven dropped to one knee at the foot of Sarah's grave and began to methodically scrape soil and vegetation from the foot area with the fresh-broken sweet gum limb. The earth was soft there, leaves having built up and rotted over the decades that had lapsed since the grave was dug. Six inches down the wooden probe found metal. He hesitated for a moment, kneeling over the grave and leaning on the sapling pole, staring at the top of a metal box buried there near the end of the civil war.

For several long minutes, he simply stood there, staring. Were it not for a late-season horsefly that terrorized him sporadically, the stillness would have been pristine. He had to open the box. He knew what was buried there, but he had no idea who might have raided it during all these years. Finally, he got down on both knees and dropped his head, not like a thirteen-year-old boy would do, fidgeting, squirming, impatient with the stillness of the singular lonely moment, but he bent like an old man remembering better times and wondering what he'd done with all that time, those years that seemed impossibly long as he was going through them but leapt by in an instant as he looked back.

Finally, he nodded slowly to himself as though he'd received an approval from some unknown source and began to use the sapling tool to scrape the dirt from the sides of the box so debris wouldn't fall inside when he pried the lid open.

It was all there—the land grant documents, the gold bars, a wedding ring, and, most importantly, a final letter from Sarah. He reached for the letter written on timeless linen and folded so many years ago, worrying that it might fall apart when he took it in his hand. For a brief time, Steven looked up to the massive oaks beyond the cemetery, thinking that he was grateful that Sarah hadn't lived long enough to see her simplistic, peaceful world desecrated with human greed. He read the letter over twice, then gently laid it back in the box, and sat down, wrapping his arms around his knees, letting his eyes close.

The east wind destroyed his peace, and Steven suddenly felt cold. He looked around but saw nothing. He wanted to cry, not from loneliness or the pain of the moment but because he understood the fragility of his existence. The part of him that lived somewhere deep inside and survived death came forth, but he finally took a deep breath, still questioning why he was alive and what he needed to do.

Tears welled in the corners of his eyes, and he sniffed, trying to stifle the lump in his throat, telling himself that he would never again fail like he'd done in these first thirteen years, confessing to himself that he'd lost the battle with himself when Dillard came. He let his head droop forward, then shook it slowly from side to side wondering how could he have allowed himself to become such a shallow human in such short a time.

Lost in deep commiseration, he didn't immediately recognize the sound of leaves rustling over his left shoulder. He jerked his head up, looking quickly in that direction, initially afraid that Robert Earl or someone had followed him up the bluff and would rob him or worse. His eyes, clear now, focused on the area where the sound seemed to be, but there was nothing. He scanned the horizon, searching back and forth. Still, nothing. Steven took short breaths, slowly searching from side to side. A squirrel jumped from limb to limb in the huge old oaks, but that was at least thirty yards away and didn't make noise. His head had been down, but he was sure of the sound. Something had walked along the edge of the bluff in front of where the house once stood.

Steven got to his feet slowly, his head up, still scanning the horizon. Gradually, he moved his hand from his side to the Colt's handle. Still, he saw nothing, heard nothing, excepting the gentle wind's occasional swishing of leaves. Slowly, he studied every suspected area—the tree trunks that could hide almost anything, the vines and brush near the sunken well, the clumps of palmetto—but he couldn't find a thing.

This was too coincidental, him opening the box and something or someone walking not far away. He touched the Colt's handle again, then let his eyes move slowly, concentrating and allowing for varying shades of light, but still, there was nothing that made sense. He'd heard something unnatural; he knew it. Still wary, he crouched, returning his mind to Sarah and the box, simultaneously swatting another ear-buzzing mosquito that obviously didn't know it was December. He took one of the twenty gold bars from the box and placed it beside him, then lowered the lid and began snapping the five catches closed.

As he pressed the last catch down, a paralyzing screeching sound seized him. Spines ran across his back, shoulder to shoulder, and he clinched his fists, readying himself to fight as every muscle tightened. The noise and shock clutched him, and he didn't think about the Colt; there was only time to freeze and get ready for the bobcat's attack. Steven turned toward the sound in time to see the muscled cat's powerful leap from the oak above on to a week-old fawn that quietly bedded under a small pine some fifteen yards away. Too late, he pulled the Colt from his belt and fired in the air, hoping to scare the big cat away, but the wails of innocent death continued for a gut-wrenching minute before the feline silenced his prey and started dragging the dead fawn toward the area where the cotton house once stood.

With the acrid smell of gunpowder lingering and still holding the gun, Steven bent down, bracing his arms on his knees, heaving huge breaths. He had sensed the danger, but he hadn't understood the looming terror and was disgusted with himself.

Steven hadn't found the danger until it was too late, and he realized that the cat could have just as easily selected him for a target, that no one would have found his body. No one knew where he was, just as he hadn't known that the fawn was curled so close by.

Steven straightened himself but let his head droop again. Their house here on the bluff had once been the site of great intellectual debates, social occasions, church services, weddings, funerals, and celebrations. Now...the bugs, the tangled underbrush, and murdering animals dominated. No one else would have seen the cemetery. It was just a patch of ground now covered with vines and briars, a virtual thicket. Leaves that steadily rotted and became rich soil covered much of the headstone rock. Anyone else would have walked right by.

He knew that he had to leave and gritted his teeth, almost holding his breath before he made his decision. He would be back, but not like this, not like the newborn fawn. Never again.

After wrapping the box with the oilskin remnants and covering it with soil that he'd packed in place, he sprinkled layers of leaves to hide the area before he bent to one knee and stared at the cut rock with Sarah's name and dates inscribed.

"Uncle Melvin told me about this place," he said. "I just wanted to come for a little while. And try to remember. That's all," he said before he turned. "I'll be back as soon as I can," he added as he took off his jacket, turning it into a sack with the heavy gold bar inside, bumping the side of his leg as he walked away. A few minutes later, he found the remnants of the old wagon road that once switch-backed down the side of the bluff and wound its way toward the footbridge.

18
CHAPTER

Steven saw the blue Chevy truck on the far side of the footbridge and froze. It wasn't Mama's car, and it wasn't Robert Earl's truck. It was Henry Watson Sr.'s truck, and he knew what that meant.

He was too late for stealth. He had absent-mindedly ambled at least ten yards from the base of the bluff out into the open ground, away from the trees and undergrowth before looking up to see the truck. He cursed himself under his breath for being so careless and walking out into the open without studying the terrain and conditions ahead of him. He knew better than that and took in a deep breath as he stared across the two hundred yards of open ground between him and the footbridge. Whoever was there with the truck on the opposite side of the creek would have seen him by now. That was clear. It was an open ground ambush, and there were at least three of them. One of them leaned his back against the passenger side front tire. He had something in his hands, but Steven couldn't tell what it was. They were waiting at the only decent creek crossing, and it would be three against one, just like Karl.

Steven stood still, thinking, contemplating, searching for options. He considered climbing the bluff and forcing them to come to him, but that would mean luring them deep into the thick brush, then flank them to the south, making a run across the open ground to get to the truck while they were searching for him up high. That seemed like a plausible solution, but it held too many variables. What if he made it to their truck and the keys weren't in the ignition? He couldn't outrun them to the road; they would get back there and use the truck to catch him. What if they were smart enough to leave one person at the truck to protect their base while the two others hunted him down? By the time he finished a fight with the one left behind, the other two would be back, and they'd have him. He couldn't outrun them, and he couldn't hide from them. Not now.

All three of them now stood at the leading edge of the footbridge, staring at him. It was Big Henry with Brad and Damian Wilson. He touched the pistol in his belt and decided to back into the brush on the side of the bluff. At least they wouldn't be able to see him there, and he could buy some time to plan.

Steven didn't turn his back to Big Henry and the Wilson brothers until he was on the old wagon road. At that point, he turned and hiked up the side of the bluff until he was half-way up, then worked his way to the north under the cover of the undergrowth until he reached the giant iron ore rock that sat almost forty feet above the creek bottom. He could easily see the Wilsons and Big Henry when he nestled behind the rock and took out the pistol. It was a very long shot for the old revolver, still slightly over one hundred yards from that angle where the rock jutted forward on the point of the bluff.

Steven pulled the hammer back, then rested his arm on the edge of the rock, tilting the barrel up just slightly to allow for the bullet's drop as he squinted, the sights aligned and steady. He took a deep breath and began to let it out as he squeezed the trigger little by little until the gun exploded, launching the bullet directly toward the footbridge and deep into the old Elm that stood on the south edge of the footbridge. Wood splinters flew and bark blasted free as the Wilsons dove for the ground and crawled toward the car. Big Henry didn't flinch, standing erect but leaning on the footbridge railing adjacent to the elm, staring at the Wilson boys.

"What in the dickens are you two doing?" he asked with that annoyed Texas twang. "Don't you know that if he'd wanted to kill us, we'd already be dead? That bullet was aimed at that elm tree, boys. Just a warning. That's all." Big Henry squished his lips together and released a breath. "This ain't gonna be easy, fellas. Little Stevie just announced that he meant…business," he said, letting the word trail as he looked across the footbridge to the big crust of rock that jutted from the bluff. "It ain't gonna be easy at all," he said under his breath where only he could hear.

Three hours later and a half mile to the south, deep in the woods, Steven sat almost invisibly under a giant pine tree whose base was shrouded with brush and vines. He swatted at another lingering mosquito, knowing that he had covered his trail and was alone on the steep slope. The afternoon sun bore down on him, and he climbed a few limbs up in the tree where he could catch any slight breeze that might cool him. Straining, he could see the Chevy truck parked by the footbridge. He was sure that they wouldn't give up, thinking that Dillard likely paid them, and they wouldn't want to swallow their pride if they went back to town without some of his blood staining their hands and shirts. Moving only when he needed to shift his weight or change his handhold, Steven waited. In two more hours, it would be dark. He could cover the one hundred and ten yards of open ground between the bluff and the creek easier then. Once he'd made it up the steep bank, he would flank Big Henry and the Wilsons and stay in the wooded areas near the road until he was back to town.

Thirty minutes after dark, he began to crawl toward the creek, dragging his homespun sack with the gold bar. He was three hundred and fifty yards south of the Chevy and the footbridge. Even though the creek was over eight foot deep at that point, the stream was only two steps wide and easily fordable. Twenty minutes into the process, Steven sat upright and began to slowly slide down the first bank, trying not to make a sound or a sudden movement that might stir a night bird and alert the Wilsons and Big Henry. Less than two minutes later, he grasped exposed tree roots and started pulling himself up the other side. His chest heaved as he reached the opposite edge and froze. There was a noise. He was sure of it, and he wedged himself in the cavity just below the bluff that had been created by the rushing high water in the spring.

"He's got to come across down here," Steven heard Big Henry say. "Spread out along the bank and be ready to use your bat."

Steven huddled in the back of the shelf with Big Henry standing almost directly over him, a full moon dawdling behind errant clouds in the eastern sky. When the moon cleared those clouds, he would be clearly visible from the opposite shore, if they went over there to look.

"Brad, come back up this way," Steven heard Big Henry say. "He won't be that far down. It's too deep down there."

Steven squirmed in his mini-cavern, hoping that he wouldn't make noise or send a rock rolling down the bank. None of them were across on the opposite shore yet. If they didn't go across and look back, he might be able to wait for them to leave.

"I ain't seen nothin', Big Henry," Brad said, standing hands on hips, staring toward the bluff across the field. "Nothin' moving. No noise. Nothin'. Why do you think he'll come across down here? We ain't really seen him in five or six hours now. Not since that shot, and we didn't really see him then."

"He's there, and he's gonna come out right through here. He ain't stupid, and somehow he knows this is the best place to get across this creek and make a run toward town."

Big Henry took a deep breath and let it out, mashing his lips together as he scowled. "That little jerk used to steal my pecans. I knew it, but I never did catch him. He ain't getting away this time. I made sure Robert Earl wouldn't come back, and I don't care if we have to wait here till dawn."

The night air seemed moist and cold to Steven. He thought about taking the bar out of his sweatshirt and putting it on but decided that it would be too risky with at least two of them standing over him. He brought his legs forward and jammed his back harder against the dirt wall behind him, hoping to fend off the cold. At least the wind couldn't get to him.

Another ten minutes passed in dark silence, but Steven knew they were still up above. Big Henry and the Wilsons were close enough that he could hear their paces in the thick grass and the occasional crunch or snap when they stepped on a fallen twig. He measured his breathing and was gritting his teeth when he felt the movement across his leg. When he heard the sound rattles, Steven lurched out of the earthen cavity, tumbling half-way down the side of the creek.

"We got him!" he heard Big Henry shout. "We got him! Get over here, Damian. Get over here now!"

Steven had only a split second to make his choice. Deciding that it was better to charge two of them rather than wait for Damian to catch up and fight three of them, he surged up the bank, churning his feet against the earth that slid beneath him. He was near the top but couldn't actually see Big Henry and Brad when the baseball bat swung with all of Brad's strength caught his left arm and shoulder then slid across, delivering the bulk of its force against the base of his neck, almost knocking him unconscious.

Instinctively, in a dazed state, Steven swung the sweatshirt in the direction of the blow with his right arm; the centrifugal force of the roundhouse swing of the gold bar caught Brad Wilson with all its weight squarely on his left ear and temple. The sound cracked like a broken branch as bones ruptured and blood droplets sprayed as though they'd been jettisoned from a water hose. Brad's eyes rolled back as his limp form tumbled forward on top of Steven just as Big Henry swung his baseball bat like a golf club catching Brad's extended leg rather than Steven. Before Big Henry could gather himself to swing again, Steven dropped the sweatshirt and took the Colt from his waistband and fired at Big Henry just two feet above.

Big Henry's knee collapsed as the lead slug shattered bone and sinew, tumbling him forward, rolling past Steven to the bottom of the creek bed as he screamed with the fear and shock that always precedes the pain.

Steven didn't hesitate. Using his good arm to grab the sweatshirt sack with the gold bar, he lurched up and over the lip of the bank, spitting blood and dirt, first crawling then running toward the Chevy truck, praying all the while that they had left the keys in the ignition and that it would start.

Seconds later, he slammed the shift lever on the steering column down into first gear as he released the depressed clutch to start forward. He was only ten yards away moving slowly when he saw Damian Wilson grabbing the tailgate, dragging behind. Steven considered firing the Colt, hoping for a lucky shot, then thought better of it and jammed the clutch and brake simultaneously. He ground the shift lever straight up into reverse and released the clutch, letting the bumper of the dark blue Chevy slam Damian into an unconscious state.

By the time Steven reached the open pipe gate that led to the hard surface road, the gray cloud in his vision dominated; his left arm dangled at his side, completely useless, and the pain from the baseball bat nearly drove him unconscious. Everything blurred. He couldn't focus his eyes.

Later, when the story was told, Steven couldn't remember the four-mile drive to town or stopping in front of Doc Raley's house, leaning forward on the steering wheel with eyes closed as he held the horn rim down, rousing everyone in the neighborhood with its constant blare. It was a little after midnight when Steven finally opened his eyes to see Mama standing over his bed in Doc Raley's office. She wore jeans and was perfectly coiffed just as she would have been to go to work every morning.

"Was it worth it, Steven?" Martha asked in that flat, disgusted tone that he hated. "Was it really worth all this?"

"There were three of them, Mama—Big Henry and the two Wilson boys."

Martha, head down, paced beside his bed. "I know all about that."

She stopped pacing and faced him. "Olin isn't sure that any of those boys are going to live, Steven. Big Henry will never walk again, and he had lost enough blood by the time they got him out of that creek that he may not make it. Neither one of the Wilsons is conscious yet. Both of them have serious head injuries. And you... you may have lost the use of your left arm. Forever. Your collarbone is broken. Your arm is broken in two places. Doc doesn't know much about your neck and shoulder yet."

She let her eyes close as she exhausted a long breath, then lowered her chin, shaking her head slightly before she looked back to him. "How could you do all this? Did you set them up? Did you lay a trap?"

"No, Mama. No," he said, half moaning. "I didn't do that."

Steven tried to shift in the bed, but his arm shot pain through him, and the base of his skull pounded. "They came after me. Dillard must have paid them."

"So why didn't you try to avoid them? You're good at that when it's convenient for you. Wouldn't it have been better to avoid all this…this horror? You could go to jail for this, Steven. Jail!"

"I did try, Mama. I did," Steven mumbled.

"You did what, Steven?"

"Tried to hide," he mumbled. "Thought I could flank them and get back to town after dark. A rattlesnake ran me out of my hiding place, and they came after me."

"A rattlesnake?" Martha asked.

Steven cut his eyes to her and nodded slightly.

"It's late in the year for a rattler to be out. Are you lying to me, Steven? Don't lie to me now. For God's sake, don't lie to me right now!"

"No, Mama. And I know it's late for rattlers." Steven let his eyes close. "It happened, Mama. I swear it."

Martha bent to the straight chair beside the bed and got her purse. "Did the rattlesnake bite you, Steven?"

"No. It was dark, and he missed when I started rolling down the bank."

Martha turned toward the door. "You think about this, Steven. Would any of this have happened if you hadn't marked Dillard with that slingshot of yours?"

Martha put her hand on the doorknob. "Everybody lost tonight, Steven. Everybody. Just pray that those other boys live and that you don't have to go to jail," she said, opening the door to leave. "Everybody lost."

Steven ground his teeth. Every part of his upper body hurt—his arm, his shoulder, his neck, and his head. Mama was blurry as she stood at the door, but he locked his jaws and swallowed hard, thinking that she was wrong. Clearly, she was wrong, and he had to do something about it. He managed to lean up on an elbow and stare at Martha.

"Mama… I want you to hear me on this."

Martha took a deep breath and held it.

"Big Henry and the Wilsons came out there to kill me." Steven coughed, sending pain darts through him again when the broken arm moved. He spat bloody phlegm in a towel. "I didn't set the trap. They did."

"But it would've never happened if you hadn't used your sling-shot on Dillard Wilson."

"That's not right, Mama. Not right at all. I didn't start all this. Dillard started all of this when he came to our house up to no good."

Steven let his words settle, staring at Martha without blinking. "Dillard started it, and I finished it. There are plenty of folks like the Wilsons and Big Henry in this world, Mama. Somebody's got to face them down and keep order. That's part of what we're sent here to do."

"How do you know it's finished, Steven? Why would you think they'll stop coming after you? Or after me?"

Steven looked away, then back to Martha. "They took a lickin', Mama. A bad lickin'. And there's more good folks in this world than there are bad folks. A lot more. And when the good people in this town find out what really happened, it won't be just us standing up against them. Not now. The bullies will back down, Mama. They ain't comin' back. And they won't try again. Not ever," he managed before collapsing to the bed, trying not to cough, struggling for breath and clarity with eyes that he wouldn't focus.

Martha stared at him, still clenching her teeth as she glared. Seconds later, she turned and left without another word.

19
CHAPTER

Forty Years Later

Steven lounged in the beige Jetson recliner with its large padded arms and pedestal base that allowed it to swivel three hundred and sixty degrees. He sometimes smoked a Cuban and sipped bourbon on Friday nights, even though the Cubans were still illegal. But there were no Cubans tonight, just a shot glass that sweated with the DC humidity. Near exhaustion, he eased his head back on the padded cushion and closed his eyes, knowing all the while that he still had to pick up Shannon from a school party at ten o'clock. She was now the same age as he'd been when he and Robert Earl first went to the Jack Tatum property where he found Sarah's grave. It was just the two of them now, excepting the housekeeper who had a room and a bath at the opposite end of the house. Tonight was his time to close his eyes and breathe, to sip the whiskey slowly and think.

Marion divorced him just after Shannon was born, telling him on a Tuesday morning as he was leaving for the office that she just didn't want to be married anymore. For her, it was that simple. They'd been married for almost fifteen years, and at first, he'd thought that he hadn't heard her correctly. Wearing the one-hundred-thirty-count Italian tailored suit, with briefcase in hand, he stared, almost dumbfounded, so she repeated it in a haughty, smug, almost cavalier way that twisted the knife that she'd already plunged into him. She was tall and pretty, a true leggy blue blood and the catch of his university class. She came from money, and he had none of that then. In those early years, his friends joked that she was far too good for him, but they'd loved and laughed for that first marital decade, and he'd assumed that they'd be together for a lifetime, even though she wasn't Sarah or Erin, and he knew that.

Steven didn't open his eyes to pull the handle for the footrest. At fifty-three and a single man for twelve years, he didn't expect to find anyone else. He cleaned the stray hair from his brush with a vacuum every month and felt his years of pain every time he bent his fragile back or reached with his left arm. He sipped the bourbon and lay his head back again, his eyes still closed, allowing himself to sink into the cloth recliner, strategically placed in a special corner of his bedroom.

He'd started the week in Paris where he kept a small apartment, had flown to Singapore to conduct a business review, caught the midnight flight to Hong Kong where he met a former colleague to discuss a new telecom venture, then made it back to London for a Thursday morning session on a potential property acquisition in the northeast quadrant, should the city be successful with its bid for the Olympics. By the time he touched down at Reagan National, he questioned why he still did it all. He longed for the sprawling house on the hill opposite the bluff where Sarah's cemetery was now fenced and manicured. He savored the sunsets on the covered porch and his precious time with Mama, who was now almost eighty and still pristine in everything she did. Hubert passed almost a decade earlier, and he knew that Martha needed him...still. No one else would ever understand the passion in his voice when he talked about the Snack Jack kids.

He was dozing in the platform rocker with the shot glass still upright in his hand when the phone rang. It was eight o'clock in DC, an hour earlier in Texas. Mama hadn't flown halfway around the world that week, and they talked on most Friday nights.

"You made it back, I see," Martha began. "Pretty fair round this week, but of course you had a head start by leaving from Paris, so you don't get credit for all of those miles."

"Humph...it was still almost enough to circle the earth, I guess," he said, pausing, trying to wake from the deep, exhausted sleep.

"Why don't you quit, baby? You don't need money. I don't need money. Neither one of us wants a fancy life anymore, and Shannon will inherit more than she can spend in ten lifetimes. Why don't you come back to Texas and just live a simple life? A better life. Be good to yourself for a change, find a nice woman and settle down."

Steven ran a hand through his long graying locks, knowing that he would enjoy that. He'd dined in many of the world's best restaurants and lived in some of the most cultural cities, but he did miss Texas. Even more than his home state, he longed for a companion, someone that could share his joys and problems, someone who would never question his sincerity or his loyalty. Shannon listened well and sometimes made comments that raised his eyebrows with subjects that he'd thought she didn't understand, but even though she'd become his good friend, he needed more than a platonic relationship. He despised going to bed alone; worse, waking to a silent house or hotel room was almost as bad as surviving in a *name-only* relationship that was long since dead. He'd come to trust Shannon, but she was barely thirteen.

Despite using all of the little-known tricks of flight, his hands and feet swelled now. They didn't do that when he'd begun this international mergers and acquisitions work in his late twenties—buying, growing, splitting, selling companies. His body routinely told him things that the doctors' tests didn't, and the swelling forced him to think of his dad who died so young with heart disease. He didn't want to quit. He was too young for that, and he believed that his business network would all fall apart without him.

"Still trying to catch up with those Snack Jack kids, Mama. They had airplanes that actually flew, you know. I'm convinced of that. And by now they probably have wives who don't flit away with the tall country club types who are good dancers and tell funny stories but don't work very much."

Martha winced, briefly holding the phone out from her ear. "Steven, Steven, Steven…when will you stop that mess and admit that you are your only real competitor? When will you stop despising those other folks? Go look in the mirror, baby. See yourself like everyone else sees you. You *are* the elite of those Snack Jack kids, and deep down where you live, you know that. You could be a model in one of those men's clothing magazines. You have friends all over the world, and your net worth is somewhere in the upper nine digits. Why can't you see yourself for once? Everybody down here talks about you all the time. Most of 'em are jealous of you living like you do, running around the world, always going first class."

"I'm just tired, Mama. Really, really tired for fifty-three. And I do have lots of enemies. Lots…of…enemies."

"Why don't you think about coming home? Run for president or maybe the senate. You'd be good at that, and the country needs high-quality folks in the government."

"Mama, the only thing that I want to be president of…is that porch down there, but Old Socks is president of that now, and he'd bite my hand off if I disturbed his afternoon nap," he said, smiling, thinking of his favorite dog. "Socks actually likes me. You know he does. I'd count him as a friend any day, but he wouldn't be happy sharing that porch with me. On the other hand, there are plenty of folks who would like to attend my funeral just to be sure that I was dead and buried."

"Why, Steven? Why? You haven't done anything illegal. And I can't imagine that you've even done anything that's unethical. That's just not you! Look at Shannon. She's just a reflection of who you are, even if she's young. Doesn't that tell you something?"

Steven stared straight ahead for a long moment. She was right, of course. Mama was rarely off target, even at eighty. Still, he'd stopped counting the weeks where he was gone for six days and only had hotel reservations for four nights. He didn't know if he could slow down long enough to actually relax. It wasn't about money or power anymore; that simply burdened him. That pace, that breadth of life was in his blood now, and he didn't know if he could quit, no matter how tired he'd become. He swallowed hard, knowing that the life he'd chosen to build was larger than himself but didn't exempt him from its pain.

"Why did Marion divorce me, Mama? I think about that almost every day. What did I do wrong? If I had those years to do over again, what would I change? And would it have made any difference to her?" He paused, thinking. "Shannon is really important to me. You and her are my only family…of course. But Shannon isn't Marion.

163

I wasn't good enough for Marion. I don't think that it was because I was too driven or that I didn't give her enough attention. I did. I really did, and I worked at that…that balance. But I just wasn't from her side of the tracks. And it wasn't all about money. We had enough of that even then. I speak three languages, play the piano, and know when to keep my opinions to myself. Believe it or not, Mama, I can even be the life of a party when I feel half decent. But she still left me." He leaned back in the big chair, then checked his watch to be certain that he wouldn't be late going to pick up Shannon.

Martha shuffled across the room and pulled the covers on her bed back, still holding the cordless phone to her ear. "Did you ever think that her leaving might have been the best thing that could have happened to you? That it might be time to recognize that you couldn't have become who you are without that pain? Everybody says that things happen for a reason, you know, and I think there's something to that. I found Hubert…or he found me in those years that were so terrible. It was just awful without your dad. You never knew how lonely I was or how scared I was."

Steven heard her sniff away the emotion through the phone.

"And that night…that night when Dillard came to collect the money that I knew I didn't have…that was the worst of it. I didn't know what was going to happen. I didn't know what I was going to do, so when I saw him through the window, I got the knife from the butcher's block and kept it hidden in the flare of my skirt. I really didn't know what I would do if he'd gotten more aggressive."

"That night changed us, didn't it, Mama? I think about it all the time and wonder if that was intended to be a test from the heavens, or was it just part of the bad things that happen to everybody, bad things that make us who we are…" Steven said, letting the last words trail. "We got through it okay, I guess, but I made too many mistakes that night."

He swallowed hard, then rolled his lips inward, feeling the emotion in his throat. "I got mad, Mama. Really mad. And I just wanted to get even. I didn't care about the consequences. I was just determined to make him pay right then and there."

Martha took a breath and paused before she spoke. "I think... I think I would have used the butcher knife," she said in her best sheepish voice, staring ahead without blinking. "Yeah... I think I would have...and that would have been worse than you using the slingshot."

Neither one of them spoke for a few seconds. They didn't need to.

Martha looked down to the oriental rug beneath her feet. "So what are you going to do, Steven? You can't keep going on like you are now. You're miserable, and we both know it. What are you going to do that'll be different? Something's got to change."

Steven let out a slow breath. He hated it when she pushed him beyond the tactical moment, especially when she was right. "Oh, Mama, life comes in seasons, I'm convinced of it. You know what the poem says, 'And he also serves those who stand and wait,'" he said, quoting Milton, then pausing again. "We wait and wait and wait for the season to change, wait and pray for our lives to get better, maybe easier or more peaceful. We wait to be ready. We don't think it will ever happen because it's been so hard for so long, and we don't think we can stand to wait anymore. And then...change just comes, a cool east wind on a sultry July night that doesn't seem possible...and it generally happens when we least expect it. We go through the drudgery of the day-by-day grind, rushing here and there, struggling with people conflicts, never-enough sleep, no peace of mind at all, and we think it's never going to change. We can't imagine how it could possibly change...how it will get better. It seems like we're stuck and that it will just never get better until we die. And then it just comes. Most of the time the change hurts, sometimes worse than we think we can stand, and it scares us; the change does. But it happens. Just like it did with us on the night that Dillard showed up."

"You didn't answer my question, Steven."

"I know, Mama. I know that. This business of being a human is pretty tricky sometimes, and I really haven't done a very good job with it," he said, looking down to the floor in front of the chair. "But right now, I have to go get Shannon," he said, pivoting. "She's the belle of the ball, Mama. She has a lot of your genetics. I had to put in a second phone line for her room so the boys wouldn't tie up the main number. And by the way, she doesn't get too excited about all that stuff. When she's had enough, she just turns the ringer off. Who does that sound like?"

Martha laughed aloud, then allowed herself a moment of pride as the moisture built in her eyes. "That's my Texas girl coming out," she said, "but she sounds like her father, not her grandmother."

"Gotta go, Mama. Got to go. Tell Socks that I might be coming home for a visit before long, and he's going to have to share that porch. Shannon has a school break in about a month. Maybe I can convince her to get out of the city and spend that time in Texas."

"That would be...nice. I hope you'll make that...happen," Martha said, hesitating. "But I do want you to think about my question, Steven. Fifty-three isn't all that young anymore, especially when you've lived like you have."

Steven put the phone back on its base and leaned forward, resting his elbows on his knees, his hands covering his eyes. She was right, of course, but he needed different people in place before he could slow down, and they weren't on the horizon just now. And... he'd been single since he was forty-one. The loneliness had almost become his crutch and paradoxically his motivation. He checked his watch again and started for the garage. He was determined that Shannon would never doubt that he would be there for her, no matter what happened.

20
CHAPTER

Steven sat in the back corner of the British Air lounge at Heathrow, struggling for a wireless Internet signal so he could send an e-mail. Groups in three different firms were waiting for him to sign a contract. He could do that electronically if he could just get a solid Wi-Fi connection. He'd tried three different carriers without getting it done, and they were about to start boarding his plane, which was at least ten minutes' walk from the lounge. They wouldn't hold an international flight, even if he were in first class.

Uncharacteristically, the lounge seemed hot and crowded. Annoyed with the wireless problem, he wanted to slam his fist on the table where his laptop sat, knowing that wouldn't resolve anything. He wiped the light sweat from his forehead and gritted his teeth. It was the same everywhere. The technology just wasn't good enough yet to get a consistent signal in a crowded place. He knew that, but it didn't matter. He could visualize all the people that were standing by in Tokyo and Paris. They needed his signature. It was a simultaneous transaction where he would buy and sell in a single moment, profiting almost eight million in an instant.

He took a deep breath and held it, tensing his shoulders as he froze in the moment, trying desperately to comprehend what had just happened. He'd never felt anything like it. Spines pricked between his shoulders as he went from frustration to a paralyzing fear and sat perfectly still, knowing that something special had just happened but completely stunned with his lack of understanding. He first turned to see if there were anyone behind him. Nothing. His back was to the wall as was his practice. Turning back, Steven took a deep breath and stared at the laptop on the table in front of him without actually seeing it.

The ruffling of his hair on the back of his head near the neck had come without warning, then sprinkled his back with the spines of ten thousand nerve endings, just as it had on the day when he'd sat at the foot of Sarah's grave, instantly knowing that someone or something was present just before the bobcat leapt on the week-old fawn. He couldn't move. There was no one behind him or near him, but someone or something wanted his attention and ruffled his hair at the nape of his neck. He didn't imagine it; it was unmistakable. For a long moment, he sat very still, almost afraid to breathe; then he looked both left and right yet again, seeing no one of consequence and no one nearby.

Thirty seconds later, his shoulders began to relax. He looked to the computer again, finally seeing the symbol for connectivity and began to pound the keys, hoping to get the e-mail out before he lost the signal again.

At the sound of the lounge attendant's voice on the speaker, he looked up and scowled. It didn't matter who she was calling; he knew it wasn't him. No one here knew him, and the sound of another human voice while he pressed to get the document done just angered him more. His face flared when he sensed someone approaching.

"Excuse me, sir," he heard her saying.

"Can you just wait a minute so I can send this email?" he asked with both defiance and irritation evident.

"I'm so very sorry, sir," she said, startled with his intensity, "but I was told that you might be Mr. Heard. Is that correct, sir?"

Steven lifted his eyes to her, trying to regain his composure. In all the years that he'd been using the lounge, no one had ever sought him out, not by name. He stopped the e-mail and looked up to her. "Yes," he said with a deep voice, steeped with classic elitism. "Yes. I'm Steven Heard. How can I help you?"

"Well...uhmmm... I am so very sorry to bother you, but... uhmmm...you have a call, sir. An urgent call, I'm told."

He nodded slightly, both acknowledging her and thanking her as he stood and took his first steps toward the desk near the back wall.

He knew it wouldn't be good news. Good news would have waited until he touched down at National. He stood stark still and stared at the Columbia blue carpet below, waiting to take the phone from the uniformed lady at the desk, wondering how would anyone knew where to find him. He'd changed his flight schedule in Hong Kong. His assistant in DC didn't even know that he was in London this early. Steven released a long sigh and reached for the phone, thinking that the woman who found him seemed so young and pretty as she stepped aside to give him privacy. He shook his head, disturbed with himself, and closed his eyes as he put the phone to his ear. "This is Steven Heard," he said, not knowing who would be on the other end.

"Mr. Steven, this is Emanuel."

"Emanuel? What's...what's happened, Emanuel?"

There was silence on the line for a full three seconds.

"I don't like having to tell you over the phone, sir, but she's gone, Mr. Steven. She's with Mr. Hubert and Mr. Jason now. It happened about fifteen minutes ago, I think. I left her a cup of tea on the nightstand this morning like I always do. She was sleeping. For some reason, I was a little worried, so I waited a few minutes and went back in to check. She wasn't breathing when I went back, just lying there with her eyes open. I tried to wake her, but she...she was just gone. I'm... I'm sorry, Mr. Steven. We're all...we're all very sorry, sir. She loved you and Miss Shannon more than life itself. I'm so very sorry, sir."

Steven's head drooped. He tried to swallow the emotion building in his throat and blinked at the moisture in his eyes. Why didn't he see this coming? Why hadn't he gotten on a plane and flown to Texas last weekend to see Mama?

"How long had she been sick, Emanuel?" he finally asked.

"Months, sir. She didn't want you to know, and she didn't want you to see her looking like she did when she got sick."

"Months," Steven repeated a little louder than a whisper. "Months?"

He exhausted another long breath, wondering how could that have been, knowing all the while that he should've seen that. He lowered his head, closing his eyes, telling himself to just take one breath at a time, then do that over and over again. She had always been there for him. How could he have been so callous to think that she would live forever? Long seconds passed before he raised his head and stared ahead in silence without blinking. His raison d'être drained from every pore. For fifty-three years, she'd been his best friend. He spoke in a hushed voice, hoping to finish the call without breaking down.

"I'll be there soon, Emanuel. Soon. Someone will call...and let you know when I'll arrive," Steven said, letting the words trail as he leaned forward to hang up the phone. Just before his hand reached the phone's base, he stopped and put it back to his ear. "Emanuel? Emanuel?"

"Yes, Mr. Steven, I'm still here."

"Good. Uhmmm...uhmmm... I thought you'd want to know... uhmm...just please let everyone know that I'll be keeping the house and farm the same as it is now...and that I'll need everyone who is working there today to continue. Could you hear me, Emanuel? No one...*no one* will lose their job."

"Yes, Mr. Steven. Thank you for that. I'll tell them, sir," he said with that mushy tone that belied a deeper toughness. "Just one more thing, Mr. Steven. There's been some folks coming around lately saying that they own the farm now and all of us will have to leave soon. These are folks that you wouldn't like much. Ms. Martha wouldn't even let them come up on the porch to talk. The word around town has been that you've had some bad financial deals in the last year and are now having money problems. Ms. Martha said there wasn't nothin' to that kind of talk, but I just thought you would want to know."

Steven took a deep breath and cinched his jaws, crossing sorrow with anger in one explosive moment. "Would the ring leaders' names be Wilson by some chance? Or maybe Watson?" Steven asked.

"Yes sir. It was. Old Dillard's been dead for over twenty years now, but them boys of his are just like him. Maybe worse."

"Thank you, Emanuel. Now I won't walk into town ill-prepared. And, Mama told you right. We don't have money problems right now." He paused, debating with himself on providing more of an explanation. "You know, Emanuel, a good many years ago,

I put both of those boys in the hospital. I was thirteen when that happened."

"Yes sir, I heard that story from your mama."

"I was lucky then, Emanuel. If it goes that way this time, they won't make that mistake again."

"No sir, I don't think they will either. They've been bothering your mama some about taking the place, and then two weeks ago, all of our paychecks bounced. None of the help would stay if they took over, not even if they begged us. They're just no-count devils, but we would all stay with you, even if you couldn't pay us for a while."

Steven ground his teeth harder and thanked Emanuel, wondering how so much cash could have disappeared without him knowing it. He assured Emanuel that they would all be paid as soon as he arrived, then hung up the phone and walked back to couch and the table where his laptop still sat open, the Internet signal lost again.

He leaned forward, trying to concentrate, then pushed back on the sofa, feeling dirty, almost greasy as though he were a fast-food fry cook at the end of a shift in July. He shook his head, trying to clear the brain fog, struggling among the Wilsons, the Internet, and the professional people standing by waiting for him, and Mama leaving. Steven let his eyes close for a brief second, visualizing Martha as she'd looked walking to work in Richland when he was just a lad, thinking that she looked so prim and proper in her solid colored suits, never showing others the fear that she must have felt with every minute that passed.

He leaned forward again, letting his head drop toward his chest before he reached back and grasped the hair at the nape of his neck. "So, Mama, found me and took the time to say *goodbye*," he said under his breath. Holding on to his hair was almost like holding her hand one last time. Tears welled, then ran down his cheeks wetting his palms as he covered his face. He tried to swallow the moisture in his throat, but it was too much, and he cried openly and unashamed, taking his handkerchief out to dry his face.

Steven sat still and stared straight ahead through the floor-to-ceiling windows and out to the tarmac. His lips remained sealed and expressionless as he visualized himself just minutes before, ready to slam his fist on the table over an Internet connection, a contract, and a lucrative transaction. He rested his chin on a tight fist and stared at the blonde mahogany table below. Mama had a small table like that, a round one supported by legs that resembled a spider. For a long while, he sat, looking down in silence, thinking that she must have been amused with him over the past several years...and paradoxically saddened.

Sitting up, he took a deep breath and considered his options, then rolled his lips and shook his head from side to side almost imperceptibly, knowing that he couldn't dodge what lay in front of him. He was the big kid now...and he had to stand straight even if he were the only one still standing. Without another wayward thought, he went to the men's room and freshened himself, then pulled his loosened tie into a proper knot, and buttoned his suit coat. As he started to the restroom exit door, he heard his name from the speaker above and walked toward the desk where he'd taken the call from Emanuel.

The attendant who had been so polite stood waiting for him. "Mr. Heard, your plane is fully boarded now. What would you like to do, sir?"

Steven thought for a moment, then took out his platinum credit card and placed it on the desk, and turned his head to the side for a brief second before returning his gaze to her. "Please release the flight, and... I need some help."

"Yes sir," she said, pushing the credit card back to him as her associate stepped away with a handheld radio to contact the gate agent.

Steven looked to her again, confused.

"Mr. Heard," she began, pausing to gather her thoughts, "we... we don't have many individuals who have flown over seven million miles with our airline group. I understand from my management that you've had an unexpected...an...uhmmm...an unexpected *loss* today. Please accept our condolences. Now...where would you like to go, sir? This one is on us."

Steven glanced down to the credit card and sniffed, his emotions mixing with the synapses that raced through the logistics at rocket speed. Finally, he looked back to the attendant. "Houston," he said, trying to swallow the lump in his throat. "Houston would be good," he added with a raspy voice. "And... I may need your help to also get my daughter there from Reagan National. It would be good, of course, if she could arrive about the same time that I get there. And I'm happy to pay for my daughter and an airline escort."

She shook her head slightly. "There'll be no charge, sir, not for anyone in your party. I'll bring you the itineraries in a few minutes. Your daughter is Shannon, I believe. Her data is already in our system, but I'll need a little time to arrange for one of our people to be her escort."

Steven nodded slightly and turned toward the sofa and his computer before stopping himself. "Ms. Burnside," he said in that soft voice, before waiting for her to look up from the monitor. "Thank you. Just...thank you."

21
CHAPTER

Steven sat on the sofa and began to consider who might be willing to get Shannon to the airport and on to Houston. She'd flown around the world several times without being late or missing connections, but for most of those flights she was with him. Steven believed that she was mature beyond her thirteen years. She'd grown up without seeing much of her mother and had become the lady of the house years ago. He trusted her. Still, he worried that she would be emotional as soon as he called. He needed a low-key approach that would be easier for Shannon to accept.

Steven studied his watch, then subtracted the five-hour time difference. He had about an hour to make his decision. It would be eight o'clock in DC by then, and he wanted to call when Shannon was dressed and ready, but before LuAnn took her to school.

He walked to the floor-to-ceiling windows and began to pace. He dreaded making the next call. Amanda Rhymes practiced law in DC the old-fashioned way. She was tough, thorough, smart, and relentless. From four different friends, he'd heard the story of her singlehandedly dismantling a four-attorney team from the West Coast who were representing a national property lender. She knew more about their client than they did and quoted a series of fifteen improper actions that they'd taken, naming dates, times, and motivational logic for each event without reviewing her notes. The Los Angeles group was ill-prepared for her photographic memory, and in the merciless settlement photographic memory. In the merciless negotiated settlement that followed, the visiting team agreed to pay her clients a total of one hundred and eighty million, plus her fees and all court costs. Amanda's son, John was Shannon's best friend and romantic interest that had begun in the third grade.

Steven flipped the phone open and closed repeatedly, despising the idea of calling Amanda to ask for her help, but he could think of no one that would be more comforting to Shannon. She occasionally traveled with John and Amanda in the summers and sometimes spent holidays at their place in Maine. Steven knew her, of course; the four of them sometimes shared dinners on weekends, but he didn't know her well, and they weren't close. She seemed to be a perfectly pleasant person, but he didn't know how she might react under the stress of imposition. He simply didn't want to make the call, and he didn't know precisely why.

Steven stopped pacing, opened his flip phone and scrolled through the Rs until he found Amanda E. Rhymes. He checked the coverage—three bars—then looked again to his watch. She would be up and going, and it would be okay to call. He knew that. The kids had been friends for so long that they all knew each other's routines. Still, Steven resisted. He simply didn't want to ask for help from Amanda. Maybe he should just ask LuAnn if she could take his car and get Shannon to the airport, or perhaps he could get to DC, and they could fly together to Houston. He knew that he could always call a limo service that would take her to the airport safely, but that seemed cold and impersonal. He closed the phone and began to pace again, not knowing for certain why he didn't want to call Amanda. She would rearrange her schedule and take care of Shannon. There was no question about that. Still, he resisted and paced.

"Mr. Heard," he heard Ms. Burnside saying as she walked toward him. "Do you think your daughter could be at National in about three hours? I know the DC traffic is fairly tough, but we'll have someone to meet her curbside and be her escort through security and all the way to Houston. She would arrive about fifteen minutes before you do…if you can make a departure from here in about thirty minutes," she asked with raised eyebrows and a furrowed brow.

Steven studied the itineraries and nodded, knowing that his hand was now forced. He told her that the plan should work. "I need ten minutes to confirm," he said. "And my flight is?"

"Just two gates down, sir. Less than five minutes' walk."

He thanked her again and opened the flip phone. He had no choice now. He had to call Amanda.

*****

The phone rang four times before she answered.

"Steven? It's early, and you're traveling this week. John mentioned Asia?"

"London...now. But...uhmmm...listen, Amanda, I really didn't want to call you; I hate to be an imposition, and I know that you're incredibly busy—"

"Steven," she said, interrupting with that firm attorney-mom tone, "you must have a large problem or you wouldn't be calling me from London at this time of the morning. I get that. Please. It's okay. What do you need me to do?"

Steven smirked just a little, looking down at the blue carpet, wondering why had he been so concerned about making the call. He released a quick breath. "I think you know how important my mother has been to Shannon and me. We have a very small family, just the three of us actually for the last decade or so. And...uhmmm... Mom passed early this morning. Uhmmm...if you can, I'd like to ask if you might be able to take Shannon to the airport and get her on a flight to Houston in a few hours."

"Done."

"Well... I didn't know if you might have court today, and—"

"Steven. It's done, and please don't argue. You don't have the time for that, and despite your reputed prowess, you'd lose that argument. Trust me. My son worships your daughter. Worships," she repeated. "And I'm rather fond of her myself. She reminds me a little of me at that age, though I was never that pretty," Amanda said, kicking her heels off as she started toward her walk-in closet to get a pair of jeans. "Just ask someone to fax me a flight itinerary and a signed one-liner giving me permission to put her on a flight...just in case. John and I will both take her to the airport. How upset is she? She thought your mother was divine."

"I haven't talked with her yet," Steven admitted. "I thought I should make the arrangements first." He hesitated. "But yes, Shannon and Granny were very close, and I think she'll be very upset."

"That seals it. She needs to be with someone that she can trust, and you're thirty-five hundred miles away. We'll handle it. Don't worry. It'll be fine."

Steven agreed and thanked her profusely, apologizing again for the imposition, then turned from the windows. For some unknown reason, the image of Dillard Wilson lying on the ground with blood oozing from the pecan slingshot flashed in his mind as he walked toward Ms. Burnside's desk. Dillard died in 1972, his scar readily visible as he lay in the coffin. For a halting second, Steven's mind froze. Was it an omen? He stared wide-eyed without seeing the table in front of him. Seconds passed as he considered calling off the twin flights to Houston, but he'd committed. People were doing extraordinary things to help him, and he'd seem foolish if he changed on such a whim. He looked again to the tarmac, thinking that he couldn't hide. He couldn't alter the plan. He could only go to Houston, then on to Richland. Still, Dillard's stark image frightened him.

Ms. Burnside faxed the name and picture of the flight attendant that would meet Shannon curbside in DC, both itineraries, and Steven's signed statement to Amanda, then received her confirmation fax in less than a minute. The plan was set. Steven had one more call to make before catching his flight.

*****

LuAnn answered the kitchen's wireless phone and carried it to Shannon.

"I'm in a hurry, Dad. What gives? You're in London, right?"

"You're always in a hurry, sweetheart. Always."

"Whose daughter am I?" she asked, smirking as she held the phone out from her ear.

She had a point. He still hadn't accepted his fifty-three years and somehow believed that he should be at least twenty years younger.

"I need you to do something for me," Steven said, taking a deep breath. "We have a situation that both of us have to deal with today."

Shannon sat on the edge of her bed, suddenly tense, waiting for an explanation.

"Granny died just before dawn this morning, and we have to get to Richland as fast as we can. There are predators and legal issues that we must address."

Keep her mind moving forward, he told himself. *Don't let her stop to react. That can come later…when I'm there.*

"I need you to pack for two weeks. Ms. Amanda and John are going to take you to the airport. Is this okay with you?"

The phone remained silent. Shannon neither whimpered nor sniffed, and Steven knew that he had to let her stop and absorb, even though he didn't want that.

"Dad…" she said as his words settled in her mind, "I… I know you think I'm young and that I don't know much, but I need to know how *you're* doing with all this? Granny was everything to you, just like you are to me. You don't have to worry about me, Dad. I get it, and I'm okay with Granny going back."

Steven felt the tears forming again and cleared his throat, trying to keep his voice clear. He never saw Martha as an older woman. In his mind, she was still that young woman who walked to work at the bank every day speaking to folks that she saw along the way. Still, he hadn't been able to see Uncle Melvin or Brother Joseph taking her through the Review Council, and that bothered him. Worse, Dillard Wilson's image flash made the spines tingle across his back yet again, and he wondered if there were trouble brewing in the heavens.

"I didn't know she was sick," he finally said. "Emanuel said that she wouldn't let him tell me. I should've been there when she died," he said, pausing. "She was always there for me. Always. And I hadn't been there enough to even know that she was dying."

"She didn't want to bother you," Shannon said. "She said it would upset you too much, that you were loaded up with other things, something about my mother, but she wouldn't tell me what. She's not bothering you for money again, is she?"

Steven hadn't seen or heard from Marion in five or six years and said as much.

"Granny called me two nights ago. She knew that she was about to leave us, but she said that this was our special secret and that she'd come out of the grave and haunt me if I told you."

"Humph…your special secret? Your special secret? That's very different than what she told me," he said, pausing. "She told me to slow down and live a little more. Find a decent woman and settle down to a simpler life. You know how she was. She spent her life trying to take care of me…and she didn't know that I was trying to take care of her at the same time. Hubert is probably still mad at me. He never got as much of her attention as he deserved, because I was always her focus. I blew it, Shannon. In the end, I wasn't there. I wasn't there for her when she needed me. I just blew it, and I'm really unhappy with myself about it."

"That's not the story I got from her, Dad. From Granny, I heard about you protecting her from Dillard Wilson and working two jobs while you were still a kid so she could have a decent life. I heard that you never had dates in high school because you were worried that she might have problems with someone like Dillard again, and you didn't want to leave her alone too long. I heard about you finding a bar of *gold*—really, Dad…*gold*—and that you used the money for a down payment on the farm, then paid for the rest of the land with the money you got by selling all those pecans that you'd picked up and stored in burlap sacks. All that when you were just seventeen? And I heard that you worried about everybody but yourself the whole time. That's…what I heard from Granny. Now…stop beating yourself up, Dad. Granny had a great life, and Uncle Melvin has already guided her through…"

Every alarm in Steven's mind went off, and he froze, staring through the full-length windows without blinking. He'd never mentioned Uncle Melvin to Shannon. He was sure of it. What did she know? How long had she been in process? His mind spun with questions as he tried to remain calm. "So…did Granny mention Uncle Melvin to you?"

"No. She didn't."

"Uhmmm…so how do you know about—"

"Dad, I'm your daughter. Your only child. Don't you think that I would have some of the same connections that you do?"

Steven looked at his watch, then turned toward Ms. Burnside who was motioning him toward the exit door. He didn't answer Shannon's question and was stunned that she was so far ahead of him, even though paradoxically behind in years. He needed time to process. Any response would be risky, and he didn't practice risk, just preparation, finite, detailed preparation.

"Shannon, I have to go. My plane has already boarded. Is it okay that Ms. Amanda and John take you to the airport?"

"Of course. Catch your plane, Dad. I'll see you in Houston." She started to press the button and hang up, then stopped herself. "And Dad… Granny was really ready to go back. You were the only reason that she stayed this long. She was very worried about you. That's why she called me. She wanted me to keep you from getting down on yourself. She told me that you would do that. Something about you were still killing yourself trying to be perfect and fighting enemies that didn't exist…"

"Gotta go, Shannon. Gotta go. We can talk in Houston and for the next couple of weeks."

"Okay, Dad. Okay. No prob. Hey, Dad… I really want to know where you got that bar of gold. Even Granny didn't know, and that was seriously cool."

Steven started for the exit door, smiling to himself through the tears that streamed down his face, taking the boarding pass that Ms. Burnside held out for him, and thanking her once again as he wiped the moisture away with his handkerchief. She'd been exceptionally good to him, more than professional. She had been genuinely nice. He half turned to get one last glimpse of her standing near the open door, waving.

Steven walked down the hallway as fast as he could, allowing himself a brief minute to think about Brad and Damian Wilson… and Big Henry. He assumed that they were simply trying to get even with him by taking advantage of an older woman without local family, just as their father and uncle would have done. He used the handkerchief again as he entered the gate area, simultaneously changing his mind on the Wilsons and Big Henry. They were up to something, probably something more sinister than he'd considered.

Steven hadn't thought about them in years anyway. They weren't part of his life, so they didn't exist, just like the bobcat pouncing on the fawn was beyond his purview and therefore didn't exist, until he'd witnessed it. He stared at the boarding gate agent, hesitating. There were too many things happening at once, and he considered that a bad sign from the heavens. He thought that this could be another test, but not now. Surely not now. It had been such a long time since he felt good about himself, and even longer since he felt consumed with spontaneous and unadulterated joy. Surely, they wouldn't come after him right after Granny passed when it was just him and Shannon. He was about to step forward when a thought landed a right-cross. Dillard would. No question. He would attack at every opportunity. And he might have some power to orchestrate now. Steven lowered his eyes, thinking, trying to remember how serious hate was treated in the heavens. It wasn't clear to him; he couldn't remember how the power and politics were managed among the plebes, and that irritated him.

The bar code reader gave his boarding pass a green light, and he almost jogged down the jetway to the 777. He had over ten hours of flight time to Houston and knew that he had to be ready by the time they touched down.

22

CHAPTER

At thirteen, Shannon was already five foot six and commanding male attention. Beanpole thin and leggy like her mother, she looked as though she could be a budding fashion model with her sandy blonde hair and the navy jacket that she wore with jeans and tan ankle boots. She ran to meet Steven just outside of the double doors that allowed international passengers to exit after claiming their luggage and clearing Customs. Steven hugged her to him for a long teary minute; then he held her out from him before pulling her back into a second hug, wondering how his little girl suddenly looked like a grown woman when he'd only been gone for a few days.

"Look at you," he said with a furrowed brow. "When did you grow up? And now I understand why John hangs around all the time."

"Just my father's daughter, I guess," she said, smiling as they embraced again.

Steven closed his eyes, still holding her. "Granny was special, sweetheart. Really special. I know she was ready to go, but it's still hard for you and me. I wish you could've known her when she was younger. She was a real looker, just like her granddaughter," he added.

"Awwgh, Dad. That's a funny word...'looker.' That must've been a sixties word. What does that mean anyway?"

"That you get a lot of looks when you walk down the street or enter a room of people. That's all. It's not a bad word, but yeah, I guess it's an old word. Well, sorta old. It could actually have been a fifties word, but that's not that so bad," he said, hesitating. "I'm not that much out of it, am I?"

Shannon hugged him again. It didn't embarrass her to hug her dad. They were friends, and she was proud of him. She looked him over as they started walking toward the Ground Transportation sign, dragging their rolling bags.

"You didn't sleep on the plane, did you?" she asked, knowing that he always slept on planes, especially at takeoff.

"That bad, huh?" he said, looking over to her.

"Uhmmm… I've definitely seen you in better shape."

Steven smiled at her monitoring of his image, tactfully trying to protect him. "We have a lot to think about right now," he said. "The bad guys are on the prowl, and have been for months, apparently. We have legal issues. A great deal of money is *missing*. And… I'm going to have a hard time driving up the road to the farm knowing that your grandmother isn't there," he said, unconsciously biting his lower lip.

Steven walked slower than usual, no airport sprints today. His head drooped, the deep sadness building in his throat. What would he have done without Shannon today? Who would he have had to talk with? For conflicting reasons, both of those thoughts rattled him.

"She was always there," he said, "even when I didn't see her for a spell. She knew me too well, always had the knack for calling me when I was really down. And she was smart enough not to try to tell me what to do but just let me wander through senseless logic until I would finally arrive at something reasonable."

He stopped at the curb and released a deep sigh. "Shakespeare believed that man is the only animal that knows he must die," he said, pausing, turning to Shannon, then looking up to the crystal blue sky. "I knew that she would go home soon. She missed Dad and Hubert more than she ever let either one of us know." He shook his head a little with disgust showing in his face. "I should've been a better son for her, more time on the porch in that old white rocking chair with her going on about things that didn't seem very important at the time. But, then, I had so many things to do, and I'm not all that proud of the way some of those things turned out. Too many mistakes. Lots of innocent people get hurt when folks like me go to business war and make mistakes. Far too many," he said, letting the words trail. "And I'd give quite a bit for just one more hour in that rocking chair with her and Old Socks in their places on that porch."

They walked on in silence. Shannon reached out and put her arm around his back at the waist as they approached the rental car kiosk.

"You're going to be okay, Dad. I promise. You're going to be just fine."

"Who's raising who now? But I must say that I really don't mind if you just want to...take charge, or something akin to that. I have lots of enemies, and they wouldn't come after you like they do with me."

Shannon laughed.

"There! Right there!" she said, pointing at him. "You said it right then."

Steven looked at her with a wrinkled, whimsical expression that bared his confusion.

"Granny told me," Shannon said, nodding in his direction. "Granny said that so long as you had an enemy, someone who threatened you, you would be just fine and that I shouldn't worry unless your life was quiet."

Steven cut his eyes toward her. "Humph...sometimes your Granny talked too much, not that she wasn't right about that. And I suppose that she also told you the story about the Snack Jack kids?"

"At least twenty times."

"Figured..." He took a deep breath. "There's something else. And...uhmmm... I hope you don't misunderstand this," he said, pausing. "There's something going on in the heavens right now. A crisis of some kind, I think. I can't be sure what it is, but...but I know that it's happening. I can feel it. And...uhmmm... I think our family is in the fray. There's just too much happening at the same time here, too many negative things popping up suddenly and without warning, and I don't mean that any of it has to do with Granny's arrival up there. I... I just sense it, and I don't know how." Steven looked over to Shannon for a reaction but didn't see anything. "Am I confusing you? Do you understand what I'm saying?" he asked.

"Yes and no. You level threes are just like that. Sometimes you sense things that others just don't."

Steven jerked toward her. In fifty-three years, no other human had referred to him as a Three, not even Mama. "So…how much do you remember? I mean, where are you…in the process?" he asked.

"Don't worry, Dad. You're way ahead of me. Way ahead. I remember some things about you from before, but I'm behind and don't really know much."

Steven furrowed his brow with raised eyebrows, wondering how much she really knew and wouldn't tell him. She'd obviously been sent by the Council, and that bothered him. Knowing that they would be together for two weeks, he decided to let the matter rest until they were settled and alone. *Plenty of time*, he told himself. *Plenty.*

What a day, he thought. Mama, the Wilsons, Big Henry, Texas, a war in the heavens, and now he'd learned that Shannon knew more about him than he imagined. He shook his head just a little, dismayed at the whirlwind that engulfed him. And in the middle of it all at thirty-five thousand feet, he signed the contract electronically and actually got the pay phone mounted on the seat back to connect and send the email. Still, he missed Mama and tried not to think about the early days when it was just the two of them. Those images brought instant tears.

"Humph…a thirty-hour day," he said under his breath. London was six hours ahead of Houston. Steven glanced at the clock in the rental car as he and Shannon exited the airport complex. It was almost five thirty, plenty of time to get to Richland before dark.

23
CHAPTER

Steven chose an S-Class Mercedes at the rental counter and looked forward to his time alone with Shannon. Once they arrived in Richland, he expected that they would be consumed with the funeral arrangements and the strange business that somehow involved the Wilsons and Big Henry. He decided to include Shannon as much as he could, hoping that she would begin to know the farm and the people, and also so that he might get private time with her. He thought that these few hours in the car would give them time to discuss Uncle Melvin as well as her usual info dump about her mother, from whom he'd now been divorced for over twelve years.

Shannon pulled her legs up on to the seat in a fold cross to sit on them. It was cool for early November, and she snuggled down with earphones and a portable CD player. Ten minutes later when they cleared the last freeway loop and turned north toward College Station, she removed the devices and turned toward her dad. "Predators and legal issues?" she asked without looking at him. "Seems pretty serious."

"Dillard Wilson has two sons who are at least as maligned as he was," Steven said, cutting his eyes to her as he drove. "Big Henry Watson has been the mayor for decades, and he hates me more than the Yankees hate the Red Socks," he said, glancing out of the side window. "We could be heading into a lions' den, and... I'm afraid that Granny may have forgotten to pay the property taxes." Steven grimaced, turning toward Shannon. "I don't understand that. It doesn't sound like Mama. There was almost a million dollars in the primary account when I checked it about six months ago."

He took a deep breath, releasing it slowly as he rolled his lips inward lightly in disgust. "They should have added funds every time they sold pecans or hay or cattle, but Emanuel told me that all of their paychecks bounced last week," he said, turning toward Shannon. "This is my fault. I haven't been studying the reports, so I can't really speculate. I just know that there's a fair amount of money missing."

Steven's eyes locked on the road ahead, but he didn't see the traffic, just the broad expanse of the creek-bottom farm with all those majestic pecan trees studding the landscape.

"Olin Jr. is the sheriff now," he said. "He's not half the man that his daddy was, but he's okay, I think. We'll start at his office tomorrow morning."

Shannon twisted in the seat to face him. "Why haven't you told me what happened between you and Mom?" she asked as she furrowed her brow and stared at him.

"Well..." Steven began, "I didn't see that one coming."

"You never really told me about that. I know about all kinds of business situations, your travels, and people all over the world...but you didn't tell me much about my own mother...and why she left you."

Steven released a heavy breath. This wasn't the discussion that he'd hoped to have. "You were too young. Still are... I think...but you do seem to be ahead of the curve on the EQ scale."

"Oh, come on, Dad. I'm a lot older now, and I probably know more than you think."

Steven turned to stare, then looked back to the almost flat but winding road in front of him. "The first few years were fine. Your mother was both pretty and...uhmmm...charming. I almost worshipped her. I was...well, just me, a Texas kid blessed with plenty of IQ points but not many close friends." He paused for a bit, thinking. "She was my life. She almost literally dominated my mind, and I... I can't adequately describe how much I adored your mother when we were young." He paused again, looking straight ahead. "Every single day, I tried to treat her like we were on our first date. But...uhhhh... that's pretty hard to maintain over the years.

"I was from a small town in Texas and didn't have family other than Granny, and she was a Marilyn blue blood with a big family and memberships in four different country clubs." He turned toward her with raised eyebrows. "I'm sure you recognize that those are diametrically opposed views of the world. And in those days, I didn't understand how important it is to see things or people…through the other person's eyes. I…uhmmm… I didn't know much about building—or losing—relationships as we look through the eyes of others…or fail to do that. You should remember that when you get married. And I promise that will be the only piece of unsolicited marital advice that I will ever give you. Lord knows I didn't do very well with marriage," he added, turning toward her with a broad smile, "except for you."

Shannon reached across, putting her hand on his forearm. "And you think I'm going to believe that's the only advice you're going to give me?" She gave him an eye roll. "You'll still be Dad when I'm married. You can't stop trying to 'help' me!" she said, laughing with him.

"Actually, I don't know why your mother first flirted with me when we were in school. I was clearly outclassed. A country kid… almost…in an Ivy League school."

Steven paused, wondering how much he should say. Shannon only saw Marion a couple of times each year, but she was still her mom. He may have been the only real parent she'd ever had, but still, he worried about compromising Marion's reputation. If something were to happen to him, Shannon had nowhere else to go, now that Martha had passed. A moment of silence paralyzed him before he recognized that Shannon was already ahead of him. She seemed more mature for her years than he'd imagined and probably knew much of the story already.

"I knew your mother wasn't happy with me. I worked all the time, trying to make my way in this world. Even in the early years, I did well enough that we had everything we needed. And…the farm was a bonus. Those pecan trees were profitable year after year. But… that wasn't enough. She needed me…and my time. She needed me to focus on her, and I didn't do both very well, even though I tried." He paused, thinking, considering how to tiptoe through the minefield that he was traversing. "So really…it wasn't her fault at all. She was who she was, and she had her needs. Max was a great dancer who came from her blue blood world; he's a charmer and a party guy who didn't have to worry about *being somebody*."

Shannon sat quietly, looking down. Steven thought she looked suddenly sad, maybe even disappointed in him. He saw her shift her feet, then look out of the passenger side window.

"How did it end?" she asked without turning to look at him.

"It was about six months after you were born. She was fully recovered from the pregnancy and looked just great, but it had been a stressful time. I knew she wasn't paying much attention to me, and I was just stupid about that. I thought it was because she was worn down in the evenings from taking care of you. I didn't know it, but she'd been spending time with Max for about three months…sometimes during the day when I was at work, and pretty much every time that I traveled."

"Were you gone a lot?"

"Nothing like the last few years, but yeah, I was gone a couple of days every week."

Shannon nodded her understanding.

"Anyway, I was leaving for the office one morning, and she stopped me in the kitchen and told me that she didn't want to be married anymore, that she was going to move out if I didn't leave. She didn't mention Max. It was another four months before I found out about that. Your mother is a great actress. If Max hadn't eventually dumped her, I wouldn't have known about him until after the divorce was complete."

"So what did you do? I mean, that day," Shannon said, turning to him. "Like, how could you go to work after that?"

Steven chuckled quietly before telling her that he didn't go to the office at all that day but went to a greasy spoon diner and stayed there until three in the afternoon. "I ate some really good food, four different desserts, and had an all-day coffee binge. I didn't want to go home. I didn't want to get a hotel room. I didn't want to leave you with her. But I had to do something, so I called Granny. She told me to hire a good attorney, then rent an apartment and some furniture before sundown. And I did that," he said, nodding just a little. "She always seemed to know what to do when I didn't."

Steven saw her mood lighten at that and believed that she was okay with the story. He drove north thinking that Dallas really would have been closer but that Houston was more comfortable...and that decision really didn't hurt them much. Another hour and a half of driving through the farm country and oil patches and they'd be in Richland.

24
CHAPTER

Shannon dozed in the evening dusk, and Steven had an open road in front of him. He'd glanced to his left to see the drilling rig with all its lights and equipment blaring. The rigs jutted from the fields and pastures creating mini-cities that buzzed around the clock, a menagerie of men and equipment sitting on a caliche pad that sometimes shook like an earthquake when the thundering force of the oil and gas first made its way to the surface. Distracted, he didn't see the one-ton dual-wheel truck approaching from farm-to-market road on his right, nor could he have determined that the truck's driver had slammed his accelerator to the floor, trying to outrun Steven so he wouldn't have to stop at the junction just ahead.

Too late, Steven's instinct turned to shock as he cut his eyes away from the drilling rig and caught motion in his periphery. His foot moved toward the brake, and he had just begun to turn the wheel away from the truck when the collision roared. Before hitting the brake, Steven had his cruise locked on seventy, but the truck had accelerated to over eighty. With a desperate gut-reaction effort, he reached across the console for Shannon, but it was too late as the noise of the impact hammered them even louder as they began the rollover, frantically trying to cling to those seconds that linger between life and death.

The truck's cow-catcher and winch on the front bumper drove straight into Shannon's passenger side door crushing it and killing her instantly, even before the rollovers began. On the second rollover, Steven's head slammed against the vertical doorpost knocking him unconscious as blood spouted from his ear like a fountain. Shattered glass mixed with blood and the airbag powder and covered both Steven and Shannon. Neither one of them moved when the car made its last turn, settling on its side thirty yards out into a soybean field. Steam and antifreeze blew from the radiator; the engine smelled of burning oil, and the plowed ground in the field was littered with metal and plastic. The Mercedes lay upside down in the field with Steven and Shannon both dangling from their seat belts. Neither of them showed any sign of life.

The next car didn't arrive for a full two minutes. A white-haired man slammed his brakes and jerked his Ford pickup to the road's shoulder as soon as he saw the Mercedes and the one-ton truck on its side in the opposite ditch. He flung his door open and ran to the Mercedes first, obviously knowing that the smaller vehicle would likely need the most help. Every door had been crushed either by the initial impact or the rollovers. In desperation, he took out his razor-sharp pocketknife, reaching through what was once the window, and began to saw away at Steven's seat belt. The good Samaritan looked up and winced seeing that the right side of Shannon's head had been bashed and her disfigured face was now a mass of blood and pulp flesh. He kept cutting Steven's seat belt, and thirty seconds later the knife finished its work as Steven fell in a heap. In a last-ditch effort, the seventy-five-year-old took off his white shirt and jammed it against Steven's ear to stem the blood. The next car skidded to a stop behind the Ford truck, and the driver jumped out, cell phone in hand, calling 9-1-1.

Steven's heart beat erratically, and he didn't understand why he couldn't move. Then he saw her. Though still unconscious, Laura was clear to him, holding Shannon close to her as they talked. Both of them seemed happy, almost giggly, and he wanted to go with them. Forty-seven years had passed since he'd last saw his guardian angel in his bedroom on the night that Dad died. He visualized himself reaching out to her, almost pleading to go with them.

Laura shook her head, pressing her lips together. "You're not ready yet, Steven," she told him. "If you don't finish, someone else will have to come here in your place."

Shannon left Laura's side, hugging him one last time. Tears filled his closed eyes and began to run down his face, diluting the rivulets of blood that still streamed. Even in his unconscious state, he knew that there was nothing left for him. Mama was gone; Shannon was gone, and the Wilsons had stolen the farm. He couldn't go on. Not now. There was no one left for him to love, no one to protect, no one to build for. He'd never been more ready to return and face the Council, no matter what the consequences were.

25

CHAPTER

Ten days and four surgeries passed, and Steven remained on the critical list in ICU, surrounded by a mass of bandages and tubes spun like a spider's web. He hadn't opened his eyes or spoken a word, and his team of doctors in the downtown Houston hospital still thought his survival was a long shot. He was cold, always cold, an almost-vegetative human without love, joy, or purpose but ever dominated by the cold that punctuated his misery.

On day 11, he moved his left leg, and the woman visiting during the scheduled hour almost leapt with both fear and joy, but that was a single incident, and the doctors wrote it off as an involuntary muscle spasm. He lay still hour after hour, day after day, his chest moving up and down so slightly that the woman stood over him straining to see if the next shallow breath would come. The doctors told her that they believed he still wanted to die and that it was his death wish that impeded his progress.

On day 15, the fluid in the tubes that ran from the base of his brain began to slow, and there was slight optimism in their tone when the doctors made rounds. Still, they told her that mental competence seemed doubtful, even if he survived.

On night 21, he opened his eyes, and when the green-scrubbed nurse came in to check, she finally understood his raspy sounds asking for water. She brought him ice chips, and he managed just one of them with her help. Then he went out again.

At the visiting hour on day 22, the unsuspecting woman signed in and started the normal trek toward the curtained ICU cubicle when the same green-scrubbed nurse, working a twelve-hour shift, saw her.

"Ma'am," she said, stopping the woman, "he looks bad, really, really bad, but his eyes are open," she said as she smiled just a little. "And I get a word or two every now and then."

Amanda's eyes began to tear as she looked down, trying to swallow the welling emotion. She didn't know why she'd come, much less why she'd stayed with Steven, but today needed to be her last day in Houston. The courts were pressuring her clients, and she had to get back to DC and go to work. "What...has he said?" she asked.

"Not much. And the tube is still in his throat. It's hard for him and almost impossible to understand." She hesitated, looking down to the green tile floor. "I get a lot of patients like him. It's hard to know how much he understands at this point. He's breathing a little better, and his eyes are open," she said, more serious now. "But I didn't want to set your expectations too high. I just can't tell much right now," she said, pausing. "And he does look really bad."

After a moment of private jubilation, Amanda thanked and hugged the nurse who looked young enough to be Shannon, if she had survived.

"He may not know you," the nurse said as she turned toward Steven's cubicle. "And he comes and goes a bit."

Amanda stopped and turned back to the curly-haired brunette who looked tired herself. "I know this will sound a little strange to you," she began, "but he didn't really know me very well anyway. I'm not really certain why I've been here for three weeks. I was just the last working number called on his phone, and the police didn't have anyone else to notify."

"Oh... I see. I'm sorry. I thought you were family. Maybe his sister," she added as Amanda turned away again.

The nurse clamped her lower lip between her teeth, then swallowed. "Uhmmm, ma'am," Amanda heard her say as she stopped again, looking over her shoulder, "visitors are sometimes the difference in living and dying for head trauma patients. They know. Even if their eyes are closed and they can't move. They know you're there, even if they can't remember you later on," she said, looking away.

"You've been the only visitor that he's had, ma'am. You and an older gentleman named Emanuel who calls every day at two o'clock."

Amanda nodded in the nurse's direction. "We shall see," she said, releasing a breath. "We shall see." Then she waved a hand in the young nurse's direction signaling both thanks and understanding before she flipped her sunglasses down to cover her red teary eyes and began to walk down the pristine hall wearing jeans, pumps and carrying her suede jacket over her left shoulder.

She might have been a fashion model or a glamorous news anchor or even a university professor. The nurse stood still watching her walk away, but never did she consider that Amanda might be one of DC's leading attorneys.

*****

Steven was sleeping when Amanda came in, and she sat in the same high-backed cushioned chair that she'd used for three weeks, waiting, hoping that he might wake and utter something that she could understand before she had to go home.

It was Shannon that she loved and had imagined being her daughter-in-law one day, and it was for Shannon that she stayed with Steven. She'd cried all the way from National to Houston Intercontinental and was unhappy with herself about that. She'd used an entire box of tissue and consumed five glasses of scotch by the time they touched down. None of that helped. She looked horrible, and even her limo driver inquired if she were okay. She wasn't, but she told him otherwise and freshened in the hospital's lobby restroom before finding her way to ICU on that first day.

For three weeks thereafter, she hadn't known if she were so upset for Steven or Shannon and John or herself. She made an initial decision to stay for a day or two to help with the funerals, not knowing if there would be two or three services. Thinking that it was the least she could do for Shannon, she convinced herself that she had to stay for the duration. The nurse's information about Steven's lack of visitors wasn't news. She knew two weeks prior that she would be the only visitor and that legal and business issues had to be addressed.

Amanda used her money to open a Houston bank account so Emanuel and the others could get paid, and on day 4, she called on Sheriff Olin Johnson Jr. and paid three years of missing property taxes. She'd advised Olin Jr. that she would call him to come to the farm and arrest Damian and Brad Wilson if they ever set foot on Steven's property again; that is, if he could find their remains when she finished with her double-barrel shotgun.

Amanda didn't make idle threats. Her grandfather owned a Montana cattle ranch where she'd been expected to do her share of the work. Up at dawn, herd cattle, keep a gun handy for snakes, big cats, and wolves that targeted the young calves. Adding the *ranch hand demeanor* to a near photographic memory, Harvard undergrad and Yale Law made her a formidable threat when she'd entered Olin Jr.'s office and suggested that he meet with the attorney who represented the Wilson brothers to arrange the return of Steven's money. She cited the statutes governing bank fraud, typically a federal crime. Olin Jr. understood. He might not have been half the man that his father had been when his dad sat at that same desk, but he did know the law. By day 12, the account showed a balance on hand of almost two million, and the Wilson brothers who had confronted Emanuel three times declaring that they owned the property were nowhere to be found.

Still, Amanda didn't know why she was compelled to stay. She could have left weeks prior. Emanuel would have arranged for an ambulance to get Steven to the farm if he survived, and she could've come back for a triple funeral if he didn't make it. John, still distraught, was back in school and seemed to be okay but texted with her several times each day. Even so, for some undefined and instinctive reason, Amanda Rhymes, who just might have just been a fashion model or a television news personality or even a renowned DC attorney, stayed in Houston for three weeks sitting in that same seasick gold chair, making every visitation period, waiting for something to happen.

Excepting the nurse's declaration, day 22 began like all the others—quiet, boring, loud humming machines, blinking lights, and Steven lying there trying to decide if he wanted to live or die.

Amanda took out a Patricia Cornwell novel and settled in the worn chair wondering if today would be her day of reckoning…if Steven would know that Shannon was gone, or would she be the one who had to tell him. Either way, she knew that someone would have that duty, and there wasn't a line of volunteers at the door.

The incoherent sound that came from Steven an hour later shocked her, and she surged to her feet.

"Wahhh…wahhh," he repeated as she scrambled for the nurse's call button, not knowing if he were mad and struggling against his restraints or a perfectly normal human coming back to life after a horrible tragedy. In either case, he scared Amanda, and she stabbed the call button repeatedly. Seconds later, the pretty green-scrubbed nurse who seemed half her age and height rushed into the cubicle.

"I don't know what he's saying," Amanda said. "And I don't know what to do."

"Wahhh," Steven muttered again.

"It's okay, ma'am. He just wants some water," she said, extending her arm toward Amanda who stood opposite her, across the bed. "When I've given him very small ice chips, he did well with them. His throat must feel horrible after all these weeks with that tube."

The nurse used a plastic spoon to scoop a tiny ice chip from a cup that sat on the bed tray and touched Steven's lips, allowing him to take it in when he was ready. "There," she said, leaning over him, "you did fine with that one. Wait just a second, and I'll get you another one."

She motioned Amanda toward the cubicle door with a head nod. "The doctors don't know if he can see. Even if he can, it may be no more than a blurb or light without any clarity, so if you give him ice, put it on his lip and let him take it in. Don't try to place it in his mouth." She hesitated, squeezing her lips together as she frowned. "And I should tell you that they're almost certain that he'll never hear again from that left ear that was crushed in the accident."

Amanda nodded, understanding, immediately wondering if Steven would ever be able to resume a normal life. She let her eyes fall, suddenly engulfed with a sad, overbearing cloud of doubt, laced with anxiety. She'd never seriously considered that he might not return to his prior self.

The nurse's paging unit strapped to her waist buzzed suddenly, and she glanced down, then back to Amanda. "Do you mind giving him a chip every now and then?" she asked, handing her the spoon and the cup of ice. "I'll be two doors down and back in just a bit."

"It's...uhmmm...not really my forte," Amanda began, "but—"

"You'll be fine, ma'am. He's a gentle soul and doesn't bite much at all. Just don't give them too fast or he'll choke. He'll probably have to learn to do everything all over again almost like a newborn, and unfortunately, that may include swallowing."

Amanda scooped a chip and touched the spoon to Steven's lower lip so he would know the chip was ready. He scarfed it down like a pro, and she began to think that her temporary duty might not be too bad. Still, Florence Nightingale, she wasn't, and she knew it well.

Steven wiggled his nose when her hand was near his face. "Aaamm? Aammmannn?" he managed.

"I'm here, Steven. Yes. It's me, and it's okay, I promise. I'm just giving you a little ice. You were thirsty."

"Aamman? Why...where?"

"Houston," she said, spooning another chip. "You were in a horrible accident, Steven."

"Wh...why? *You?*" he asked, barely able to get the words out. "Shan—? Mama?"

Amanda almost answered, then stopped herself. She didn't want to sugarcoat or mislead, and she worried about the shock of him knowing too much too soon. He'd finally started to come out of it, and she wouldn't do anything to cause a relapse. "You've been in a coma, Steven...for almost three weeks," she added without mentioning Shannon or Martha.

Steven winced, closing his eyes so tight that wrinkles formed around both sockets. "Head...hurts. Leg, killing me," he said with sounds that barely cleared as words.

"You've had several surgeries, Steven. I'll ask for more pain medicine," she said, pressing the call button.

Like the courtroom attorney that she'd become, Amanda used the time between ice chips to think, to plan what she wanted to say. She thought that her first answers must have seemed harsh or abrupt as she replayed them to herself. She knew that she needed to soften her words and her tone. "Steven…can you hear me, dear?" she asked.

He blinked his eyes, closing them again as he nodded slightly and took a shallow breath.

"Good. Good," she repeated as she paused, swallowing. "I really don't…*enjoy*…having to tell you things just now, and I'm not completely certain that you can hear me—"

"Little," he managed.

"Okay, good," she said, slower now. "I need to tell you that you're better today than you've been in three weeks, but you're still in pretty bad shape and that there's no one else here," she said, narrowing her eyes as she waited a second before continuing. "Do you know who I am, Steven?"

He nodded again without opening his eyes. "Ammann?" he asked again. "You're…here?"

She sighed, thinking that she was still moving him too fast, and spooned another ice chip, placing it on his lower lip.

"Mama… Dad now," he volunteered without her prompting. "Hubert too. Happy," he added before turning his head on the pillow and slipping into a deep sleep.

Amanda stood over him, gazing. For some undefined reason, she was no longer afraid of him. He was back now, no longer in that territory between earth and the heavens. For those weeks when she didn't know if the man before her still had a soul or not, he scared her. That elusive, undefinable man who lingered on that bed with all those tubes and monitors seemed inanimate, and she had no experience with a person in that state. She didn't know what she would do if he had risen from the bed and demanded something…anything. Neither could she comprehend the softness of eyelids that needed to be closed on that last day. Back then, she had no concept of the death process, and it frightened her. But now that she wouldn't have to find out, she was relieved.

Amanda sat in the high-backed chair and took out her phone, calling her DC assistant. "Pat, I'm going to be a few more days," she said unapologetically and somewhat gruff. "I know that I need to get back there, but he's alive now…barely. We will only have two funerals, and I'm going to help with that…no matter what." She hesitated, listening to her assistant's protests. "No, I'm staying down here," she said. "For Shannon's sake. I'll let you know when to get John down here for the funeral," she added before she clicked the phone.

On day 25, the primary physician took the tube from his throat, and Steven winced as he managed to bend at the waist when the bed tilted up.

"Well…" Amanda said, doing her best to be cheerful as she entered the cubicle afterward. "You get a private room today and a hearing aid for your good ear. I'm sure you're delighted about that," she said, smirking.

"Can't wait," Steven said, turning his head away. "I didn't know that I would turn into an old man that can't walk and can't hear in less than a month's time."

Amanda raised both of her hands, shaking both the forefinger and index finger of both hands in his direction. "I'll leave now if you want me to," she said in that stern, take-no-prisoners voice.

"No. No. God only knows where I'd be if you hadn't come along. This is all my fault, not yours. I didn't mean to feel sorry for myself at your expense."

"How in the world could any of this be your fault? That guy came out of nowhere at eighty miles an hour and rammed you."

Steven turned back to her and fidgeted with the call button as he looked down. "I had the choice of flying to Dallas or Houston. If I'd taken Dallas, none of this would have happened."

"Good God, you're impossible. Next you're going to tell me that you should've known that there would be a civil war in Bosnia and gotten there in time to stop that too."

Steven didn't answer.

Amanda moved to the side of the bed near his head. "I know all this hurts you deep within," she said, briefly rubbing her eyes. "I can't conceive of your agony; it must be horrible, just horrible. But it wasn't your fault, Steven. You didn't make a mistake that killed your mother or Shannon."

"Not recently," he said, sulking.

Amanda twisted her head, squinting, not understanding what he was telling her.

"I was told this would be a very rough life a long time ago," he said, obviously annoyed. "But I never imagined that everyone around me would also be hurt or killed." He looked toward the window, seeing the bright blue sky for the first time in a month.

"I have no idea what you're saying," Amanda said, shaking her head a little. "But we have real work to do, and you can't duck it now. You're going to live, Steven... Like it or not, you're going to live. If you'll just do what they tell you to do in therapy, you'll learn to walk again. And you'll certainly hear better if you wear the hearing aid. I ordered the best grade and brand on the planet."

"I suppose you think I'm just a selfish jerk, don't you?" Steven asked.

"No... I don't. You're just struggling the same as anybody else would, even though you don't seem to think you're like any other human," she said, scowling. "And... I do recognize that this is probably the best disposition that I could rightfully expect at the moment. Your whole world is a mess. I get that."

Steven grimaced and gave her a slight nod, then lowered his head, and closed his eyes before opening them again and looking back to her. "I... I do know how to behave, you know," he said. "Especially in the presence of a lady. It's just that...that I have a good bit of pain right now, and...and I'm more than a little unhappy... with me. Not *for* me...but *with* me. It has nothing to do with you. How could I possibly be unhappy with you? Apparently, you've done everything imaginable to help me, and you've had to manage it all by yourself. So, yes, I've just proven beyond a shadow of a doubt that I am indeed an absolute jerk."

Amanda put her hand on her forehead and rubbed before running her fingers through her hair, thinking that she'd been on the road too long, especially for hospital duty with someone that she really didn't know very well.

"Humph…" she heard Steven mutter as she looked up. "Mama used to do that."

"Huh?" Amanda asked, staring at him.

"Running your fingers through your hair, then pushing it back some. When she was frustrated and bone-tired, she did that."

"Well… I'm not your mother."

Steven nodded.

"No," he said, pausing. "You're not, and I should just say *thank you* for all that you've done for me and beg your forgiveness for my unpleasant disposition."

Amanda looked up, staring at him without blinking. He still looked horrible…for him. It was going to take more than a few days for him to look better, and she wrestled with the idea of going back to DC then returning for the funeral when he was stronger but thought better of it. There didn't seem to be a good solution. She took a deep breath and took his hand in hers. "How bad is the pain?" she asked.

Steven turned his head to the side seeing the mass of tubes and monitors, then looked back to her. "Did they cut my leg off in the last hour?"

"No, but you won't ever breeze through airport metal detectors again." She released his hand but continued to look at him. "Lots of screws and plates, I'm told. Probably a little super glue to go with them. I'll ask them to bring you a pain shot in a minute."

Steven tried to lift a hand waving the idea off but didn't get the hand to move much. "Think I'll pass and try to stick it out, unless Doc says I have to. I need my head in gear, and those things really put me away."

Amanda nodded her agreement. "Look…uhmmm… I really don't want to press you, but it's been over three weeks since your mother died and Shannon passed in the wreck. We…kinda need to have a funeral, Steven…as soon as you're up to it. Is it okay for me to begin making the arrangements?"

Steven took a long time to answer, then swallowed to clear the yuck in his throat as he opened his eyes. "It's not the physical stuff that worries me about getting ready. But…yeah," he managed just above a whisper. "Please…please do that," he said, pausing again to breathe. "When do the doctors think I can transfer to the farm?"

"Not too much longer," she said, "but you do have more surgeries coming. I didn't want to tell you that, but we might as well be straight about things." She hesitated, looking toward the window, then released a sigh before she turned back to Steven. "Look, I need you to know something. I came here hoping to get some peace about Shannon. You were the only conduit for me to connect with her, so I stayed. You didn't have anyone else, and I knew that I could push my work out some."

She paused, standing a little straighter. "You actually helped me, Steven, even though you couldn't see me or talk with me; you helped me. I'm okay with what happened to Shannon now. Don't like it. I think somebody yanked part of my heart out, but I'm better about it now, probably because I watched you struggle to stay alive for so long."

"I knew you were there when I was in the coma, but I didn't really know it was you," Steven said. "I guess I should say that I knew someone was there. I tried to speak. I tried to move in the bed. I could hear your discussions with the nurses. I tried to open my eyes…but I couldn't do anything."

Amanda didn't press further. Despite the pain, Steven dropped into a deep sleep with her standing at the bed rail looking down on him, still wondering how she'd positioned herself in this miasma of death and recovery. It didn't really make sense that she should be there. Even for Shannon. A few minutes passed before she sat in the high-back padded chair and took a pen from her purse to begin making funeral notes.

26
CHAPTER

Steven took a sedative on day 32 and slept for most of the ambulance ride from Houston to the Richland farm. Amanda and Emanuel spent the previous day clearing Martha's things from the master bedroom and outfitting it with a hospital bed, a motorized wheelchair, and all the things that Steven would need for a lengthy recovery. The week prior, Emanuel had a wheelchair ramp built so the high brick steps wouldn't be a problem when they brought the gurney in. And much to his dislike, Socks got a long hot bath, so he could become an indoor dog, at least for part of the time.

Steven struggled with being in Mama's room. If they hadn't done so much work to get it ready for him, he might have asked to move back to his room, even though it was much smaller and not central to the house. The ambulance personnel left the door open when they'd wheeled him in and transferred him from the gurney to the bed. That helped, of course, but it was still Mama's room, and he was invading her space. He toyed with the idea of asking Emanuel to move him until he saw Socks lumbering toward him, followed by a green-scrubbed nurse, Amanda, and Emanuel.

Emanuel looked older, much older, but then Steven thought he should. He hadn't been to the farm in months, and even though the Emanuel had full authority to run the place, he'd almost singly carried the burden of also being Mama's caretaker and confidante. Now a month into Martha's death, he still had a grandmother-granddaughter funeral, Steven's recovery, amateurish local threats, and a woman who had become the family's guardian angel in residence.

Steven studied him as the huddle of folks walked in. Worst of all, it was clear to him that Emanuel was deeply saddened by Mama's death. His normal starched self appeared down and almost droopy. He knew that Emanuel didn't have family in the area and had been steadfastly loyal to Martha and him for decades. He was clearly the reason that the farm still worked. More than that, Mama had always insisted that he give Emanuel acreage when she died so he could build a home and have a place for his own family one day, if he preferred that. Steven nodded almost imperceptibly as the group walked toward him, silently vowing that he would do more than that.

In that space of seconds between the door and his bed, the void swept Steven's singular moment of confidence away, pushing him back into the hot tar pits of panic and despair as though he were a falling leaf without the means to be alive again in the spring. He took a shallow breath, then released it slowly. Shannon should have been there, smiling, walking with that bit of bounce in her step, and bringing joy to his homecoming. He didn't want to be a victim, just like he'd tried not to cry when the Snack Jack plane shamed him into the same despair that now engulfed him. The family had no heir, no one to come behind him and take the constant stress of balancing between taking care of others and growing the dream. He needed Shannon. Right then. He tried to swallow the pain and smile as they took their last steps and stood beside him.

Steven looked to his side seeing Socks' paws up on the bed rail with his tail wagging. He reached down and started rubbing the big dog's head, almost baby talking with his buddy, knowing all the while that he'd never get this kind of companionship in a hospital.

"Is...is that okay?" he heard Amanda asking.

"He's probably out of danger now," the nurse said. "And Socks will do him more good than harm. He should just wash his hands pretty often," she added, checking the monitors.

Steven looked again to Emanuel and Amanda, thinking how different they were—race, sex, family background, and education—and yet so strong together, each carrying his share of the load and focused on helping him, one reaching out through him for Mama and the other doing the same for Shannon. It seemed to Steven that the Almighty had held all of them in reserve for these many years, then brought them forward together at just the right time. He looked again to Socks then back to Emanuel and Amanda and half smiled.

"You two seem to have thought of everything. I wasn't expecting to get indoor time with Socks," he said, looking up to Emanuel and Amanda. "Mama's room. Pretty high cotton. Not sure she'd think I'm worthy of that."

"That was Miss Amanda's doing," Emanuel said in that deep baritone. "But I'm thinking Miss Martha would be quite pleased to see you in here."

"You're closer to him now," Amanda said, nodding toward Emanuel. "Not down on the end by yourself and isolated like you've been all these years. Plus, it won't be so far to the kitchen when you're up and around."

"Which will be soon!" he said, trying to bull his way through Shannon's absence and the depression. "The IV is out, and you can forget about that wheelchair over there. Just keep that cane hanging on the bed rail," he said, turning to Emanuel.

"I'm going to be here for a while, probably a long while," he added with a furrowed brow. "I don't want that to change anything. You run the place. Take care of the folks and let me know what you need whenever you need it. You and Mama took care of things for decades. I don't want to mess that up."

Emanuel nodded, accepting the compliment with grace, as always. "I'll let you know what's going on from time to time, just like I did for Miss Martha," he said, the gray so evident in his coiffed locks and mustache, the lines more prevalent than Steven had seen.

"Now…" Amanda began, putting her hands on her hips, "my turn. We…all three of us…have to plan a funeral. It's not something that any of us want to do, but we have to."

"Small," Steven said immediately. "And make it a Methodist funeral. I presume you've already done the caskets, vaults, and all that."

In her ultra-efficient way, Amanda had met with the mortuary management and covered that weeks prior, and she said as much.

Steven saw Emanuel shifting his weight as he looked down. "Emanuel...what did I say that's bothering you?" Steven asked.

"It's the *small* part, Mr. Steven," he said, pausing. "Miss Martha lived in this county for eighty-five years. She was a very generous woman. Churches that couldn't afford the things they needed got new pews and carpet. Kids that had nothing got Christmas presents and big meals. And only she knows who owed her how much cash money that she loaned interest free for cars to get fixed or roofs to get patched. I don't really think she cared if she were ever repaid. There are lots of folks that don't have very much in this world that will want to come and pay their respects." He looked up to Steven with a half-smile. "And she knew lots of big folks, most of whom were scared of her. They'll want to come too," he added.

Steven hadn't considered either of those groups, and Emanuel was right, of course. He agreed to an open funeral but asked that they keep it to just a graveside service.

He turned to Amanda. "Will John be able to come?"

"Of course. I don't know about Shannon's other DC friends, but he'll be here."

"Good. He can have my room and stay here. I don't need it anymore."

Emanuel shuffled his feet again and swallowed hard. "Where?" Emanuel asked. "Family cemetery on the bluff or town?"

Steven took a deep breath. He'd debated this since regaining consciousness and understood what had happened. It was far easier to use the town cemetery. They had a large plot there, and his dad had been laid to rest there. It would be easier to visit in town, but Hubert's grave was on the bluff along with all the older graves. The farm had been special to Hubert, a place of peace for him and Martha in the middle of so much madness elsewhere. Steven studied his hands, thinking. "Family," he said finally. "Family."

"We'll get it ready," Emanuel said, happy with Steven's answer, knowing that Martha wouldn't be too far away and that he could go visit in private when he liked.

"That road going up the side of the bluff may need a little attention, but the fellas will take care of it. And, I'll call the golf course and rent about twenty carts. We shouldn't put too much weight on that old footbridge that crosses the creek. Those cedar and hickory logs have been here longer than I have."

Steven agreed with all of that and half-smiled about the bridge. He knew about those logs.

"When?" he heard Amanda ask.

"Three days," Steven shot back immediately, seeing her smirk with a wrinkled brow. He knew she questioned that he could be ready by then. "It's Biblical, and I know we've been waiting for weeks, but the *process* to bury is typically three days. That will also be on Friday, which is perfect. I'll be ready by then," he added with a lowered chin and wrinkles on his brow. "Promise."

Amanda shook her head and frowned a little. "Don't you think you should give yourself another week to recover and prepare?"

"Probably," Steven agreed. "Probably. But we have to end it. Mama would expect us to do it that way, and for once in my life, I'm not going to disappoint her."

Amanda squiggled her lips from side to side, looking down. "Well… I do need to get back to DC, I guess," she said, agreeing.

27
CHAPTER

A heavy fog covered the sprawling field below the house early on Friday morning. Only the naked tops of the pecan trees poked through the white haze appearing like long lines of modern sculpture jutting through an ocean of snow. As had become their custom, Steven, who reluctantly accepted his frailty, sat in his wheelchair on the long covered porch with Socks at his side to watch the sun come up. Shortly thereafter, Emanuel arrived with tea for both of them.

"I think we're going to have a hard day today, Mr. Steven," Emanuel said as he pulled the white wooden rocker near the wheelchair and sat down.

"Lots of pain," Steven said, pausing. "Of multiple varieties."

Emanuel nodded his agreement without speaking. Steven still refused to take anything stronger than an aspirin for the spears that shot through his leg intermittently and without warning. There didn't seem to be any position that would bring relief to his left knee, and reconstructive surgery was scheduled for the following Wednesday.

Steven looked over to Emanuel, seeing the quiet, gentle man with his scruff beard and unflappable disposition and realized that he and Mama must have had tea on the porch routinely. She would never have been able to run the place without him. The farm's equipment was complex and overbearing in size. Even the midsized tractors had tires that were taller than Steven, and the hydraulic cylinders that were used to move heavy loads were sometimes larger in diameter than his thighs. Emanuel dealt with chemicals, people, soil and weather conditions, conservation practices, and constantly changing markets every day. Steven managed a tight-lipped smile, thinking that Emanuel was almost toying with variables that would have challenged a chess master on his best day. Somehow he'd managed to work through it all and refused to let it disturb his placid demeanor. Steven turned back to the foggy field.

"Do you miss her?" Steven asked after sipping his tea.

Emanuel rolled his lips inward and nodded slowly. "Your mother and Mr. Hubert were really good to me. They were…legends…of a sort. At least for me. Now it's just me that remains of the three of us."

Emanuel began to rock slowly, still holding his cup with both hands and staring across the foggy meadow. "Mr. Hubert was easy to get along with, and your mama, she was the real boss around here. We solved some terrible problems sitting on this porch in the early mornings. I do miss both of them."

He paused to take another sip. "Even when they struggled to walk down here from the main door, they were both stronger than I was. And I never had to worry about them not being there for me when we had troubles," he said, sipping the tea again. "It's hard now. I have to do everything that they used to do, and…uhmmm… I have to be the one that solves the hard problems for everyone else, like they did for me. They were…real legends indeed, and I do miss them."

"She thought highly of you, sometimes better of you than she did of me, I think." Steven chuckled softly. "She told me once that she should have had more kids. I was out of school and gone from here, not visiting nearly often enough to suit her. But you *were* here, and you did take care of her. I'm obliged to you for that, Emanuel. Always."

"It was my pleasure, sir. My pleasure. You don't meet many folks in this life that are the type of person that she was, not many at all." He took a deep breath and released it. "My pleasure."

They sat quietly, listening to Socks snore and watching the Mallards come and go from the seven-acre lake on the north end. Steven knew plenty of people that would pay thousands for a single morning on the porch like this. Both he and Emanuel fully understood why.

"Mr. Steven," Emanuel began when they were done with tea and ready to go in and get dressed for the funeral, "there is just one thing that I need to mention…because I think it could be trouble. And I don't think Miss Amanda knows this yet. She may. She's an awfully smart woman, and I wouldn't be surprised if she didn't find out in the night like I did."

Steven twisted toward Emanuel, frowning in his mystery.

"Ms. Marion arrived in Houston about four o'clock yesterday afternoon. Is there anything *special* that you'd like me to do about that?"

Steven's body tensed as he white-knuckled the wheelchair arms. He understood what Emanuel meant with the word "special." A few seconds passed before his hands relaxed, his annoyance having peaked and subsided. He tucked his lower lip between his teeth before he turned to Emanuel. "Let her come," he said almost too quietly. "Help her with logistics and accommodations if she needs it. Treat her well. I haven't seen her in years, but she was Shannon's mother, at least according to our legal guidelines."

Emanuel frowned as he looked down on Steven sitting in the wheelchair, his chin resting on his hand, staring at the raw wooden boards of the porch's floor.

"You know, it didn't go well the last time Ms. Marion came to the farm. She complained for the entire visit, scolding everyone as though they were failing to meet her expectations. She even went into Rosa's kitchen to badger her about the Southwestern seasonings," Emanuel said, frowning. "Most of the staff from those days still live and work here at the farm. None of them will be happy to see Ms. Marion."

"I know," Steven said, nodding slightly. "I was most embarrassed with her behavior back then. But… I think we have to let her come, and if she's coming, we must be kind to her…and pray for the best."

*****

Emanuel helped Steven get into the tailored suit and prepare for his first public appearance since the accident. Amanda used a smattering of her makeup to help cover the fledgling scars. His hair was too long, but he didn't care about that, thinking that it might actually make him seem a little younger. By ten o'clock when the ministers arrived on the bluff, he was ready and positioned under the sixty-foot-by-eighty-foot tent that covered much of the small cemetery where he'd rediscovered Sarah's grave forty years prior. Emanuel and Amanda stood beside him as he chatted with people that he hadn't seen in decades, most of whom wanted to know if he still had his slingshot.

Emanuel touched his shoulder and cleared his throat, and Steven smelled Marion's perfume, that sweet, thick fragrance so popular in the eighties. He turned as much as he could in the wheelchair.

"Hello, love. How are you?" he asked with a bubbly sense of boldness that he didn't actually feel.

"Ahhh…that's my guy," Marion said, bending to hug him and give him a peck on both cheeks. "I'm… I'm doing really well…except for losing our dear little Shannon, of course."

"And you look it, my dear," Steven said. "My gosh. I don't know how you've frozen your age in the mid-twenties, but it's amazing. Just amazing. Every woman in America would be jealous if they could get a look at you," he said, almost ill with his own syrupy praise.

Steven made a mental note that she didn't ask about his health or situation and thought she'd probably have been happier if she were attending a triple funeral.

He knew that Marion had little interest in memorializing a daughter that she rarely saw and that her crazy-like-a-fox motif was anything but accidental. He was without natural heirs, which meant that she had a better chance to garner a larger portion of his wealth than others who were more distant.

Emanuel, perfectly dressed and coiffed, stood erect behind Steven. He leaned forward slightly, extending his brown hand. "It's so very nice to see you again, Ms. Marion. It's been quite a while since you visited us here on the farm."

"Yes…uhmmm… I'm delighted…to see you again as well," she said without referring to Emanuel by name.

Steven couldn't turn enough to see either Amanda or Emanuel but watched Marion's face pale, knowing that she was struggling to recall who the elegant Hispanic man with Steven might be.

"You remember Emanuel," Steven said, smiling. "And this is Amanda from Washington. Her son John and Shannon have been close friends for the last seven to eight years. John's plane was a little late, and he's at the house changing now."

Marion nodded to Emanuel who did the same, acknowledging her also with his tight-lipped smile that implied everything that he thought of her, but acknowledged nothing.

Marion turned to Amanda, extending her hand as she would with anyone in polite society. "Thank you for coming," Marion said as though she were the natural first lady of the event. "And thank you for all that you must have done for my Shannon through those years," she added.

"My pleasure," Amanda said, stone-faced. "She was a sweet young lady. John and I both miss her terribly."

"She's also the best attorney in all of DC," Steven said, flashing a smile. "Razor-sharp," he added. "Razor-sharp."

"Hardly," Amanda responded, cringing as she turned to the side. "But thank you for the thought."

Marion didn't flinch or acknowledge Steven's comment. Ever adept, she pivoted, holding her arms out to Steven, then stepping back. "Let me get a good look at you," she said as she stepped back further. "It's been a while, and you've had a bad time of it, I hear."

"A bad time indeed," he said.

Marion gave him a broad smile, then shook her head just slightly, feigning adulation. "But you look so unbelievably good. How old are you now? Forty something? It must be somewhere in that range." She released a deep sigh. "What a fool I was. You really do look good, even now, after all you've been through. My...my. I'm so very sorry, dear. You must be incredibly lonely after losing both Martha and my cute little Shannon."

"I've seen better days," he said, noticing in his periphery that the black-robed ministers had arrived and were proceeding to the front of the tent where two polished mahogany caskets sat side by side adjacent to the graves. Steven nodded toward the clergy.

"I should go speak with them for a minute," he said to Marion, using the wheelchair's joystick to turn. "I'll catch up with you in bit," he added, smiling as he rolled away on the outdoor carpet with Emanuel and Amanda following close behind.

*****

The service was brief—twenty minutes, scripture, comments from both ministers with glowing remarks about Martha's generosity in the community, and words of consolation for Shannon being taken too soon. Steven felt emotion rising in his throat during the second prayer but choked it back. When the baritone from the Houston Metropolitan Opera sang *On Eagles Wings* a cappella, his eyes began to tear with the song's power, but he brushed the moisture away and looked across the area toward Sarah's grave, thinking what a place this had been for his family. He swallowed hard when he felt Amanda's touch of support on his shoulder, wondering where he would have been without her help. He nodded and moved his wheelchair forward to face the crowd when the senior minister with the long red Methodist cross embroidered on his robe nodded in his direction.

Steven thought Olin Jr. looked tired, old for his years. All the staff from the farm and their families were there, standing patiently, waiting for him to speak. Near the back on the left side stood the Wilson boys, both overweight and a little discombobulated, much as their father had been. Big Henry stood in the back, alone near the corner of the tent, leaning heavily on a cane, his knee never having recovered from the gunshot.

Amanda stood erect, now with her arm draped across John's shoulders and a wad of tissue in her other hand. Steven felt her pain and tears in his, wondering if his sorrow were for losing Shannon or for himself, in her absence. The source didn't really matter to him, but it still didn't seem fair, to her or to him, though he'd tried to dull his sorrow with the self-consuming anger of losing a child. Any child. She was special, at least to him. He shuddered at the thought of going on without her, drawing his shoulders forward, tensing a damaged body that was already in pain, then let his eyes continue to roam.

A young sandy-haired boy with a leather bomber, jeans, and boots stood in the very back by himself. The lad stood straight with his arms across his chest and had green eyes that pierced. Steven almost passed him by, then let his eyes go back to that serious face. He thought the young man would be about the same age that he'd been forty years prior when he'd rediscovered the bluff. He didn't know the lad and made a mental note to ask Emanuel later. Still, that piercing stare disturbed him, and he moved on with reluctance.

Most of the prominent families from town were well represented. At least seventy people had braved the cold, gray morning to pay their respects. He thought that Mama would be happy with this, and Shannon would have been pleased that John and Amanda had come.

Steven thanked them for braving the weather, then apologized for asking them to come out to the cemetery at the farm, explaining that the spot had a special significance to the family, and that he believed that Martha would have wanted to be laid to rest here. He praised all of the staff, thanking them for taking such good care of Martha before telling two small stories of her younger years, when it was just the two of them, before Hubert. He had trouble memorializing Shannon and stopped twice to look down, brush away tears, and swallow the emotion that pounded him like an incessant tide on Scotland's rocky cliffs. In the end, he asked for a moment of silence, after which he said the Lord's Prayer aloud with the group joining. The ministers then finished with a benediction, and it was over, as much as the public portion would ever be over.

Steven spoke informally with the guests for another thirty minutes before they loaded into Emanuel's golf carts to go back to the house where a large lunch waited. It didn't seem odd when Steven stopped the wheelchair at the tent's edge to hold an intense chat with Marion, who dabbed her eyes sporadically, then hugged him far longer than friendship would allow. She was over-the-top when she kissed him on the forehead, pulling him forward and into her chest.

Some who witnessed the discussion and subsequent affection even commented at lunch that they hoped such a gorgeous couple might get back together and settle down on the farm.

Steven stopped the wheelchair near the last golf cart, turning it back where he could see the polished caskets and the old graves behind, knowing that he would never again see this image. He clamped his lower lip between his teeth and tried to control the escalating emotion. One of the sawed rectangular iron ore rocks stood just beyond the fresh caskets, marking Sarah's grave. A moment later, he lowered his chin to his chest and closed his eyes thinking that he had no chance to find her now. There simply wasn't enough time left. Seconds later, he used all of his available strength to stand from the wheelchair and ease himself on to the golf cart's second row of seats where Amanda and John waited.

28

CHAPTER

Big Henry Watson sat alone in the back of the room filled with round-of-eight tables that jutted from Rosa's kitchen then spilled out to the south end of the covered porch. His thick wooden cane hung from the back of the white slatted chair that stood adjacent to him while he sipped a cup of strong black coffee. Steven had just finished telling the story about Dillard's coil wire for two of Martha's United Methodist Women friends when he saw Big Henry sitting alone. He turned his head away, closing his eyes briefly before cutting his eyes back to Big Henry and reaching for the wheelchair's joystick.

On this particular day when his life resembled a boil swelled with infectious yuck and pulsating agony, Steven didn't want to talk to Big Henry. Not today. He hadn't seen him for over thirty years, and when he'd run into him at the gas station on that day three decades past, Big Henry didn't speak or look in his direction, refusing to acknowledge that the renter's kid who stole his pecans had become an East Coast money baron that Texas' new governor once hosted for a private dinner and a poker game at the mansion. Steven hesitated with the joystick, dreading yet another confrontation but longing for an answer to a forty-year-old question. He let out a shallow breath of moral acquiescence and began to maneuver the wheelchair through the maze of tables and chairs with the joystick.

"Big Henry," Steven said with that deep, firm voice that he reserved for moments of uncertainty like this.

"Steven," Big Henry said as he pushed the chair with his cane aside, making room for the wheelchair. "Join me. But maybe I need to ask Junior to be sure you aren't packing heat this time," he said, trying for humor that didn't work.

Steven sipped his beverage then turned toward Big Henry. "How'd you know, Big Henry?" Steven asked. "That's what I want to know. That day down by the footbridge. How did you know where I was? And that I was alone?"

Big Henry, who was still almost six foot seven and twice Steven's size, leaned forward placing an elbow on the table then rested his balding head in his massive palms. "Robert Earl came to the soda fountain bar at the drugstore. Damian and I were in there drinking a cherry Coke and watching Sandy Richardson breathe in one of those tight sweaters that she used to wear. We overheard Robert Earl saying that he'd left you out here by yourself," he said pausing, brushing a hand back and forth over his upper lip as he stared straight ahead without looking at Steven. "It was too much of a temptation. Uncle Dillard had promised us twenty dollars each if we whipped you; thirty, if we scarred you." Big Henry looked over to Steven who still sat in the wheelchair. "That was big money back then."

"Forty years ago," Steven said in a flat monotone. "That... yeah...that was big money."

"I should've known better," Big Henry said. "It was Damian's idea, but I had hated you since the day when we were five and you wouldn't let me have all of my pecans, grinding that one in the ground like you did. You were an arrogant little cuss, and I didn't think you had anything to be arrogant about, living in that rent house, especially after your daddy died. I thought I'd go along with Damian and maybe get even," he said, pausing. "Never figured it would be my last day to get around without that cane over there."

Steven nodded without speaking for a minute, still staring straight ahead before he narrowed his eyes and turned toward Big Henry. "You never looked to see who I was," he said. "You looked at the house we had, the clothes that I wore, my appearance...how much money we had or didn't have. You knew that you were bigger than I was, and faster. That's how you sized me up. You never bothered to try to find out what I was made of." Steven paused and looked away before continuing, "You probably size folks up the same way today. Most people do."

"Humph…" Big Henry muttered as he looked across the room. "I suppose you might be right about that, Steven."

Steven didn't trust Big Henry when they were boys, even before the fight on the creek, and he couldn't imagine that a butterfly would ever emerge from the caterpillar that was their relationship.

"You know, Big Henry, I've actually thought about you and the Wilson boys a good bit over the years," Steven said as Big Henry turned toward him, his brow furrowed. "No, it's true. I have." Big Henry narrowed his eyes, almost squinting. "Every time I lift my carry-on to put it in the overhead bin, that shoulder that you and Brad knocked out of the socket reminds me of you fellas. Those tendons are still rolled back in opposite directions in that shoulder, and it hurts like the devil from time to time."

Big Henry turned away, shaking his head a little. "Why'd you have to shoot me in the knee? There wasn't any call for that. Hell, now I'm an old man at fifty-three. I weigh close to three hundred pounds because I can't get around and do anything. Never played another down of football, and Daddy had two universities watching me, even back then."

Steven smirked, shaking his head. "I seem to recall that you and the Wilsons came after me, and that it was three on one," he said.

"But you didn't have to shoot me and leave me to bleed out and die."

Steven looked over to Big Henry and stared before he took a deep breath and let it out slowly. "Isn't that exactly what you fellas planned for me? All three of you had baseball bats. You broke my arm, knocked that shoulder out. Your intentions were pretty clear, Big Henry."

"They were until you hit Brad with that sack or whatever it was. Must have been some lead in that thing. Busted his jaw, his nose, even his eye socket. Cracked his skull. Hadn't been right in the head since. Never will be."

"He shouldn't have stomped on that busted arm after he broke it. The bone was already through the skin. He knew better than that."

Big Henry squirmed in the terry-cloth-covered folding chair, leaning forward to straighten his bad knee. Steven thought he looked old, much older than fifty-three; his fingers were even discolored from chain-smoking, and the tiny veins stood out, crisscrossing the skin below his cheekbones like St. Augustine runners matted below the blades of grass.

"He stomped you. I know he did. And that wasn't right. We just got riled up, and it got out of hand. That's all it was," Big Henry said.

"Maybe to you," Steven said, "but not me. I had a compound fracture, a shoulder out of its socket, and ruptured tendons. All of you were swinging baseball bats, and I was rolling around on the ground with an arm that didn't work. Don't tell me it just got out of hand. You came out there to beat me to death and leave me for the buzzards. You should be happy to be alive right now, Big Henry, even with that knee like it is. If you didn't have such a strong guardian angel, you would have come out of that creek in a pine box, and you know it."

Steven grimaced and shook his head. "Senseless. Look at what you fools did. I've got a bad shoulder that can't be fixed. You've got a knee that won't let you move much. Brad is addled and basically useless for anything of consequence. And Damian is afraid of his shadow. For what? A few dollars? Pride? Senseless!"

Big Henry sat still, looking at Steven before he rolled his lips and nodded. "How'd you get that gun anyway? None of us boys had guns back then."

"It was my daddy's gun. I'd been target shooting. Robert Earl probably didn't mention that," Steven paused, glaring at Big Henry.

Big Henry still looked away and didn't respond.

"Why'd you come today, Big Henry? You and Mama weren't exactly close, and you've never even met my daughter."

"Figured I needed to come see you. You could call it part of my mayoral duties, or you could just say that I needed to come."

Big Henry reached for his cane and used his arm to help push himself up, standing to look down on Steven. He squished his lips together, then brushed his hand across his stubbled chin. "I deserved this knee, Steven. I don't know how you pulled that old gun out all of a sudden with a busted-up arm and shoulder, but I deserved it. I went along with the Wilson boys, and I shouldn't have done that." He paused, glancing toward Emanuel who stared at both of them. "But you don't deserve that chair you're in, and you didn't deserve to lose your little girl like you did." He shifted his weight, hesitating. "I guess that's why I came today. To say that."

Steven nodded, looking down, accepting the pseudo apology in silence as Big Henry turned back quickly, lifting his cane toward Steven who wasn't looking.

"Just one more thing, in case you've been wondering."

Steven looked up, his brow wrinkled.

"If you choose to stay down here, you won't have any trouble from the locals. I've already put the word out. I don't look like much of a threat to anybody these days, but folks do listen to me, for whatever reason. The Wilsons are broke, and nobody pays any attention to them anymore. Damian is scared to death of you anyway, and Brad... Brad is just addled. That lady lawyer friend of yours had Olin Jr. thinking she was going to arrest *him*. I think he aged twenty years in the hour that he spent with her."

Big Henry paused, thinking, hesitating. "And as much as I hate to say it, Steven, you turned out to be sort of a legend around here. Everybody tells stories about your deals and money things that you do all over the world. We're not backward down here anymore. We have the Internet. We know about you." He stopped, releasing a breath. "As for me, well, I'm just an overgrown small-town mayor who's got lots of property but no money...and a bad leg." Big Henry turned again to leave.

"Get your knee fixed, Big Henry," Steven said. "You've got plenty of years left, if you'll do that."

"Can't," Big Henry said. "Insurance won't cover something done so long ago, and I haven't got the money otherwise."

Steven stared straight ahead, unblinking. "I'll pay, Big Henry," he said in a somber, quiet voice. "I'll pay the bill."

"You know I can't let you do that. Word would get around. Nobody would see me struggle to get in and out of my truck. They wouldn't feel sorry for me, and I probably wouldn't get re-elected. No sir. Can't do that at all," he said, half smiling.

Steven nodded, snickering under his breath.

"You get out of that chair now, Steven. Don't let it beat you back," Big Henry almost shouted over his shoulder as he made his way through the crowded round tables and covered chairs.

Steven caught Emanuel's eye and nodded toward Big Henry, mouthing that it was okay. Emanuel understood and hurried to assist Big Henry down the wheelchair ramp and over to his pickup.

"What was that all about?" he asked Steven when they were both on the porch watching the Ford truck drive away.

"I think…he came to apologize for something that happened about forty years ago, right down there, near the footbridge."

"Did he?" Emanuel asked, hesitating. "I mean, did he actually apologize? If he did, that would be the first time anybody ever got an apology from Big Henry Watson."

Steven offered a wry smile without looking up to Emanuel. "Not really," he said softly, letting the smile spread to a full-fledged smirk. "But he tried. That's worth something, I guess."

29
CHAPTER

Steven leaned on the polished wooden cane just before daylight the next morning. His vision seemed better; the fog in his eyes remained, but the gray cloud wasn't as heavy or as thick as it had been in the hospital. The eyesight was worrisome, but the left knee that bent at an odd angle in the crash stabbed him with sharp pain and frightened him more. He didn't look forward to the surgery or the rehab, but on this early morning, Steven didn't want to consider that. Facing the east with a view across the flat land below, he eased into his favorite porch lounge chair and waited for the sunrise with Socks stretched out near his feet.

Had he been able to see through the dark and the gray morning fog, he would have been surprised to see a heavy white frost blanketing the panorama before him with the late November cold. He pulled the thick porch blanket over him and settled back into the outdoor recliner. Emanuel would bring tea soon. He could doze a little until then, if the pain didn't rob him of that little bit of pleasure.

Steven twisted in the chair taking the pressure off his left side, then smiled as he thought of Laura and Shannon giggling like preteens on a Saturday night sleepover. He couldn't remember how they left him; the head trauma robbed him of that, but he did recall Laura's exact words, and they worried him more than his loss of vision and hearing. The thought that he wasn't *ready yet* and that someone else would have to come in his place if he left now troubled him. The most frightening word in all of it was "ready."

He couldn't be more ready to go back. Surely, the Council would recognize that. He'd tried hard, but failed with all the big ones—marriage, fatherhood, compassion, and love...real love beyond Mama and Shannon. He'd spent his years building, doing, and gathering things and wealth to insulate him from the pain and fear of his younger years, and now that it was too late to revert, he finally understood the paradox. Steven straightened himself in the chair, looking across the meadow, thinking that he had more ability and confidence when he was thirteen than he did at fifty-three. With eyes that were barely open, he understood that all the pastoral beauty that lay in front of him would fade within a few years of his passing, just as the farm had done once before, and that haunted him further.

He squished his lips together, narrowing his eyes before he closed them, allowing his head to droop toward his chest, still thinking. It was the fear that haunted him most...still. He'd been afraid of Dillard Wilson, so he planned the attack long before the drunken boar showed up that night. He was afraid of being poor, so he'd become a multi-millionaire. He was afraid of being run over by the likes of Big Henry, so he'd built a political and financial fort that would stand challenges. But now he didn't have Mama or Shannon. His body was beat-up, and he'd convinced himself that he didn't have a future and that there was no one coming behind him. Maybe Mama was right when she told him that he needed to slow down and live now, if it weren't too late. Maybe she was right about all those things she said near the end.

Steven pushed himself up in the chair, covering his eyes with the palms of his hands. If pain were his primary teacher, how could he not be *ready*. He'd lost Marion when they were both young because he wasn't good enough for her, and now Mama and Shannon left on the same day. That surely wasn't an accident, and now there was no one left. He dropped his hands, wondering why had it been so hard and why did the agony begin when he was so young. Surely, he'd suffered enough to learn whatever the Council intended for him to have gotten out of this life. How could he not be *ready*?

"Nobody...left," he mumbled just louder than a whisper before exhausting a deep breath. "Nobody at all."

He lay back in the chair again and pulled the blanket up, covering his face. There was still time to doze before the others would come out.

As he closed his eyes, he wondered what she meant by "someone else will have to come in your place." Would someone else's life be cut short because he failed to get ready? He'd struggled between the demands of both self and soul, trying to please both like everyone else...and had nothing to show for it, nothing that would stand the test of time, nothing that would be important to the Council. Thomas, the red-robed fella on the end of the Council row who seemed to hate him, would get the last laugh after all.

Twenty minutes later as the sun broke the horizon he heard footsteps coming down the covered porch and opened his eyes. He couldn't turn his head; the pain was too intense.

"Morning," he heard Amanda saying. "Did you sleep out here all night, or are you just one of these Texas before-daylight risers?"

Steven hadn't expected her to be up and dressed so early.

"A little of both, I guess," he managed, taking the tea from the tray. "Mama taught Emanuel how to get the tea just right. Some of the best hotels and restaurants in the world don't do tea well. They don't get the water hot enough, and they don't let it steep long enough"

"So...how'd you really do last night?" Amanda asked with raised eyebrows, ignoring his attempt to pivot with the dissertation on making tea. "The night after a funeral sometimes doesn't go well," she added, looking down on him. "Do I get a truthful statement...or do I get an 'I don't want to talk about it answer'...again?"

Steven looked over his cup, watching her take her coffee from the tray.

"A fair amount of pain, and it just doesn't seem to let up," he said, rolling his lips inward. "Add a healthy dose of brain fog to go along with that." He took a deep breath and released it. "Not a lot of sleep."

She sipped her black coffee before cutting her eyes over to him.

"You were right on the cusp of making yesterday a triple funeral, you know. Three and a half weeks isn't exactly a lengthy recovery period, considering what happened. But... I can't blame you for wanting to fast forward six months and have a good bit of this behind you."

She put her cup on the small table near his cup and pulled another porch lounge chair alongside, then gathered her porch blanket.

"It's fairly impressive seeing a DC lady dressed and ready this early on a Texas morning. Hair, makeup, the whole deal. Not exactly an easy thing, and I do recognize that we guys have it far simpler," Steven said.

"Travel day," she said without looking at him. "Not that I want to. But the clients are screaming at me on email and by text. The judges are upset with having to juggle their calendars, and I think even John might even be missing me a little," she added with a half eye roll.

"Understand," Steven said, trying not to show emotion, knowing that he would miss her badly. "I...owe you," he said, glancing down. "But I think you probably know that already...and that you're far too considerate to bring that up with someone in my current state."

Amanda didn't answer but stared across the broad meadow with its lush grass and massive pecan trees. The early frost had done its work, and the grass emitted that musty, sweet smell of fresh-cut hay, lovely in its dying days. She took a deep breath. "No..." she said with a lengthy pause, "no...you don't. I like it down here. A lot. It reminds me of Grandfather's place up in Montana. It's easier to see yourself here. Not so many demanding distractions to drive your mind away from life itself." She hesitated, then sipped the coffee. "DC is a pretty rough town sometimes, especially if you're a single mom trying to pretend that she can do everything perfectly...all at once."

She looked over toward Steven who gave her mental space with his brief silence. "I guess I've never been one to shy away from self-imposed stress...or ambition," she added.

"Humph... From what I hear, you've handled yourself pretty well in DC," Steven said after he swallowed the tea that carried warmth all the way down.

Still, she didn't look at him but continued to gaze across the valley, sipping her coffee. "The professional stuff...yeah, maybe, at least some of the time. But that's not what counts in the end. We both know that. All that other stuff—being compassionate, staying poised in the middle of the everyday *human grind*, putting up with people who don't respect themselves, much less me…and perseverance, always perseverance—those things count in the end. That, and getting John through the hard years. That really pays too." She paused, the bright sun now shining on her face. "I haven't always done so well with that side of things."

"You did with me. You didn't have to come down here. You didn't have to stay so long." He paused. "And somehow, I think I knew it was you sitting in that weird chair in the ICU. I knew, but I couldn't say anything, and I couldn't move. Then when I woke up, I lost it all…somehow. Strange. Really strange."

Steven took a large swallow of the tea, then tucked his hands under the thick blanket. The frost wasn't melting yet. "Why are you still a single mom, Amanda? You've got it all," he added with raised eyebrows.

"Hardly," she said, smirking.

"No, really. You've got a practice that every attorney dreams of building, the DC connections, the IQ points, the appearance, the education. Everything. And I do recognize and acknowledge that we haven't spent much time together, so I don't really have the privilege of making a comment like that, but some things are just obvious." Steven wanted to go further but worried that he may have gone too far already.

She turned toward him quickly and stared before she sighed. "I could say the same about you, couldn't I? And ask you the same question."

"Humph…guess I led with my chin on that one, didn't I? And I really don't need any more bruises just now," Steven said.

"Divorce is painful, isn't it?" she asked rhetorically, not expecting him to answer. "And I don't just mean the financial part or custody or property settlement. It just hurts. Deep down where you really live, it just hurts. Doesn't matter who started it or who did what in the heat of passion; both sides get hurt. Sometimes it's worth it, I guess, but I swore that I'd never put John through that again."

She took a deep breath and let it go. "And so far... I've managed to run off eight-to-ten very nice guys, in about the same number of years. So far," she repeated.

Neither one of them said anything for a few minutes as they sipped the beverages, watching the sun rise over the far hill. Like a duck's feet underwater, Steven paddled through panic trying to remain poised and silent. Beneath the surface, his mind raced through scenarios to justify the mixed emotions that swamped him. He put his cup down, concluding that Amanda saw much of herself in Shannon and was simply devastated by the idea that Shannon had been taken from her. She hadn't asked him for the crash's brutal play-by-play, and he didn't know that he could discuss it anyway. It was too hard, and it was too soon. If he'd just been three seconds slower. Not even that much, just one full second slower and Shannon would still be with him, and with Amanda.

Despite his dependency and emotional roller coaster, Steven had concluded that Amanda just missed Shannon and felt sorry for him, that she would have felt guilt had she left him alone to deal with losing Shannon, the funerals, the Wilsons, and all the burdens of a premature passing. He was suddenly sure of it. Only then did his panic subside. He couldn't lose this fledgling relationship with Amanda. That couldn't be. He'd never been her primary interest anyway. It was just Shannon that she mourned, he concluded.

"I thought you handled the situation with Marion well," Amanda said, letting her eyes move slowly down the hill and over the meadow. "She's a beautiful woman. Still looks like she's thirty. Definitely not fifty. Pleasant, classy. Better than me, that's for certain."

"She...came for money," Steven said in that soft but definitive tone after waiting for a second. "She wasn't a mom for Shannon. Granny or maybe you were much closer to being Shannon's mom. But I knew she'd show up with a hand out. It's not the first time she's done that. Always tactfully, but she has to ask. She doesn't work very much and still expects to live well."

He sipped the tea, pausing. "Four years ago, I made her the beneficiary on Shannon's life insurance. I never really believed she'd collect, and Marion didn't know that I'd done that until yesterday."

He paused again, briefly closing his eyes. "So, she had every reason to be pleasant. She'll pick up almost two million in tax-free cash because I drove just a little too fast, or a little too slow, however you choose to look at it."

"Stop that," Amanda said with disdain in her tone. "Don't go there. Just don't. You can't punish yourself, and it's definitely not credible for you to consider yourself as a victim. You didn't do anything wrong, and you're *way too smart* to go down that rabbit hole. You just have to pull it together and go on. 'Living ain't easy,' as the song says, but what choice do you have? And…and I do know just how *harsh* that sounded by the way."

Amanda twisted in the porch lounge chair to face Steven, releasing a deep breath of disgust. "She didn't come just for money, Steven. We both know that. She came for you. All of you. And why wouldn't she? You fell for her once. You were young, and we're all big kids now, but those early emotions don't really go away. She wanted a second chance, and that was abundantly clear. She definitely didn't come to mourn for my little buddy. Shannon despised that woman."

Steven raised a hand to interrupt and argue the point but then thought better of it, recognizing that she just might be correct.

"And…that's why I said you handled that well," Amanda said. "You didn't fall for her, hardly gave her the time of day, even though she sat beside you at the graveside. And you have to admit that she is an incredibly attractive woman," she said, nodding to herself. "She looked great. Absolutely great. And I expect she spent last night in a Houston hotel beating herself up for not being able to get your attention. And…she probably hates *me* already, even though I don't think I said an unkind word to her all day…which is sometimes pretty hard for me to do."

Knowing that she might jerk it away, Steven took a risk and reached across the small table between their chairs, taking her hand in his, then looked into her eyes. "Thank you," he said quietly. "For everything. I would have been in real trouble without you. No one else came to check on me in ICU. No one else could've put the Wilsons in their place and gotten the money back and then planned a double funeral." He paused, looking away. "No one else would've had strength to talk with me the way you just did."

Amanda moistened her lips and nodded.

"Just...thank you," he said again before releasing her hand.

Amanda hesitated, swallowed hard, and looked at him eye to eye. "You have to finish, Steven. I know how difficult this must be for you right now. You lost your two best friends on the same day, and there's nobody...nobody that can fill that void, because no one else shared all those years with you. Deep inside, you must be absolutely miserable, and even though you might not think so, I do understand that you probably want to just quit on life. You might not think that I have the right to understand that, but I do. Trust me. I do.

"You probably have emotional explosions blowing up every few seconds," she continued. "It has to be really hard for you to maintain control, but you're the only one who can deal with it." She breathed heavily and raised her eyebrows. "But hear well on me on this. Please. Finish. You've been prepared, and you can't just give up."

Steven didn't flinch as he stared down the hill almost without blinking. He'd already given up, and he'd already prayed to die. Begged for it.

"Steven? Are you listening?" He nodded, almost imperceptibly. "Sometimes I can't tell if you're really hearing me, and I know you're struggling, even though you won't say much. There's only one thing that I want you to remember, and I want you to think about this because...because I've never said this to another human."

Steven wished he'd taken the pain pills when he slowly turned his head to face her.

"You...you're the only person that I've ever known who had a chance to really be *somebody*. Somebody who could actually make this a much better place, not just earn a lot of money and live a comfortable life. Plenty of people can do that."

Amanda paused, putting her hand to her mouth for a second. "And I mean that. You have that kind of talent. I'm not even in your league, and we both know it. You walk into a room in DC and everybody turns to look; then they start to whisper and begin to slowly gravitate toward you as though you have some special magnetism.

I get *looks*, lots of *looks*, but not for the same reason you do. You can't give up, Steven. Not now. You just can't. If you were to do that, Shannon would be incredibly upset, and your mother would be downright mad at you. You don't owe me. Not me. Not one little thing. But you *do owe them*, and we both know that too."

Steven looked up to her and nodded again, this time noticeably, with tears welling.

"The problem is," he began before he stopped to squish his lips together, thinking. "The problem is that I don't have any fight left in me. None. Just none.

"When I started to work on this farm forty years ago, I had nothing…but I had something that I needed to prove to myself and also to a few people around here," he added, pausing to take a minute to look across the hillside where the frost had now begun to melt. "Now all that's missing. Deep down within, I have this hollow, listless feeling. I don't have any heirs. No family at all. Not now. It's difficult to explain to anyone else just how debilitating that position is." He paused, looking away for a second. "The person you knew in DC doesn't really exist right now. The farm, this house, all of it will be in complete disarray ten to twenty years from the day Emanuel and I die. The briars and scrub brush will take over the fields; the trees will go untrimmed and begin to break down. Without people to work and take care of things, it will all go back to wilderness."

"I didn't intend that you commit to working or managing the farm," Amanda said. "Just don't give up. Don't sit on this porch day after day and stop doing things in the world beyond…beyond here."

Steven nodded, then released a deep breath. "If I knew that there were someone coming behind me to shoulder the load, then maybe I could get going. But she died about a month ago."

"No. Absolutely not. You're not getting away with this," Amanda said. "You're not going to be a voluntary victim. That isn't going to fly with me, Steven. If there weren't something important left for you to do, why would you still be alive?"

Steven stared at her without speaking before he looked away. "I'd hate to face off with you at summation," he said, trying for a half-smile, before his eyes drifted again.

"Likewise," she said. "Likewise. But right now I have to start the process of getting back to D.C," she added, standing.

"What time do you fly?"

"Ten," she said with a grimace, before beginning to walk down the porch to get her things.

Steven let her take a few steps.

"Amanda?" He swallowed hard, almost terrified to ask the question that he knew he must ask. For once in his life, he could not let the moment pass without having the backbone to take the risk. No matter what the consequences might be, he simply had to know.

She stopped, looking over her shoulder.

"The E...my contact information has you as Amanda E. Rhymes. What does the E stand for?"

"Oh, thank God... Thank God," she said, obviously relieved and almost laughing as she turned fully toward him. "You looked so serious, and I was so worried that you were going to ask me something that I wasn't ready to answer, something that would immediately damage this budding relationship." She released a huge sigh and smiled as she took another half-step in his direction. "It's Erin. A family name, of course. One of my great-grandmothers also had that name. Mother always called me Amanda, and I never really understood why. I'd bet there haven't been ten people to ask that question in my lifetime."

Steven stared at her, trying to keep his chest from heaving as he offered a polite, tight-lipped smile, fighting himself to maintain composure and stem the tide of emotion that thundered through him.

"Erin," he said with that faint but husky voice. "A pretty name... very pretty indeed," he added with as much stoic solemnity as he could manage.

About the Author

J. Ronald Clements writes fiction based on the life events and fears of everyday people who are torn between the realistic problems of human existence and a desperate lack of heavenly understanding.

Blessed with a rich array of personal experiences, Mr. Clements was in Germany on the night that the Berlin Wall fell, was once held hostage at an Egyptian military camp in the Sahara, has been harassed by the police in China, and—in addition to multiple USA locations—has lived in Paris for four years and Singapore for two. His day jobs included being a farmer, a teacher, and a senior executive in high-tech electronics, aerospace, and the oil and gas industries. He is a staunch Methodist, an Osteen-Lakewood advocate, and also a Gideon.

He currently resides in the red hills of North Louisiana with his family.